THE

ART OF

BEING

LEWIS

A Novel by

DANIEL GOODWIN

Cormorant Books

Canada Council Conseil des Arts
for the Arts du Canada

 ONTARIO ARTS COUNCIL
CONSEIL DES ARTS DE L'ONTARIO
an Ontario government agency
un organisme du gouvernement de l'Ontario

 ONTARIO ONTARIO
CREATES CRÉATIF

 Canadian Patrimoine
Heritage canadien

Canadä

The publisher gratefully acknowledges the support of the Canada Council for the Arts
and the Ontario Arts Council for its publishing program. We acknowledge the financial
support of the Government of Canada through the Canada Book Fund (CBF) for our
publishing activities, and the Government of Ontario through Ontario Creates, an agency
of the Ontario Ministry of Culture, and the Ontario Book Publishing Tax Credit Program.

LIBRARY AND ARCHIVES CANADA CATALOGUING IN PUBLICATION

Goodwin, Daniel, 1970– author
The art of being Lewis / Daniel Goodwin.

Issued in print and electronic formats.
ISBN 978-1-77086-529-7 (softcover).--ISBN 978-1-77086-530-3 (html)

1. Title.

PS8613.O6485A78 2019   C813'.6   C2018-900028-7
                                        C2018-900029-5

Cover design: angeljohnguerra.com
Interior text design: Tannice Goddard, tannicegdesigns.ca
Printer: Friesens

Printed and bound in Canada.

CORMORANT BOOKS INC.
260 SPADINA AVENUE, SUITE 502, TORONTO, ON M5T 2E4
www.cormorantbooks.com

For my family.

PART ONE

Rationalism is the enemy of art,
though necessary as a basis for architecture.
— ARTHUR ERICKSON

1

LEWIS WAKES UP early, hoping the day will be sunny and warm for the ribbon cutting. But when he tiptoes to the window of his room in the Westin Nova Scotian to quietly draw the drapes, he sees the Atlantic Canadian weather is in no way complying with his desires. The late July day is just barely dawning and already at 6:15 the sky threatens rain. Even worse, the fog blowing in off the Halifax harbour is heavy.

Despite Lewis's best efforts, the thick drapes rustle loudly, and Laura is already stirring before he turns away from the window. He freezes and watches his wife of fifteen years slowly wake up. Her eyes haven't been open more than a few seconds, and already she can see the disappointment on Lewis's face, the way his mouth is sagging slightly at the right corner. But Laura doesn't let Lewis infect her waking mood. She glances at the weather outside and, with a smile and a quick tilt of her head toward the empty pillow beside her, summons him back to bed.

WHEN LEWIS GREETS Drescher an hour and a half later over breakfast in the little organic restaurant in the Halifax Seaport Farmers'

Market, the rain has already started. It is heavy Atlantic Coast rain and appears to be falling horizontally off the harbour. But Drescher doesn't care to notice as he picks up his breakfast tray and chooses a seat right near the window overlooking the pier. Laura and Drescher's wife, Miriam, are still waiting for their meals at the counter and talking with great animation about something far more interesting than the weather. Lewis doesn't know what is so entertaining. He's too distracted by the rain smashing against the window right beside his face, but Drescher doesn't mind. In fact, he seems cheered by the semi-hurricane scene unfolding just on the other side of the glass. For the wind has picked up off the ocean and is carrying the impossibly large drops inland. It's an unusual reaction — or non-reaction — to the terrible weather on the morning when their latest design is about to be officially shown to the world.

"Do you think anybody will show up?" Lewis asks.

Drescher shrugs and smiles, and not for the first time Lewis notices his partner has a very charming smile. "Might keep some of the media away. But who the fuck needs them? As long as the Macdonalds are happy as a passel of pigs in shit." Like most professionals, Drescher has an ambivalent relationship with his clients. Lewis makes a mental note to look up the word *passel* and comforts himself with the following thought: as profane and ungrammatical as Drescher is in private, he will be urbane and eloquent once he takes the podium. Drescher takes a bite of his heavily buttered toast, wipes a smudge from his chin, and adds, "Besides, we designed it with these kinds of days in mind. Worse, actually."

AT 10:00 A.M., LEWIS finds himself standing to Drescher's left beside the podium in the pouring rain. The hotel umbrella doesn't seem to be adequately shielding Lewis's shoulders or his legs. His height doesn't help, but neither does the wind. Drescher is holding his umbrella at a jaunty angle, like Fred Astaire in one of his dance routines. There are a few media types in attendance, but only one TV crew is present. Yet Drescher can't seem to stop himself from smiling. The crowd itself is large enough. The Macdonalds are out in force, and the premier and half his staff. Every elected official in Halifax, representing all three levels of government, seems to have shown up for the official opening of the Macdonald Arts and Culture Building, the latest addition to the Halifax waterfront. Lewis recognizes almost the full provincial cabinet. Each member wants to be seen playing a part in this generous cultural gift. Every local and regional architecture firm is represented. Drescher is a role model to them all. Lewis is disappointed by the lack of media turnout, but Drescher keeps smiling.

Lewis catches Laura's eye. She is standing two rows back from the front. She gets to see her husband often enough and doesn't want to spoil anyone's view, so she has let some of the local politicians elbow their way into the first two rows. Like Lewis, she is tall. Miriam has to lift her head to whisper something in Laura's ear. Both women laugh, and Lewis assumes he is the object of their amusement. Perhaps he is looking far too serious when he should be happy and relaxed. After all, the Macdonald Arts and Culture Building, or MAC as it has already affectionately been christened by proud Haligonians, is a Drescher and Morton building. The name on the firm might still only be Drescher & Drescher, and Leon Drescher might have done the lion's share of the design for the $100-million building, but many of the touches that have already been nominated for international awards are Lewis's. And architecture is an art of accumulated detail.

SPEECHES GENERALLY SHOULD be brief, especially when the audience is cold and wet, but family patriarch and cultural benefactor Darren Macdonald likes to talk. This is his moment in his second career as philanthropist, and no amount of rain is going to rush him. Besides, Lewis remembers, long before their client built a typical Atlantic Canadian family-owned billion-dollar empire — spanning transportation, construction, and fish farming — he got his start on the family fishing boat. Seventy-year-old Darren Macdonald is used to rain.

Thankfully for the audience, Darren Macdonald has the Atlantic Canadian gift for plain-spoken, colourful speech. And everyone appreciates a hometown boy who loves his city almost as much as he adores his wife. He speaks with simple eloquence about Margaret and Halifax and his desire to pay tribute to both with a multi-purpose space for the performing arts and a place to train young people to participate in them.

He reminisces about starting out on his career in business: "When I got the chance to buy this parcel of empty land on the waterfront — for a good price, I have to tell you — everybody, including Margaret even, wondered what the devil I was up to. But I knew one day I would build something special for my city and for my Margaret."

And he speaks touchingly about his beloved Margaret's early career as a ballet dancer. He even tells a funny, self-deprecating anecdote about one of their first dates when he asked her to a community dance and found out she could dance circles around him. "And fifty years later she continues to do so," he concludes to loud applause. Standing to his left, Mrs. Margaret Macdonald, still slender at sixty-eight, smiles affectionately.

The premier speaks next, and then it is Drescher's turn. Lewis and Drescher always work together on designs, but it is Drescher who brings in the commissions and speaks at ribbon cuttings. Leon Drescher has always been the front man. He gives the same speech he delivers at every opening, but each time the audience is sufficiently different, and Drescher is a good speaker so it always succeeds. It's the same speech Drescher gave Lewis when he interviewed him straight out of the McGill School of Architecture eighteen years ago. Despite his newly minted degree, at the time Lewis thought he was qualified to do nothing outside of university, and he was looking to escape his memories of Montreal. Lewis was impressed by Drescher then, and the feeling has never left him. Drescher at fifty is only — and, somehow surprisingly to Lewis, always — ten years older than him, but a generation ahead of him in world view, experience, and self-confidence.

After four years of architecture school, it was Drescher who taught Lewis how to draft, how to work with clients, how to think. Drescher immersed Lewis in all the complexities behind the decisions made by their predecessors hundreds and, in many cases, thousands of years before. This wall a certain height, this tower's walls a particular thickness, this orientation of a room to the rising or the setting sun. Stairs that curved at this, not that, angle. A banquet hall that was 150 feet long, not one more nor less. The brightness at which the sun shone through the bedroom at dawn. The infinite ways that finite space could be enclosed. "This is how architecture differs from sculpture, Lewis. It is not about displacing space. It is about enclosing it."

Drescher is about to give his "What is architecture" speech. A lesser architect, that is to say every single architect in attendance and most in the profession, would speak at length about the building and the client and let the audience in on some of the more benign mysteries of the design process. Drescher touches on each of these subjects in turn, but he is perfunctory and brief.

When describing the building he kicks off with the requisite Maritimes tour guide's joke: "If you could see through the fog, this is what you would see." But he saves his passion and eloquence for the speech he can deliver without any effort. The fog is so heavy now that the outlines of the building are just barely discernible when Lewis quickly glances behind. But Drescher is undeterred. And the audience doesn't look uneasy.

"Architecture, my friends, is one of the few activities that separates us from animals and from chaos. Architecture is considered one of the prerequisites of civilization, even more so than a written language." As Drescher warms to his topic, he lets the umbrella slip even further from a vertical axis. The rain is hitting him straight in the face now, but it doesn't detract from his well-chosen words or his appearance.

Like Lewis, Drescher is tall and thin. But unlike Lewis, with his incongruous brown eyes and blond hair, everything about Leon Drescher's appearance fits tightly together. Drescher is silver-haired, wears tailored suits, thinks tailored thoughts, and speaks tailored speech when he chooses to. He smokes expensive cigars and hums melodiously along to classical music while driving his ridiculously short commute to work in his BMW 750 from his Victorian mansion on Mount Pleasant Avenue overlooking the industrial heart of Saint John.

When Lewis first moved from Montreal to Saint John to take the job, it was Drescher who introduced him to the refined joys of season tickets to Symphony New Brunswick, which plays regularly in the Italian Renaissance–inspired Imperial Theatre designed by Philadelphia architect Albert Westover. Unlike Lewis, Drescher always projects confidence, whether making a pitch to a client or opening a building that nobody can see.

"So while the dirty hordes who overran Rome in the fourth

and fifth centuries might have had a complex social structure and a language to go with it, they will be forever condemned in history books and human memory as barbarians because they left behind no buildings, no architectural record that they were here and expected to be here in the future.

"The Aztecs, on the other hand, with their crazy" — Drescher has never heard of political correctness — "and elaborate ceremonies culminating regularly in mass human sacrifices that included removing still-beating hearts, had no real written language. Yet they are considered a civilization because they were able to build in stone, including the massive, awe-inspiring temples atop which many of their human sacrifices transpired." Drescher pauses for effect. "That, my friends, is the power of architecture." And the audience, convinced by now if they weren't before that they are in the presence of true genius, applauds even more heartily than they did for favourite son Darren Macdonald.

THE TWO COUPLES drove up to the ribbon cutting together the day before in Drescher's spacious BMW. On the four-hour drive to Halifax, the two men sat together up front while Laura and Miriam sat in back, and they keep to the same arrangement on the return trip later that day after the opening of the MAC Building. The fog lifts as they leave the outskirts of the city, only to worsen again as they climb toward the Cobequid Pass. It is one of the most dangerous stretches of highway in Nova Scotia, but Drescher only accelerates as the big car moves into the fog. Miriam doesn't seem to mind, and if Laura does she doesn't say anything. Lewis has always trusted Drescher's driving, no matter how fast.

"The Germans get up to amazing things with their fog lights, Lewis." Lewis nods in appreciation as he checks the speedometer. Drescher is hovering above 135 kilometres an hour and is still picking up speed. But the car is so well-designed it feels like they are standing still. Drescher looks relaxed. He has loosened his tie. Laura and Miriam are laughing in the back. Lewis still has no idea what is funny, but it seems they haven't stopped laughing since they left Halifax. Lewis wonders how their rib cages can take the constant pounding. As Drescher slows down for the toll booth and roots around for four dollars, he says, "Meant to tell you something."

He hands the toonies to the attendant and speeds off. Drescher doesn't speak again for twenty kilometres. He covers the distance quickly, but still Lewis waits patiently for him to continue. Later, Lewis will reflect that Drescher chooses a moment when Laura and Miriam are talking even more loudly than usual in the back. The car is so quiet there is little highway noise to drown out Drescher's voice. And Drescher's voice is just a little lower than normal. Only later, when he thinks back to the conversation, will Lewis recall that despite being in the privacy of his own car, Drescher speaks in grammatical sentences. And doesn't once swear.

"We're probably going to be served with a legal action." Drescher glances over to gauge Lewis's reaction, but Lewis doesn't have enough information yet to have one. Who is the "we" is the only thought running through his mind at the moment. The firm? He and Drescher? Miriam and Drescher? He waits for Drescher to elaborate. Another fifteen kilometres go by. "I'm told it will be for the building we just opened today."

Lewis is confused. The Macdonalds are happy with the building. But maybe they are facing legal action on the land or from the builder that has nothing to do with the design. Perhaps Drescher is using the "we" because he identifies with the client in this case. Lewis asks his first question. "Are the Macdonalds in trouble?"

Drescher doesn't look over at Lewis this time. He accelerates yet again, if that is possible. Lewis checks the speedometer. They have passed 145 kilometres per hour. But he still doesn't feel the speed. "No, it's nothing like that." Drescher shrugs his shoulders, and his right hand comes off the wheel with his palm facing upwards. "Some architect may claim we infringed copyright on minor aspects of the design."

Lewis relaxes a bit in his soft leather seat. Drescher's and his designs are so prominent and distinctive in Atlantic Canada and parts of New England that they attract the architectural profession's version of wackos. Obscure architects barely scraping by, sometimes living in their parents' basements, who once doodled on a scrap of paper and who imagine they see, through the clouded failure in their own eyes, echoes of their half-baked ideas in the steel and glass and concrete manifestations of his and Drescher's vision. They've been served three times before. Each time the judge threw out the case before it had time to get started.

The rest of the drive is uneventful. The women keep talking and laughing, but the two men sit together in comfortable silence. After sharing his news, Drescher slows down and drives the rest of the way only twenty kilometres above the speed limit. Lewis closes his eyes, and in his mind the fog clears and he sees the Macdonald Arts and Culture Building clearly.

2

AFTERWARDS, LEWIS IS never sure how things might have been any different. It's not as if Drescher was in any position to reach out himself. Yet Lewis finds himself feeling slightly resentful that it is Laura and not him who gets the call less than a week after their trip to Halifax for the MAC ribbon cutting. The accident occurred at 10:00 p.m. the night before, and Miriam was notified just before midnight, but Drescher's newly minted widow waits until 7:00 a.m. the next morning to call Laura. Four-year-old Samuel and the baby, Skye, are miraculously still sleeping, but the two older children, Judah and Alexandra, are already up and eating. Laura is making healthy school lunches when the phone rings, so she nearly doesn't answer it. But she does.

Lewis is in the kitchen helping Laura with the lunches, fumbling with the plastic wrap she hates. He can see immediately from Laura's face as she walks back into the kitchen holding the phone tightly to her ear that the news isn't good. This is confirmed when Laura says, "Oh my God, Miriam, I'm so sorry," every time it is her turn to speak. And then, "How can we help," followed by two more, "Oh, I'm so sorry"s.

When Laura gets off the phone, her face is altered.

"What is it?" Lewis asks.

Thankfully, Laura looks nothing like Lewis's father, Mordecai. But when Laura turns to him after speaking with Miriam, Lewis sees hints of Mordecai about to give him news of his mother when he was in grade six. The effect is so powerful that Lewis has to remind himself that Miranda is long gone. The bad news he is about to hear concerns Drescher.

Like Mordecai, Laura doesn't believe in being indirect. "Drescher had an accident. He's dead, Lewis." Laura reaches out to give him a hug. Despite the warmth and strength of his wife's long arms, the room starts to spin around Lewis and his legs get weak. Lewis has to sit down at one of the kitchen table chairs. Laura gently lets go and sits down beside him.

At first Laura talks to the floor. She is talking half to herself. "Poor, poor Miriam. The first thing she said when I picked up was, 'I didn't want to wake you.' It sounds like she was up all night. The police called her just before midnight, and she had to go to the hospital to identify the body. She was in no state to drive, so she took a taxi home. I don't know why she waited so long to call."

Lewis still doesn't know what has happened. Laura seems to be losing her train of thought. Now that she has delivered the basic news, that Leon Drescher is no longer alive, she seems reluctant to reveal the details. Lewis waits patiently, as he did when he was a boy and his father, Mordecai, was explaining things.

Laura seems to remember that Lewis is waiting to hear about Drescher. But instead, she asks Lewis a question: "Lewis, did Leon call you last night? Was he planning to visit at all?"

Lewis shakes his head. Now he is looking at the floor. Words are hard to come by. "No call."

Laura nods as if this makes perfect sense, as if she is making a mental note. "I didn't think so, but Miriam asked me to check with you." That out of the way, she tells Lewis the story she has just heard. "Last night Drescher left home a little before ten. He gave Miriam a kiss and said he was going out for a little drive." Everyone knows that he did this from time to time. Drescher always claimed there was nothing like driving at night to help him think through design problems. He got into his car, the BMW 750, and drove away.

"Fifteen minutes later, a man out walking his dog along Rothesay Road saw Drescher's car speeding down Fox Farm toward the river. He heard the car first. It was so loud." Laura pauses as if this fact is significant. "When he looked up, he realized the car was going too fast. The police told Miriam the man estimated Drescher reached the intersection at the bottom of the hill at over ninety kilometres an hour." Laura doesn't have to say that was far too fast to stop at the stop sign. She looks at Judah and Alexandra, who are halfway through their organic oatmeal. "Luckily, at that hour Rothesay Road was quiet and there weren't any other cars. Drescher's car went right across the road, over the tracks, and landed in the river. Fifty feet from shore." Laura pauses as if she can't believe what she is relating. "The water's apparently already deep at that distance. The witness called 911 immediately, but you know the car: it sank quickly. The ambulance and fire department were there in ten minutes, but Drescher was already dead.

"He was still strapped in, Lewis. He never even had time to unbuckle and try to escape from the sinking car." Laura looks stricken. Lewis knows she is sad about Drescher but thinking mostly about Miriam. Before too long she will start to think about what it means for Lewis.

As for Lewis, he is silent. Drescher is dead. Lewis's mind is not able to formulate any questions.

THE FIRST TIME Lewis's mother, Miranda, attempted to commit suicide he was at school. Grade six. Lewis found out when he came home and his maternal grandmother met him at the door. "Your mother's in the hospital," was all *Bubbe* Rivke said in her Yiddish-inflected accent before she offered him her homemade honey cake and a glass of chocolate milk.

Lewis asked if he could visit Miranda, and *Bubbe* Rivke said tomorrow. "Your father's there now."

When Lewis's father, Mordecai, came home that evening, he poured himself a glass of twenty-four-year-old whisky, made a cup of tea for Lewis, and the two of them sat down together at the dining room table, a wedding gift from *Bubbe* Rivke and *Zayde* Saul. Mordecai looked pale and tired, which was unusual for him. And Lewis noticed that Mordecai wasn't smiling, which normally he was.

When Lewis thought about his parents, he saw Mordecai as a pirate who couldn't stop laughing and Miranda as a wealthy merchant's artistic daughter who had run off to be with him. Mordecai had swarthy skin, longish wavy black hair, and a neatly trimmed mustache and goatee. He was often mistaken for Spanish, and the older he got, the longer he wore his hair. Miranda was the opposite. She had translucent skin, the palest blue eyes Lewis had ever seen, and golden hair. She was beautiful, but Lewis couldn't help thinking she looked like she had been dipped in bleach. Lewis got his brown eyes from Mordecai and his blond hair from Miranda. It was as though God hadn't been able to make up His mind whether to make Lewis dark or light.

"As you know, Lew," Mordecai began, all his usual splendid humour and joy drained from his face, replaced by a tired, understated calmness, "your mother has not been feeling very well the last few months."

It seemed to Lewis that Miranda had been spending most of her time lying in bed, reading or sleeping. Sometimes she would wander downstairs in her nightgown and an old sweater and sit in her favourite armchair, where she would pretend to read the paper or watch TV, but really she was looking inward, at what exactly Lewis didn't know. She would often start to cry easily and for no reason. She had given up drawing and painting weeks earlier, and had stopped cooking regularly for the family. Mordecai had been pitching in with some of his staples: sandwiches, fried steak, hamburgers, and mashed potatoes.

"She's in the hospital now, where she will get treatment and hopefully she will feel better."

"What happened to her?" It wasn't a rhetorical question, as it might have been for another eleven-year-old speaking to his parents. One of the qualities Lewis most admired, and sometimes most feared, in his father, Mordecai, and mother, Miranda, was their shared inability to dissemble, to treat him as a child, to leave out inconvenient bits of truth when speaking to him. Ever since Lewis could remember, he knew he could ask Mordecai or Miranda any question and he would always receive a no-holds-barred, grown-up answer. It was reassuring and frightening at the same time, the way his parents never censored their conversations with him or in front of him.

Mordecai took a swig of whisky. Lewis noticed how golden the liquid appeared in Mordecai's glass. "She swallowed her rings — both wedding and engagement — and then overdosed on the sleeping pills and tranquilizers she has been taking over the last while."

Miranda was a painter, not a jeweller, but she had designed her engagement ring herself and had found a jeweller down on the Main to execute her vision. It was a solid gold band with a series of small gold stakes protruding from the top, like a flower or starburst. Lewis wondered if it had hurt Miranda's throat as it went down. "Is Mom okay?"

"Physically, yes. The rings are still in her stomach, but the doctors pumped out most of the medication. It was enough to hurt her but not kill her. The emotional and mental recovery will take longer."

"Do you know how long?"

Mordecai reached over to tousle Lewis's hair and reassure him with his touch. His hand was warm on Lewis's forehead. "I don't, Lew. But I know I will visit her every day. We can go together tomorrow. Did you want to do anything tonight, play chess or go for a walk?" But Lewis just wanted to pick up a sketch pad and drawing charcoal and forget what he had just heard.

3

IN THE WEEK following Drescher's death, everyone at the firm gathers at the water cooler and in the conference rooms to pay their respects. Fully grown, unemotional men who only ever cried when they created perfect buildings, structures that married ancient principles with the transitory demands and desires of their clients, have tears in their eagle eyes. Everyone tells their favourite stories, like the time Drescher flew the entire senior team to London to take a personal tour, delivered by one of the U.K.'s leading architects, of Westminster Abbey, one of Drescher's favourite churches.

Like Lewis, Drescher was Jewish, and he had a Jew's genetic distrust of graven images. But in spite of that, or perhaps because of it, churches were the apex of architecture for Drescher. In a church — that is, a proper church built before the twentieth century ruined everything — each element of design flows together not just for a purpose but to create an emotion. A church is not simply a place to pray, to relate to God. Through the inspired shaping of space, narrowing in places and widening in others; the use of specific, relatively timeless materials, stone and wood and gold;

the various aesthetic tributes paid to both the living and the dead in what was there and what was not; the way light crossed through the stained, bright, age-distorted, slowly yet still always flowing glass; the way the ceilings soar and seem to float — in all of this, a church is an architectural miracle. A church is designed to bring all who enter that space a little closer to God so when they leave they have not just entered and exited a building but are now different human beings.

TWO DAYS AFTER Drescher's funeral, the lawyers and accountants materialize out of nowhere like ghosts trailing in the wake of the dead. They wear dark suits, ties, and carry briefcases. Real briefcases, hard and dark with metal clasps and hinges, not the soft tan leather bags with magnetized straps that Drescher, and so by osmosis also Lewis, favoured.

Although Lewis is sure each lawyer or accountant is a normal person outside of work, with a spouse, children, friends, and hobbies, they don't smile in the hallways, and they look the other way when any of the partners says hello or attempts to make small talk. They commandeer Drescher's office and the largest conference room and spend their days poring over files, working on their slim laptops, and huddling in private conversations, even when they are alone with each other behind closed doors.

After a week of confusing limbo, the one with the greyest hair, hazel eyes, and pale, almost translucent skin calls a meeting of the firm's partners. He says, "Good morning" with such certainty that he appears to Lewis like a medieval crusading knight with obsessive-compulsive disorder bent on rescuing Jerusalem from the infidels. But he is so pale that despite his determination he looks only half alive: Lewis decides he is a ghostly knight temporarily returned from the dead to fulfill his fated role in a difficult quest.

"Thank you for being here. As you know, Mr. Drescher passed away suddenly just over a week ago. Being partners in the firm, you are all aware of the two-tiered partnership model that Mr. Drescher employed to structure the firm. Each of you holds equity, but Mr. Drescher held the majority and controlling class of shares. Two months before his death, Mr. Drescher reached an agreement with us to prepare his controlling shares in the firm for sale."

Lewis feels the oxygen go out of the room. Everyone seems to collapse inwardly in place. The ghostly crusading lawyer with the pale skin continues. "In preparation for the sale, which I feel obligated to inform you is imminent, we must ensure the firm is in as strong a position as possible. That is why we are asking everyone to immediately stop spending any money and doing any work. Until the firm is sold, nobody is to have any further communication with anyone outside the firm, including with any clients, without approval from one of us," he says as he gestures to the four other lawyers or accountants with him. None of his colleagues nod or smile or look anyone in the eye. "We will keep you fully informed as things progress. Any questions?"

Only Randall raises his hand: "What do we tell clients about not being able to do any work, and second, how long do we expect it will take to sell the controlling Drescher shares of the company?"

"And you are?" the pale crusading accountant/lawyer asks. Randall says his name, and the pale one nods and answers. "We will provide you with talking points tomorrow. As for the sale, we don't believe it will take more than two to three weeks, at the outside. We already have a very motivated buyer. You must have done good work." It is a half-hearted attempt at a compliment, but nobody at Drescher & Drescher is in the mood to accept it.

It is also at this meeting after Drescher's death that Lewis first hears more about the lawsuit that Drescher mentioned on the drive back from Halifax. The partners assume the meeting is over, but as they are about to stand up the pale crusader says, "Before we break today, there is one more thing." The room goes silent. "Some of you may have heard about *the lawsuit*." The partners cast sideways glances around the room at everyone else and try to guess who is in the know. Nobody reveals anything. Each partner assumes everyone else is in the inner circle. None of them realizes this the first any of them have ever heard of it, except for Lewis. Lewis looks down at his hands.

Mr. Crusader plows ahead. "Naturally, it is paramount that none of you speak publicly about *the lawsuit*. Any questions?"

It is, of course, Randall who speaks up. "What, if I may ask, is the lawsuit in regards to?" Randall knows better — he attended an expensive private school where he learned proper grammar in a real English class rather than simply exploring his feelings and getting comfortable with self-expression in "Language Arts" — but he has no shame today about ending his sentence with a preposition. He is doing it on purpose. He knows that many lawyers abhor technically poor grammar. It affects something in their souls. "I haven't heard anything about this *alleged* lawsuit. Has anyone else?" Randall looks around the room. They all shake their heads, but just barely. Nobody wants to stand out. Lewis stares at the floor.

"Very well then," the crusading lawyer says, "we will bring you up to speed, but I must first remind everyone of the absolute sensitivity and strictly confidential nature of this matter." Pause. Quick scan around the room. "Does everyone agree to be firmly bound by the rules of strict confidentiality?" It sounds to Lewis like a sadomasochistic romance. Tentative nods around the room. "Okay. I'd like to ask Michael Milkman to say a few words. Michael is a senior litigator with Parson Levine, where he leads their national intellectual property practice. He is based out of Toronto but will be spending a significant portion of his time in Saint John while preparing our defence."

Milkman stands up and moves without hurry to the front of the room. His Zegna suit moves well with him. He is dark and thin and gracefully bears a resemblance to a young, taller Al Pacino. He gives you the sense that he is aware of the resemblance but is too grounded to play it up. Although he does absolutely nothing to play it down either. He waits until he is firmly planted on his two feet at the front of the room, but even then he doesn't start to speak right away.

As all the architects struggle not to look at each other, Milkman looks at each one in turn. Mr. Ghostly Crusader has to slide his chair over to the side and turn it around so he doesn't have his back to him. Milkman gives everyone a knowing smile, as if they are all the honourable members of a jury he has personally selected. He chooses to start off with a rhetorical question. You can see it in his eyes. He has attended the lecture in which budding lawyers are instructed never to ask a question to which they don't already know the answer.

"Would anyone in the room be familiar with Maurits Abercrom?" Michael Milkman might look like Al Pacino, but he doesn't sound like him. No trace of an Italian accent. Well-modulated vowels. He sounds Toronto.

There is only silence at first. Every architect has heard of Abercrom, and anyone graduating from architecture school in the last twenty years has studied his work and read his essays, but nobody wants to acknowledge the condescension implicit in the question. Milkman waits, his smile staying fresh. Finally, Randall breaks the silence.

"Of course we have. One of the most famous architects in the U.S. Designs skyscrapers and expensive homes." Good old Randall.

Sentence fragments deliberately spoken.

Abercrom is firmly in the stratosphere of those architects, like Frank Lloyd Wright, who are known equally for the buildings they design for clients and the homes they design for themselves. Open Windows is the name Abercrom bestowed upon his beachfront mansion on Long Island. The windows alone had cost a million. There were one hundred of them, and Abercrom used a special glass pioneered by NASA that created the illusion of having no windowpane at all. The glass was specially designed to protect against the bleaching effects of the sun because Abercrom is also a renowned collector of Renaissance and late twentieth century art. Abercrom is not a wacko. He doesn't live in his parents' basement. Lewis is paying close attention now.

"Exactly. I think the best word to describe him is *celebrated*. He is one of the wealthiest and most successful architects in the world." Dramatic pause. It appears that Michael Milkman can't turn off his mode of jury address. Subtle reduction in volume. "Mr. Abercrom has very recently undertaken legal action against Drescher & Drescher, alleging that Mr. Drescher misappropriated one of his designs. Or, in simple terms, he is alleging copyright infringement." Milkman pauses to subtly enjoy the effect of his words on the room. "The plaintiff claims he shared this design casually in conversation with Mr. Drescher over lunch when they both happened to be vacationing at the Fairmont Southampton in Bermuda. The two men were exchanging views on how to represent natural forms in concrete. To illustrate a point he was making, Mr. Abercrom claims he drew a design on a piece of Fairmont Southampton stationery. Mr. Abercrom is alleging that Mr. Drescher illegally claimed this design as his own and infringed on Mr. Abercrom's copyright by using the design for the new Macdonald Arts and Culture Building in Halifax."

Lewis isn't quite sure if he hears a collective gasp around the room or if it is just his sharp intake of breath. Even though only Drescher and Lewis worked on the design, all the partners feel responsible by proximity for the firm's latest award-winning building. A stunning design of red sedimentary rock, molded concrete, blue slate, and glass, MAC was designed to represent waves coming ashore. It has already been compared to the iconic concrete interlocking shells of the Sydney Opera House, but not in a derivative way. It stands on its own. It was one of Drescher's favourite designs. Nobody says anything.

Milkman remains standing but lays down the law. In addition to reporting to the lawyers/accountants any and all incoming calls from clients, and no longer working on any projects or proactively speaking to any clients without Milkman's written permission, nobody is allowed to speak or make any other communications, written or otherwise, about Drescher.

When asked why, all Milkman will say is that it's privileged information and could negatively impact the lawsuit, the very future of Drescher & Drescher as a firm, and by extension each of their personal futures as well. "And of course, any of you who worked on the MAC Building are now under a strict preservation order for any and all documentation related to the design. This includes emails, blueprints, meeting minutes, etc. You must retain everything." Everyone studiously avoids making eye contact with Lewis. Along with Drescher, Lewis is the only member of the firm who would have worked on the design.

The pale crusader now feels obliged to stand in order to bring the meeting to a satisfactory close. "Well, then," he says, and in a low voice befitting his status as a ghost in Lewis's imagination, he concludes with, "That is all for today."

Within minutes of exiting the meeting, the partners sound like pre-adolescents whispering about their favourite villain from the Harry Potter books or observant Jews conferring about their loved and hated Old Testament G-d whose name they cannot speak aloud. All they can talk about for the next two days is the possibility that "He who shall not be named" could be an intellectual thief, a liar, and a blackguard. A fraud. An intellectual property felon. The firm quickly breaks into two camps. The first will not even entertain the thought that the Leon Drescher they knew could have stolen another architect's design. Impossible, they say. Would never happen. Not even in anyone's dreams. It violates every principle of the universe they hold dear.

The second camp, however, in hushed conversations in the corners of the office or the washroom, will softly moot it among the realm of possibility. "You can never really know someone," they say gently to each other.

For his part, Lewis is almost certain that Drescher never would have stolen another architect's design. Aside from his disdain for speed limits, Drescher was one of the most ethical men that Lewis has ever known. Besides, even if he wasn't, he never would have had to steal an idea. He always had the best ones himself. But in a small, rational part of Lewis's brain that he struggles valiantly to ignore, he begins to doubt, and that is because he remembers how the MAC design came about.

EXACTLY TWO WEEKS after that first meeting with the lawyers, the managing shares of the firm are sold to a global architectural holding company based in London, and a new managing partner is installed. In one of the very early days of the new ownership, Lewis walks into the lunchroom and sees the back of a man he doesn't recognize, slightly bent over, looking for something in the fridge. Lewis assumes this stranger is from outside the firm, visiting the office for a meeting.

The man must have heard Lewis enter the kitchen because he starts speaking but doesn't turn around: "Is there any milk? I can't seem to find any milk." The accent is high Eton-Cambridge. Silky. Posh. Based on Lewis's view of his back, the man is tall with the straightest and broadest shoulders Lewis has ever seen tucked into a light blue Hugo Boss suit, his long blond hair spilling over his collar.

Lewis walks over to the counter and opens the second, smaller fridge. "Here you go."

The stranger stands up and somehow without managing to make eye contact he accepts the milk that Lewis offers with a perfunctory, "Thank you." But Lewis notices that the man's bluish green eyes are disconcertingly the colour of Lake Louise, which Lewis saw eight years earlier on a trip west with Laura and the one child they had then.

Lewis doesn't know it at the time, but this is his first introduction to Edward Montcalm, the new managing partner. When Lewis is formally introduced to Montcalm the following day, he can't help comparing Montcalm's appearance to that of his predecessor. Drescher was tall and thin. He wore his silver hair short and neatly parted on the side. Montcalm is tall and big and blond, his long hair combed straight back and tousled.

4

IT DOESN'T TAKE Montcalm long to remodel Drescher's office. In less than two weeks it is done. The wide pine floorboards are covered with slate and Persian rugs, the landscapes and portraits by Canadian artists replaced by American abstracts that Lewis's mother, Miranda, would have hated, the old, modest mahogany desk with its scarred and ink-stained surface on which Drescher sketched a thousand designs shipped out in favour of a gleaming ebony ode to European machismo.

On his first time in the updated office, as he looks around, Lewis can't help thinking of his mother, and a smile he is only half aware of slowly illuminates his face. Miranda would have called Montcalm a *philistine*. And she would have dragged out the vowels. A philistine, for Miranda, was the worst insult she could bestow on another human being. At its core it meant someone who cared more about money than art. But in Miranda's eyes the word denoted several other specific failings. These included hanging print copies of boringly famous paintings instead of original art on the walls of one's home or, even worse, choosing art to match the colour of the walls or furniture. Lewis is not as judgmental as his mother, but he does have strong opinions in his chosen profession.

Take one of modern residential architecture's true abominations: the split-level house, which ruled in the 1950s and 1960s as a popularization and bastardization of a Frank Lloyd Wright concept of adapting the house to the land and further dividing the parts of a home where people lived and slept. The split-level is the absolute nadir of modern architectural taste as far as Lewis is concerned, as well as his favourite symbol of the modern world's solipsism and materialism. Lewis cannot enter a split-level dwelling without feeling dizzy and disoriented, without experiencing an existential sense of mental nausea. It violates thousands of years of architectural principles and designs to enter a home and be welcomed not by an open space but by an impossibly small landing leading upwards and downwards at the same time. The split-level dwelling is the physical world's manifestation of a split personality, an architectural limbo, neither heaven nor hell, where the soul stops, startled. Lewis will never admit it to anyone, not even Laura, but he can't, on some level that goes deeper than any principle he can ever consciously articulate, ever be truly friends with anyone who lives in a split-level home. The modern split-level is a highly visible symptom of a breakdown in the culture. It is a repudiation of the past and the idea of a well-ordered mind. It is an assault on the beauty of space.

Montcalm also changes the location of his desk from the corner to in front of the window that you immediately face when you enter the office. In the late afternoon, when the sun is low, you are at a distinct disadvantage, staring into the perfect silhouette of Montcalm's face while you struggle to keep your eyes from watering. Drescher used his desk to work, but whenever he was meeting with anyone they sat down together at the round table in the other corner near the window. The table was large enough to comfortably seat six, but more than ten often crowded around to discuss new designs or opportunities. Drescher jokingly referred to these gatherings as High Councils of the Knights of the Round Table, and Lewis appreciated the mythological allusion with a boyish enthusiasm. After Montcalm's office makeover, the round table disappears. Montcalm prefers to sit behind his desk, and Lewis thinks of it as the non-burning version of the fire one of the medieval popes kept flaming between himself and all visitors during outbreaks of the plague.

Drescher's battered floor-to-ceiling bookcase with its collection of architecture classics, novels, poetry collections, and history books — many first and signed editions — is consigned to an auctioneer and rare book dealer to fetch the best possible price. In its place, Montcalm has a shelf installed on the windowsill behind his office, containing less than fifteen books. On that first visit to Montcalm's remodelled office, Lewis notes with some perverse sense of satisfaction that only two of the volumes are about architecture. The others are the various interchangeable heady gospels of the modern executive, promising speedy enlightenment under such titles as *Leading by Example* or *Leading in Times of Change* or *Fundamentals of Finance for Architects*, *The Secrets of Managing Time*, *The World Is Five Dimensional*, *The Power of Integrity in Business*, and so on. Some books are structured around interviews, many employ fables to make their point, and some unabashedly surf the latest trends, like crowd-sourcing and social media, as if media were never social before. Lewis thinks of Stalin erasing Lenin from the history books, toppling his statue in town squares. Within a few weeks, it is as if Drescher never existed at the firm that still bears his name.

The second sign of Drescher's existence to disappear, after the redesign of his office, is the collection of architectural models of his favourite designs: temples to business, the arts, academia, and sports. Suddenly they are gone. Perhaps the most jarring change of all concerns the removal of any trace of Drescher from the firm's lobby. Drescher filled the lobby with small sculptures of animals, mostly Inuit carvings that he bought himself on trips to the North; a specially commissioned, lavishly illustrated picture book of the firm's most celebrated buildings; and a white and green marble chess set on the coffee table. These icons disappear, along with the black and white photos of Drescher with various clients. These photos are higher-end versions of the photos of movie stars, musicians, and athletes that used to grace the neighbourhood delis in downtown Montreal and New York City. Drescher's photographs are quickly replaced by a nearly poster-sized photo of Montcalm playing soccer and a bronze soccer ball mounted on a massive pedestal. The bronze sphere is a trophy from an amateur tournament Montcalm once played in, but he had the oak pedestal custom designed to display it.

Montcalm is crazy for soccer, or "football" as he calls it, as it doesn't take long for the partners at Drescher & Drescher to discover. The second clue to Montcalm's obsession with soccer, after the appearance of the soccer action photo and the bronze soccer ball, is that Montcalm wears soccer jerseys to the office on Casual Day Fridays. Drescher always wore a Harry Rosen bespoke suit, but in one of his few nods to sartorial modernity he loosened up enough on Fridays to remove his tie.

The third clue is the big-screen TV that Montcalm installs in the waiting area outside his office. Ostensibly it is to show new designs and provide a continuous loop of virtual architectural tours of the world's great buildings to keep everyone, partners or clients, perpetually inspired by the world of architectural possibilities that exist outside Atlantic Canada. However, the partners begin to realize the TV is increasingly tuned to international soccer matches. Montcalm pops out of his office to get a coffee and then lingers for a while in front of the screen on his way back. In the beginning he stands and watches, but after his first week in the role he is taking the time to sit.

There is a fourth clue, in case anyone misses the fact Montcalm really likes soccer. In fact, Montcalm thinks soccer is not just a personal pursuit or a mere — albeit insanely popular and global — sport. Montcalm believes soccer holds extra meaning as an all-encompassing metaphor for life and business. The fourth clue is the series of soccer matches that Montcalm's assistant, Lucie, begins to organize for partners and their families on Saturday mornings. Lucie is from Paris, and Montcalm imported her the week after he gave Drescher's long-time assistant, Janet, her walking papers.

The firm's partner soccer matches are held at one of the local fields in Rothesay or Quispamsis, and Montcalm always has an ample supply of food and drinks and a special game organized for the children while their fathers embarrass themselves on the "football" field to various degrees. One or two of the partners played soccer or another team sport in high school or university, but the rest of them are either non-athletes or coordination-challenged devotees of individual sports. Morris Kanofsky, the firm's director of human resources, has no doubt explained to Montcalm that he can't force his partners to take to the soccer pitch, and Montcalm takes great pains to explain his approach with a self-deprecating smile at partner meetings: "Our firm soccer matches are completely voluntary —" dramatic pause "— but I expect one hundred percent participation."

Lewis actually likes soccer. He thinks it a relatively non-violent sport with some grace and non-exclusionary in an economic sense in that it requires almost no equipment. But as a matter of principle and out of some loyalty to Drescher, Lewis refuses to participate in any of Montcalm's organized soccer matches. Drescher was not just the managing partner but the majority and controlling shareholder in the firm. Although he personally had many and varied personal interests, ranging from hiking to art collecting to classical music to amateur race car driving, Lewis admires the fact that Drescher never — not once, not ever — imposed his own personal interests on his partners and associate architects as if he were the resident lord of the manor.

Lewis comes up with various excuses to miss the soccer games (or are they *matches*?) including scheduled children's activities and helping Laura with chores around the house. Lewis even begins to seriously consider joining the Saint John synagogue, which stubbornly persists in the face of a tiny and declining local Jewish community, and attending religiously so he would have an airtight alibi on Saturday mornings.

The soccer games on their own are unsettling for Lewis, but even more disturbing to him is how some of the partners, men whom Lewis always respected, who never in their entire professional lives expressed any interest in soccer — in fact, some made condescending comparisons of the sport to North American football — now find ways to work the sport into their water cooler conversations or meetings with Montcalm. Within a month, the majority of the partners at Drescher & Drescher have become red-blooded, faux-European soccer aficionados. Where once they argued the merits of postmodernism over neomodernism, Lewis's fellow partners now debate with the same egghead gusto the strengths and weaknesses of a particular striker or the strategic merits of the Italian versus the German approach to the game.

The partners develop an interest in soccer as rapidly as they abandon Drescher's trademark fusion of modernism and post-modernism for the neofuturist architectural style that Montcalm champions. In his first meeting with the partners, almost in the same breath where he extolls the virtues of soccer, Montcalm cites Robert Venturi's putdown of fellow architect Mies van der Rohe's modernist philosophy — to "Less is more" Venturi retorted "Less is a bore" — before offering his own attempted contribution to architectural soundbites: "Po-mo? Slo-mo. The future is hu-mo." As in, neofuturism puts people back in the centre of things. But although none of the partners believes Montcalm's made-up abbreviated words, they are all too cowed to say anything. So they nod appreciatively whenever he speaks. Men who for their entire professional lives lived and breathed Drescher's heady architectural brand of strange bedfellows — the austere aesthetic of modernism married to the expressive freedom of postmodernism — now turn their backs on all of it like an outmoded suit, awkward with wide lapels or baggy pants.

However, the pièce de résistance, and the fifth and final clue that Montcalm is soccer mad, is the picture of himself playing the game that he carries everywhere with him saved on his BlackBerry. At first he shows it to only the most senior partners. But after a couple of months, everyone in the office has seen it, from the junior associates to the secretaries to even a young summer student who always dreamed of interning at Drescher & Drescher ever since he drafted his first line drawing of his local school.

The Photo, as it comes to be known, shows Montcalm flying down the midfield, gorgeous golden hair trailing behind him, back-lit with the sun so that he looks like the athletic version of one of those Renaissance portraits of Saint Francis of Assisi. His arms are pumping and his right leg outstretched. He has just scored what

Montcalm never hesitates to tell whomever he is showing the photo to was the game's winning goal.

Everyone carries photos with them, but the kicker for Lewis, pardon the pun, is that Montcalm is shirtless in *The Photo*, his chest the perfect chest of a younger man, muscled and hard, ridiculously defined, his biceps bulging, his torso mysteriously hairless, like the picture of the hero on the cover of a Harlequin romance.

"Not bad for forty-seven," Montcalm will say modestly as he hands the BlackBerry to whomever his victim of the day is, and that person will politely murmur their assent.

When one of the senior partners first tells Lewis about being shown *The Photo*, he says half jokingly, half not: "You know, Lewis, I always hoped to be sexually harassed at the office; I just never expected it would be by another man."

After Lewis makes a sarcastic remark to one of the other partners, a man whom Lewis has always considered a friend at work, about the firm's sudden interest in soccer, the other partner doesn't even bother to be diplomatic in his reply or look up while he shakes sugar into his coffee. "Oh, come on, Lewis, you might as well get with the program. Drescher's dead. He's never coming back."

When Lewis is first shown *The Photo*, he doesn't know what to say. Perhaps he smiles politely. He isn't quite sure what his face is projecting because seeing Montcalm half-naked reminds him of his mother. It's not that they look anything alike. It's just that both seem to exhibit the same attitude to nudity.

AS A CHILD, Lewis was very conscious that Miranda was not only an occasional model for some of her artist friends, like the increasingly famous and flamboyant Montreal painter André Johnson, but was an artist in her own right. Miranda didn't sell or exhibit her work, but she was constantly drawing or painting. Memorably for the young Lewis, Miranda always brought him along for the adventure. Chez Nick was her favourite neighbourhood café, where she would drink coffee all morning and draw the patrons: reading their newspapers, sipping their coffees, nibbling their pastries, chatting with their friends.

Most of Miranda's subjects never realized they were the focus of her drawing. But occasionally someone, usually sitting alone, reading no book or newspaper, talking to no one, thinking perhaps of nothing, would notice the blond, brightly dressed woman — peasant skirt, long asymmetrical earrings, scarf or shawl, bangles on wrists — sitting by one of the windows where the light was good.

"Never underestimate the importance of light, Lewis," Miranda would whisper as she touched her pencils or charcoal to the page. "It is almost everything." Miranda didn't just observe her subjects but stared at them with a child's intensity, pencil or charcoal in hand, attempting to capture not their physical likenesses — that would be too boring — but their character, if not their souls, within the two-dimensional space of her sketchbook.

Every so often, one of Miranda's non-consenting models, perhaps unusually sensitive, or depressed, or simply irritable, would get up from their table, taking a break from their latte or *pain au chocolat*, shamble over to Miranda, and, while Lewis looked on, mesmerized, interrupt his mother's concentration and ask her to please desist. "*Arrêtez, s'il vous plaît.*" Or, "Please, can't you see I am trying to eat, to relax." Or, "*Je ne veux pas qu'une femme me dessine. S'il vous plaît,*" emphatically said, with perhaps a hand gesture in case Miranda still didn't get it.

In most of these instances, when she was asked, Miranda would stop. But sometimes she was obstinate and would tell her subject that *she* wouldn't mind if someone was drawing her, that it was a free country and if they didn't like it they could leave, couldn't they. And sometimes the person would retreat sadly to their table and perhaps shift position so they were facing the other way and Miranda would have to give up; other times they would just pay their bill and leave.

One day, a particularly stubborn older man asked Miranda to please desist from drawing him. When she refused, he returned to his seat after picking up a napkin from another table. He sat down, pulled a black and gold Mont Blanc fountain pen out of his tailored tweed jacket, and began to draw Miranda, staring at her with a gaze so bold it nearly forced her to turn away. When it was time to leave, this man dropped his work of art on the table at which Miranda and Lewis sat with a flourish, and with his name, Louis St. Pierre, in expressive calligraphy at the bottom. The man had quickly drawn a caricature of a witch. Miranda's features were recognizable but exaggerated, with enlarged eyes and dilated pupils that leapt off the page. Miranda turned the napkin around so she could see the drawing right side up and said, partly to herself, partly for Lewis's benefit, "Not bad, not bad. He has talent." And she resumed her sketching, this time of someone else.

Miranda liked to draw patrons in Nick's café, and she painted her family at home, but when she wasn't doing either she was one of those painters who had a single-minded devotion to a particular subject, the way some artists become famous for painting only dead fish on silver platters, or faceless swimmers in green water, or antique cars, or the same breast-like mountains and vaginal lakes over and over again. In Miranda's case, her preferred subject was herself. And to Lewis's childhood chagrin, Miranda liked to paint herself naked. Always naked, with never the barest suggestion of clothing on the canvas: not a hat, sock, shoes, or handkerchief. "Without artifice," as Miranda put it. "Only the truth." And never once in the same pose, and never with the same facial expression.

Lewis once asked Miranda why she looked different in each painting. He was only thinking about her face because that was all he tried to notice, looking upwards to the ceiling in each painting so he could see only her face and not her naked body. Miranda replied that each face represented a different side of her personality. "The intellectual. The artist. The mother. The daughter. The wife. The sister. The citizen. The consumer. The Jewess. The liberated woman. The slave to the patriarchy."

Once, when Lewis was fourteen, his friend John was visiting and John took a left turn instead of a right on his way to the upstairs bathroom. Fifteen minutes later, John wandered back down to the kitchen, where Lewis had finished most of the cookies they had been eating, with a glazed and envious look in his eyes. Lewis was worried. He thought John had experienced a terrible stomach upset and was not able to eat any more cookies.

"Lewis, why didn't you ever tell me?"

"Tell you what?"

"Yeah, right. Your dad has the most amazing room. The one full of paintings of naked women. Women standing up, sitting down. Legs crossed, legs open. Turning around. Looking at you. Looking away from you. Looking happy. Looking sad. Looking smart. Looking not. You should charge admission."

Lewis felt sick. The cookie tasted like sand. He looked down at the floor. "Those are paintings of my mother. By my mother."

John's expression was blank for a moment. "Oh." Then he smiled. Judging from the way his face was illuminated, the thought didn't seem to faze John at all.

5

"LEWIS, DID YOU ever work with Mr. Drescher on the Macdonald Arts and Culture Building?"

Lewis's meeting with Michael Milkman has been scheduled for a week, and M&M knows what Lewis is going to say. To cheer up Lewis ahead of his interview, Randall made some inquiries and filled Lewis in on Michael Milkman's nickname on the legal circuit. "He's known, among both defenders and prosecutors and even some judges, as 'M&M.' After the candy. The ones with peanuts. He's hard on the outside and equally hard on the inside."

Lewis can't get the mental image of a package of M&Ms out of his head as he answers the question: "Yes, I did."

"And during that time, did you ever sense that Mr. Drescher might have had access to a previously existing — that is, copyright infringed — design?"

"No, I did not."

"Is there anything else you would like to add that might shed some light on this situation?"

"No."

"I thought you should be aware that legal counsel for Mr. Abercrom has decided to name you in the lawsuit on the assumption — logical enough, it seems to me — that as Mr. Drescher's creative partner you would have collaborated fully with Mr. Drescher on this design. That is so, isn't it? You worked with Mr. Drescher on the MAC Building." These are not questions. The answers are already known.

Lewis wants to say that while he enhanced the design later, it was Drescher who came up with the essential design. But out of loyalty to Drescher he answers the question narrowly. "Yes. That is true."

"And you are confident that the design was original."

"Yes."

LEWIS'S DEFAULT PUBLIC position is to defend Drescher's integrity against all doubters, who are increasing in number by the day. But inwardly Lewis is not so certain. The genesis of the MAC design was not straightforward.

Drescher and Lewis met three times with Darren and Margaret Macdonald. Drescher and Lewis knew exactly what their client intended the building to be used for — a multi-purpose space for the performing arts and a place to train young people to participate in them — and where the building was to be located: on an undeveloped parcel of land on the waterfront on the edge of downtown Halifax, near Point Pleasant Park. And both were clear on the extent of seventy-year-old family patriarch Darren Macdonald's twin personal ambitions: to pay tribute to his wife's early career as a ballet dancer and to put his family's stamp on the city and province where they had made their fortune in transportation, construction, and latterly fish farming.

But despite Darren Macdonald's passion and his clarity of

purpose, neither Drescher nor Lewis could generate a design. For once, inspiration deserted them. They each came up with a few half-hearted ideas that they embarrassedly shared with the other over coffee at Starbucks, but both agreed they weren't hitting the mark. Feeling frustrated and seeking to break out of this rare creative slump, Drescher decamped to his favourite hotel, the Fairmont Southampton in Bermuda, for a week of R&R and hopefully inspiration by the pool.

Lewis didn't receive a single email from Drescher during the whole time he was away, which was highly unusual. But when Drescher returned, looking tanned, fit, and well-rested, he called Lewis into his office first thing on Monday and articulated in less than two minutes the essential elements of what would become the award-winning design for MAC: a soaring building shaped to resemble powerful waves breaking against a shoreline cliff.

Lewis immediately recognized the genius behind the concept and added several modifications — what he modestly called "details" — that took the design to new heights. It was Lewis's idea to use jagged sheets of blue slate set against the concrete mass to evoke the ocean, and to incorporate the red sedimentary conglomerate rock widely found on the Maritime coast to symbolize the cliffs. Various architectural juries around the world praised the way the two men paid tribute to the natural beauty of the Nova Scotia coastline. Local newspapers boasted how Drescher & Drescher had created a new natural wonder for perennially insecure East Coasters to call their own. And Darren Macdonald was effusive in his praise and gratitude. The ribbon wasn't cut before the referrals started pouring in.

TWO DAYS AFTER Lewis's laconic meeting with "M&M," Montcalm asks Lewis to come to his office. Montcalm sits behind his desk, looking both patient and fluid, the default demeanour of the athlete at rest. As usual, he doesn't look Lewis in the eye but appears to stare both inwardly and past him, as if Lewis is an intrusion to his grand thoughts that have to be managed like everything else in his life: his career, his soccer, no doubt his wives. Montcalm is on his third, if Lewis has heard correctly.

"Lewis," Montcalm begins, "thank you for coming. I want to speak with you about your standing at the firm." Montcalm calls most of the other partners by their last names, but he insists on calling Lewis by his first. He always makes it sound aggressively formal.

"Given the latest developments in the lawsuit alleging copyright infringement, in which, as you know, you are now named equally as a plaintiff along with Drescher; and given that Drescher is dead and you are still alive" — Montcalm somehow manages in his beautiful accent to make this last observation appear unfortunate — "we must take some new actions to protect the legal position of the firm." Pause. "It is with some degree of sadness, therefore, that we must ask you to step away from all commissions you were working on with Drescher." Montcalm's placid expression indicates that this decision saddens him not in the least. As usual, his beautiful Lake Louise eyes are focused on a point past Lewis, at the upper corner of the wall.

Lewis nods. Those commissions happen to be the only ones he was working on. He and Drescher were a team. Drescher brought in the clients and Lewis worked with him on their designs. Since Drescher's death, Lewis has had no new commissions.

"And until the lawsuit is resolved, you mustn't speak about it or even about any of your work with Drescher with anyone." What, then, will Lewis talk about? His work with Drescher was his life. But there is more. "Nor, I am afraid, will you be able to take on any new work until the legal matters are resolved." Montcalm continues to speak to the wall. "We would really like you to continue with the firm. And we'll take care of you. But you must appreciate our position."

Lewis swallows. He observes the physical existence of his intestines. Now he too is not looking directly at the other human being in front of him. He worries his voice will carry too much emotion. "What will I do?"

"I'm not sure yet. You won't have to come into the office during this time. You can if you want, naturally, but you don't have to. You can take as much time as you like, as long as you don't work on any Drescher & Drescher projects."

"How long until the legal action is resolved?"

"Well, nobody really knows. But Milkman estimates two to three years is a likely scenario." Lewis thinks he detects the slightest hint of amusement behind Montcalm's mountain lake eyes, but then it passes and he wears an expression of solicitude on his perfect face as he continues to gaze beyond Lewis.

This is the first time Lewis has ever found himself in any sort of legal predicament. Just like someone with a doctor in the family can easily call for free medical advice, most people in Lewis's position would call their father. Mordecai is a lawyer. But Mordecai is a different kind of lawyer, and Lewis doesn't want Mordecai's help, so he holds back.

BY THE TIME Mordecai was trying to get into McGill, in 1948, he only had to do a bit better than most other applicants, including the many returning veterans. He didn't have to earn a grade average ten percent higher than non-Jewish students because by then the Holocaust had made McGill's admissions quota for Jewish students seem quaint and impolite. Mordecai graduated top of his class and was accepted into McGill's law school, where he decisively took the gold medal.

But when Mordecai graduated with a law degree in 1955, in a Quebec still ruled by Duplessis, he found that when it came to finding an articling position at one of the big establishment firms in Montreal, a respectable British-sounding name only went so far. His McGill law degree and the name "Morton" was good enough on paper to get him interviews with some of the English, Irish, Scottish, and even the newer French firms. But neither academic pedigree nor surname were sufficient once Mordecai showed up in person with his olive skin, wavy black hair, very un-Anglo-Saxon eyes, and the slightest trace of an Eastern European accent that somehow the five-year-old immigrant had never managed to completely lose. Keen interest in his credentials quickly turned tepid in person.

There was, however, one prestigious law firm that enthusiastically looked past Mordecai's stubborn Jewishness, or perhaps never saw it in the first place. Abbatelli Gatti Neroni was a firm of loud-speaking, hand-waving, irreverent Italians where Mordecai felt right at home from the moment he walked through the door for his first interview. Admittedly, all the partners were Catholics, but in other, more important, aspects they were the same as him. The lawyers at AGN didn't fit the Anglo-Saxon legal mould. They weren't embarrassed by other men who talked loudly, swore in meetings, and gave each other hugs and even on occasion kisses on both cheeks.

Six months later, by the time the partners trusted Mordecai enough to introduce him to the firm's main clients, Mordecai felt like he was back among family. AGN started to fill in for the Romanian *shtetl* that he would never forget, even though — or perhaps because — almost everyone in his family who stayed behind ended up being deported to an extermination camp or else had to strip, dig their own graves, and conveniently fall in after being shot. Around the same time that Hollywood super-agent Lew Wasserman was coining his aphorism about making it in a gentile world, "Dress British, think Yiddish," Mordecai Morton was making a good living, supporting his family, and succeeding beyond his wildest dreams by "Thinking Yiddish, dressing Wise Guy." Although, good team player and self-made man that he was, he would never admit it. Not even to his own flesh and blood.

Years later, one of Lewis's university classmates, the son of a celebrated Montreal Crown prosecutor, cornered him late one night at a McGill student ghetto party after too much cheap beer and asked him how Mordecai could have worked for decades as legal counsel for one of Montreal's most infamous organized crime families. Lewis spilled his beer, sputtered some half-hearted denial, and soon after left the party without saying goodbye to the host. But the question was all the worse because Lewis had always suspected it but never had the courage to ask. Nothing else had ever been off limits with Mordecai — no movies, books, or topics were ever inappropriate subjects of conversation — but somehow Lewis had always known never to ask too much about Mordecai's work.

It was only after Miranda's fourth suicide attempt that Lewis decided he had to fully understand his father. So, one day at the breakfast table, as the sun shone through the windows almost directly into Mordecai's eyes, Lewis asked him point-blank with the earnest rudeness of the young, "Dad, so is it true you work for the mob?"

Mordecai didn't reply at first. He didn't even look up at Lewis. He went on buttering his toast. For the first time in his life, Mordecai refused to answer one of Lewis's questions. But Mordecai's expression didn't change. He didn't look surprised. When he finally finished smearing the butter and looked across the marble-topped table, Mordecai studied Lewis the way he had often watched Miranda when he was visiting her in the hospital. "I have to leave for work now," was all he said.

When Lewis got home from class and Mordecai returned from work, they made supper together, which had become a habit during Miranda's last hospitalization. They didn't speak much that night. Mordecai didn't answer Lewis's question from the morning, and Lewis didn't re-ask it. But the next day, over breakfast, Lewis asked Mordecai again if he worked for the mob. Again, Lewis watched Mordecai's expression, which remained placid, and once more Mordecai refused to answer. This went on for three days.

On the fourth day Mordecai put down the toast he had been bringing to his lips and wagged his finger at Lewis, like Clinton before his speaking coach told him it looked aggressive and that he should instead hold his hand like a fist with a straight thumb. "*Alleged*, Lewis. *Alleged* crime families. Under the rule of law, everyone's entitled to the presumption of innocence, and not one member of the Family" — despite his protestations, Mordecai still capitalized the noun when he spoke — "was ever convicted of a crime. It's important to be precise in your language, even if you are studying to be an architect."

By the fourth day, Lewis had known what Mordecai's answer was going to be and had thought of his response. "Dad, we're taught Jews are supposed to be 'a light unto the Gentiles.' How do you square that with working for the mob?" At least Lewis was self-aware enough at the time to know how much he sounded like a moralistic undergraduate.

Mordecai took a quick bite of rapidly cooling toast, as if to fortify himself for this conversation with his son that he had put off for so long that he eventually came to believe he would never need to have it. "First of all, Lew, I don't work for the 'mob' as you so politely put it. I work for Mr. Tony and Mr. Massimo. The Messanas are successful businessmen and more importantly Canadian citizens and above all human beings: you can't reduce them to a pejorative label. Second of all, morality is important, don't get me wrong: it's essential to take care of your family and friends and generally be a good person."

Mordecai was now unconsciously brandishing his half-eaten piece of toast like a sword. "However, if you don't learn how to defend yourself and figure out who your friends are, you end up like the six million lights unto the gentiles who went up in smoke over Europe. Survival, Lew, trumps approval every time. Every time. Take Israel: Israel's in a constant state of war, and when you're at war, you don't always get to do the nicest things. It's not like the Boy Scouts or American football with referees. If Israel has to protect itself and gets criticized by dictators in a few barbaric cesspools playacting at being civilized countries, so be it. It's better than the alternative, which for Israel is to put its hands behind its back, get the shit kicked out of it, and then have a few sensitive, educated, intellectual souls write about how sad it is that another million Jews just got wiped off the face of the map." Lewis didn't have any more questions, but Mordecai still pre-empted them when he stood up and said, "I've got to go to work now."

Mordecai would never admit it, not even to his own *mischpocheh*, his flesh and blood, because to do so would acknowledge what he had been doing in the first place. But in the year before Lewis started university, several years before Mordecai would retire to long lazy days of pinochle and leisurely workouts down the hill at the Westmount YMCA interspersed with bouts of loud, passionate conversation with the other oldsters about hockey, politics, business, and the various ailments and desires of old men, Mordecai had embarked upon his greatest professional goal, what he called only in the supreme privacy of his own mind his legal magnum opus.

By the time Lewis graduated as an architect, Mordecai would have masterminded, like a modern Moses who got to enter the land of milk and honey, the Messana family's flawless social migration from Montreal mobsters to well-respected pillars of the community. Within the time it took someone to earn two university degrees, the Messanas would be transformed from outlaws into owners of legitimate businesses, philanthropists, über-honourable men with style and gravitas whose wives served on the boards of McGill and the Montreal Children's Hospital and whose sons and daughters studied diligently to become doctors, lawyers, and MBAS, and who married well and who raised children with whom they could speak freely about how they earned their money. In the space of eight years, Mordecai would single-handedly accomplish what it had taken armies of lawyers to do for other famous Montreal families. The achievement would become Mordecai's most enduring, if by necessity unspoken and unshared, source of professional pride.

But in Lewis's young and uncompromising eyes, not only was his father firmly outside the pale of twentieth-century Canadian morality, and not only was he failing a basic principle of human relations by letting Lewis hear first about his secret life from a stranger, most damningly Mordecai had not been able to prevent Miranda from sinking into a fourth and final suicidal depression.

6

UP UNTIL DRESCHER'S death, Lewis always assumed he would retire from Drescher & Drescher somewhere around the age of seventy. Lewis didn't found the firm — Drescher had done that twenty-five years ago right out of Dalhousie's architecture school — but Lewis took to it immediately. It became a second home. Even Drescher's choice of name for the firm meant something to Lewis. There was never another Drescher — no brother, father, or son — but Drescher liked the sound and the look of the doubling of his name separated by the ampersand. It sounded more traditional and substantial. It inspired confidence in clients. And in Lewis.

In his orderly projection of the future, Lewis would go out on his own terms with a blowout retirement party, a substantial going-away gift, tear-inducing toasts, and witty and poignant anecdotes recounted by his comrades in arms, his partners in making the world a more beautiful and orderly place. Retiring at sixty-five was for sissies and people who hated their jobs. And retiring earlier, say fifty-five, was for fools. Of course, even after retirement Lewis would never entirely withdraw from the business of the firm:

he would be given a spacious and distinguished office to which he would return two or three times a week to make calls, write emails, draw up provisional designs on napkins, and generally be available to mentor the younger staff.

Lewis sometimes thought he would continue working full-time indefinitely and end up happily like Richard (Dick) Harrison, who, following his "retirement" at seventy-five, had come in to the office four days a week until he was ninety-two, only to drop dead one day of a heart attack behind his drafting desk as he was working on a commission for a client. That thought was comforting to Lewis, far superior to the stories he heard every week about poor schmucks who hated their jobs but who single-mindedly worked their whole lives in order to retire in their fifties, only to get the big C six months later and literally disappear before everyone's eyes with dizzying speed.

But after his conversation with Montcalm, Lewis turns his back on the firm and the life he has built for himself within its walls. He stops going into the office. He is too embarrassed about having nothing to do. Now with Drescher's death, an impending lawsuit, and a sentence of internal exile at the firm, Lewis has nothing to occupy his mind. He takes up walking by the river on Rothesay Road to relax. Sometimes with the family dog Rufus, a border collie with wise brown eyes, and other times on his own. And when Lewis isn't walking he is networking. He has gotten it into his mind that he has to find a position at another firm. So, although Lewis has never cultivated professional contacts outside the firm, he emails the handful of architects that he knows socially or has met at conferences and asks them out to lunch.

Alex Flandergast is the first to reply. His email is short and full of promise, like he is. Flandergast is soft and round and short and pinkish. He is always in good humour. Always ready with an anecdote or inoffensive joke. Flandergast is the principal of Eastern Architecture, a boutique architecture firm that builds commercial and residential buildings in Nova Scotia. Flandergast has close ties to much of the business elite in Halifax, mostly due to the good luck of having married a Simcoe, in his case one Jane Linda Marie Simcoe.

Mother and Father Simcoe still own Simcoe Department Store and have been fruitful in their domestic life as well as in business, having birthed ten children who all went on to become lawyers or doctors or accountants or engineers or entrepreneurs. Lewis got to know Flandergast when they were both hired at Drescher & Drescher out of A-school. After three years of apprenticeship, Flandergast went off, mostly at his entrepreneurial wife's urging, to found his own firm, while Lewis, ever the loyal soldier, stayed and ended up where he was now, in a vast professional no man's land.

After expressing the requisite, and perhaps even genuine, surprise at Lewis's carefully confided news that he may be looking to leave Drescher & Drescher, over lunch at Billy's Seafood Market, Flandergast chuckles politely and nods encouragingly. "Look, Lewis, I don't have anything open right now for someone of your seniority and calibre, but let's definitely stay in touch." It isn't until he's halfway through his delicious cedar plank salmon that Flandergast asks, without looking up from his plate, "So, what's this I hear about a lawsuit?" Flandergast must know that Lewis won't be able to comment, but he asks anyway. Miraculously, Maurits Abercrom's legal action hasn't yet hit the papers, but it's clearly the most open professional secret in town. Lewis loses much of his appetite as he mutters something about not being able to speak about the matter because it is before the courts. The rest of the lunch is gently forced. Flandergast offers to pay but

Lewis insists on taking care of the bill, seeing it as a sign of benevolence and optimism.

A LUNCH THE next day with Jeff Dolan, managing partner at another Saint John–based leading regional architectural firm, seems infinitely more promising. Lewis has known Dolan since his early years at Drescher & Drescher. They met at a cocktail party, hit it off, and stayed in touch over the years. Dolan is tall, lean, and athletic. He is also clever, confident, and always full of bright plans for the future. Unlike Lewis, Dolan sails and golfs. Lewis has never seen him without a tan or a witty retort. He is one of those men who always likes to tease and be teased. But a straight shooter, who always tells it like it is.

After the awkward lunch with Flandergast, Lewis doesn't quite know what he is supposed to say or how he is supposed to sound. Lewis decides he is expected to come across as sophisticated and indirect. He alludes to what is happening at Drescher & Drescher and how he is looking for "a change." He is considering "all his options." Does Dolan know of any "available opportunities"? Dolan obviously knows how the game is played because he jumps skillfully at the opening, asking Lewis if he has ever considered Dolan's firm.

Lewis, flattered, smiles and says the prospect of joining Dolan's firm would be "very interesting" and "worth another conversation."

For his part, Dolan is "very interested" in bringing Lewis on as another partner in the firm. "To be honest, Lewis, I've always thought you were under-appreciated at D&D. I've often thought it would be wonderful to work together."

Over coffees that same week, it is apparent that Dolan has big plans for Lewis: "Big buildings, big commissions." Lewis will come in as a "full partner." Dolan wants to grow the firm's commercial building business. He and Lewis spend time at various coffee shops plotting out everything. Dolan wants Lewis to take over a new client service group filled to bursting with bright young architects. Lewis will be their mentor. Teach them everything he knows. Dolan will continue to be the front man. Bring in the clients. It will be just like working at Drescher & Drescher. The two of them even talk through the range of investment Lewis will have to make to come on as a full partner. The money he expects to take out of Drescher & Drescher once he sells his partnership will cover it with a bit left over.

BECAUSE OF ALL these enthusiastic coffee chats, Lewis is surprised, in fact his very breath is taken away, when Dolan calls him one evening the following week to tell him that the very next day his firm will be filing for bankruptcy because of unpaid bills for some major work they have been doing in Florida. In an early casualty of the burgeoning American housing crisis, two major clients who had over-extended themselves were vaporized almost literally overnight, and thousands of miles away Dolan is left holding the bag.

There is no more firm. No new partner role for Lewis to run to.

Lewis closes his eyes. When he opens them seconds later, the world is still there. Lewis is still holding the phone. Dolan is still waiting for him to speak. Lewis is polite, and besides, he doesn't know what to say. Lewis feels too embarrassed to become angry because that would be an admission of how naive he has been. So instead he says all the right things to comfort Dolan, who has just seen the value of his retirement savings collapse like a house of cards.

Lewis sleeps terribly that night, if what he manages between waking up every hour can be called sleep. He has nothing better to do during the coming day, so he decides that after dropping off the kids at the bus he will go for a walk.

7

LEWIS'S ELDEST SON, Judah, has recently turned twelve. Grade seven. Just a year older than Lewis was when Miranda overdosed for the first time. Unlike Lewis, Judah is calm and rational and self-sufficient. He hardly ever asks for help or advice. He plays sports, has many friends, and does his homework — quite well, if school report cards and enthusiastic comments at parent-teacher interviews are to be believed. Very soon he will have to decide if he wants a bar mitzvah. Even though Laura never converted, Judah can be Jewish if he wants, at least in Reform Judaism. Judah certainly doesn't need Lewis to walk him down to the bus that takes him to junior high. But Lewis walks Alexandra down the hill every day, and Judah politely tags along. Lewis could stay home and let Judah take Alexandra, but he thinks walking a six-year-old child down to Rothesay Road is too large a responsibility to put on a twelve-year-old's shoulders, no matter how mature he is. And Lewis likes the short walk.

So far, less than two weeks into his life as an underemployed architect, neither Judah nor Alexandra are asking why Lewis is walking them to the bus every day and picking them up when they return from school. The boys — Judah and four-year-old Samuel whom Lewis drives to nursery school in the afternoons — are, or at least seem to be, oblivious. They go to school, play with their friends, read their books, play their games, and have their tea and conversations about the day with Laura when they come home from school without ever asking any questions or expressing any concerns about Lewis's client-less state. For them it is completely normal that their father is around the house more. They don't appear to have noticed Lewis's odd mixture of despondency and manic energy.

Perhaps as he stands on the brink of middle age Lewis is becoming adept at hiding his feelings — from his children at least — and putting on a stoic front, like a cowboy in a John Wayne movie or one of those cool heroes in action moves who is able to nonchalantly crack witty jokes as he is about to be thrown out of a helicopter or shot with a machine gun. But Lewis doesn't think so. His boys are simply confident and oblivious. Lewis both envies and pities their embryonic masculine insensitivity to their surroundings, the feelings of others, and the future.

He hopes the boys will easily carry on when he loses his architecture licence or goes to jail. The baby, Skye, will have to get to know him on prison visits. But Alexandra is another matter. She hasn't asked him anything yet, but she is starting to look at him differently, as if she knows something about him she is unwilling to publicly admit to. The other night when he went to tuck her in and kiss her goodnight she nodded sagely for no apparent reason. Lewis always thinks of her as at least fourteen years old because of her argumentative skills, sense of humour, and outsized personality. She is indomitable, and she both shames and inspires Lewis by the way she never gives up, never admits defeat, never shows fear in the face of punishment.

When she is caught sneaking chocolates Laura is saving for company or refuses to put on her warm coat to go outside, when she throws a fit in defiance of her mother — she has a soft spot for Lewis and rarely gets angry with him — and when Laura calls in Lewis and when he has to reluctantly punish her by sending her to her room or taking away a favoured doll or video, Alexandra never backs down or whimpers or offers an abject apology and pleads for a reduced sentence. She never appeals to Lewis's pity or affection. She cold-heartedly disavows any attachment to what is being taken away and loudly utters her familiar and invariably rousing refrain: "I don't care."

Lewis can't help being inspired by her example and stoical philosophy in light of his current situation. Even when he is punishing his second child and oldest daughter, Lewis has to fight the urge to smile in front of her as he secretly and silently cheers on her steadfast defiance, her refusal to fear and be sad and blame herself for the circumstances in which she finds herself. Because of this, Lewis is always surprised when Alexandra comes over and hugs him and he looks down at her and realizes she is so small. He looks down at her today as he holds her hand, and by the way she looks up at him quickly and smiles encouragingly before turning away he knows that she has reached certain conclusions about his increased presence around the house.

Usually Judah listens to his iPod while they wait for the bus, but today he pulls his earbuds out as they reach Rothesay Road and asks Lewis a direct question. It is a simple one and largely rhetorical, but Lewis is pleased that his soon-to-be-teenage son is asking him anything. "Can I go over to Rob's house after school? We're going to play video games."

Rob is one of Judah's good friends. He lives near the school. From overhearing Judah ask Laura the same question over breakfast on several previous occasions, Lewis knows what the answer is.

"Of course. As long as you call us when you get to his house."

Lewis is happy that his son's questions are so easily answered.

THE DAY AFTER her first suicide attempt, the eleven-year-old Lewis and Mordecai visited Miranda in Intensive Care at the Montreal General Hospital, where she was under twenty-four-hour observation. The hospital smelled sickly sweet to Lewis, and as he caught glimpses of patients lying on beds or shuffling down the hall he wondered what had brought them there and whether they were going to die. Miranda was hooked up to an intravenous, and a black strap ran across her chest and her legs. At first Lewis thought she had been physically injured and the straps were part of the medical treatment, like a flexible, open-air cast. But he quickly realized Miranda was being restrained so she wouldn't hurt herself further. And so she couldn't escape.

When Miranda noticed Lewis she took his hand and pulled him down to kiss her. Her blond hair was disheveled, and her skin was paler than usual. Some liquid had dried opaquely on her mouth, and Lewis felt some of it stick to his lips. There was a bitter smell about her face. Miranda, who always appeared to Lewis as supremely confident and in control as Mordecai, started crying. She held Lewis's hand tightly and said, "I'm sorry, I'm so sorry, I'm sorry. You must be so disappointed in me, Lewis, I'm so sorry." A nurse came over to make sure everything was okay, and Lewis felt embarrassed about feeling embarrassed by his mother.

Mordecai gently moved Lewis away and took his place, holding Miranda's hand and gently stroking her hair. "There, there," he whispered, "there, there." Lewis had never heard anyone use that expression outside of a book before, and it sounded funny and old-fashioned coming from Mordecai. After Miranda stopped crying, Mordecai began to tell her about what was in the news, what the weather was like, and what he was going to make for dinner that night.

Three days later, Miranda was moved out of Intensive Care to the psychiatric ward, where she would remain for seven months. During that time, Mordecai visited her every single day. In the beginning, Lewis also visited regularly. On some days Miranda was calm, her eyes clear, her body relaxed. On these days the Morton family talked about many things: Miranda's art, family, the news. On other days her hands shook, her eyes were full of imagined fears, and she couldn't manage a conversation, let alone a work of art. As Miranda was speaking, her voice might trail off mid-sentence and she would stare at something imaginary behind Mordecai's or Lewis's heads, her right hand moving back and forth so she looked like a blind queen waving to the crowds from her carriage. Other times Lewis or Mordecai might be speaking, and Miranda would raise her hand as if to silence them. She would plead with them, tears in her eyes, to stop tormenting her with whatever they had been talking about.

After a few weeks, as the doctors experimented with different types and doses of medication, Miranda seemed to worsen rather than begin to recover. Her hands shook more, her speech was slurred, and she shuffled from her room to the common visiting room as if her legs weighed a thousand pounds, even though she was tall and thin and had lost a lot of weight. Many of the visits were spent holding hands, without any conversation.

Throughout these visits, Mordecai's spirits never seemed to weaken. He would be invariably cheery, greet Miranda with a kiss, say hello to all the other patients and staff he saw in the hallway. He would tell stories and jokes, and beginning the third week of Miranda's hospitalization, he brought a book to read to her. He would read about ten pages at a sitting. Lewis was never sure if Miranda was listening, but she seemed calmed by Mordecai's reading voice.

Lewis thought Mordecai's choice of book, *War and Peace*, was a little ambitious because he assumed Miranda would be home long before Mordecai finished the novel, but after she had been in hospital for two months, and Mordecai was on page 420, he appreciated his father's foresight. "It's a good book for her," Mordecai once said as the two of them drove home together after a visit, "not only because it is so beautiful and long but because there are so many characters and events for her to follow. It's good for her mind."

War and Peace was one of Mordecai's favourite novels. Lewis would never go on to read the book, always associating it with his mother's first hospitalization, but every lawyer Lewis would ever meet, starting with Mordecai, seemed to have a soft spot for it. Maybe it featured lawyers in a positive light. Or maybe it was so long and complex it reminded lawyers of a good legal brief. Four months after he began, Mordecai would finish reading *War and Peace* to Miranda, who would remain hospitalized for another four weeks before being discharged slowly over the course of a couple of months.

The discharge process started with Miranda's doctor letting her out for the day under the supervision of her family. Lewis and Mordecai often took Miranda for a drive or a walk at Beaver Lake on Mount Royal or Westmount Park down the street from their house on Arlington. From these day outings, Miranda graduated to spending a night at home, working her way up to three nights in a row. Then, one day, after a little over eight weeks of temporary releases, Miranda was suddenly home for good.

"For good," in this case, turned out to be two years. There would be two more failed suicide attempts before Lewis was out of high school — close calls, but both, by definition, half-hearted and ambivalent. Each of these occurred within weeks of Miranda deciding to stop taking her antidepressants because they were dulling her artistic perceptions and interfering with her painting, her sensory experience of the world.

By the third breakdown, Lewis and Mordecai could read the signs. Miranda would begin to have difficulty with a painting she was working on. Her colours would fade, the composition would sag, and the paintbrush would shake in her hand. She couldn't concentrate and would get nervous, angry, or weepy at the slightest things, like Mordecai being late for supper. She would forget to take her pills, lose the bottle, or experiment with infrequent and lesser doses. This would go on for about a month.

And then she would overdose.

8

LEWIS DOESN'T LIKE to walk aimlessly. That would be too relaxing, and Lewis can't calm down sufficiently to relax. He needs a purpose, a destination. So, he decides he will walk Rufus the three and a half kilometres to the Tim Hortons in Quispamsis, the next town over from Rothesay. Both are suburbs of Saint John masquerading as standalone towns nestled in the Kennebecasis River Valley, each with their own mayor. But where Rothesay is genuine country-lane Victorian, Quispamsis is late twentieth century subdivision. Lewis doesn't leave before 9:00 a.m. — when the Valley commuters have made their fifteen-minute drive into Saint John, twenty minutes if the traffic is heavy — so anybody driving is less likely to see him walking alone with his dog when he should be hidden away at the drafting table.

Laura is already at her computer, dreaming up her latest brilliant marketing plan. This time she's working for one of Lewis's favourite organizations: Symphony New Brunswick. As Lewis bends over to give her a kiss on the top of her head and tell her he's going out for a walk, Laura doesn't take her eyes off the screen but asks, "Where are you going?"

"I think I'll go to the Tim Hortons in Quispamsis." Unlike almost everybody else in Atlantic Canada, Lewis insists on referring to the ubiquitous coffee chain by its full name. He never says "Tim's" and would never be caught dead saying "Timmy's." Lewis is a Starbucks man at heart, but there isn't one within walking distance. So, he settles for Tim Hortons.

Laura turns around now. She is the one sitting and Lewis is tall, but she tilts her head forward and lowers her jaw so it looks somehow like she is the one talking down to him. "Make sure you go to the bathroom before you leave."

Coffee goes through Lewis like a sieve. Last summer he and Laura walked to Tim Hortons with Rufus. As usual, Lewis had to order the largest coffee. On the way out, Laura suggested Lewis go to the bathroom, but Lewis assured her that he was fine. They started walking and hadn't gone more than two blocks when Lewis got the first inkling he might have to pee. At this point they were still in the small-town commercial district where Quispamsis ends and Rothesay begins, and Lewis could have stopped at the Irving gas station to use one of their unnaturally clean bathrooms, or washrooms as they insist on politely calling them in Atlantic Canada. But he thought he would be fine.

By the time they were halfway between the Irving — as the omnipresent blue and white gas stations owned by the family with the same name are known — and their house, Lewis was in such pain that everything else had ceased to exist for him in any meaningful way. Lewis insisted on pulling Rufus along with an abrupt "Leave it" every time he wanted to sniff the grass or lift his leg, which Lewis in his condition took as a deliberate provocation.

As they approached the East Riverside-Kingshurst Park on the other side of Rothesay Road, Rufus began to whine and wag his tail because he hoped Lewis would cross with him as he always did.

When Lewis pulled Rufus roughly back, Laura knew something was wrong. And when she looked at Lewis's face and saw the way he was walking, both quickly and as if holding back, she knew what it was. They were about ten minutes from home but only a hundred metres from Tom and Maura's house. Laura pointed at it and said, "Let's stop. I'm sure Maura's home." But Lewis waved the suggestion away as if he had no time for it and said he would be fine. His breathing and walking became more rapid and laboured. When they reached their street, Lewis hurried up the hill in something approximating a run, fumbled for an agonizing ten seconds with the door key because at this point he could barely see, and nearly tripped as he unzipped his pants while running to the bathroom.

Lewis smiles at the memory. "Of course," he says and kisses Laura again, this time on the lips. Laura's mouth remains tight. And she watches Lewis leave the room before she returns to her computer screen.

THE WALK TO Tim Hortons is uneventful. At least Rufus enjoys himself. Saint John is relatively small, and whenever a car goes by Lewis assumes the driver knows him and is watching him, so he slows his walk and lifts his chin. He wants to appear cheerful and nonchalant, in control, as if it's his choice that he's out walking his dog when he should be at work. And in a way, he supposes, it is. He isn't allowed to work on any files, but he could have gone into the office. He doesn't want anyone driving by to think he's lonely, so he makes a point of talking cheerfully to Rufus when he sees a car coming or hears one behind him.

Not surprisingly, the walk goes by in a blur. Lewis ties Rufus up outside and takes his place in line, which reaches almost to the door. Once inside, Lewis relaxes just a little because he doesn't know anybody who hangs out at the Quispamsis Tim Hortons. He is content to anonymously wait in line and enjoy the smell of baked sugar and cheap coffee. The crowd filling most of the small tables is predictably retired, underemployed, and outwardly happy. The line is long but fast. Lewis orders a large coffee and donut, manages to uncharacteristically enjoy both without thinking too much about anything — neither the lawsuit nor Montcalm enters stage left in his mind — and before he knows it he's back outside untying Rufus's leash and beginning the walk home.

It's only when he's five minutes past the Irving that Lewis remembers Laura's warning, and by this time he already has to pee. He doesn't want to turn back at this point. He thinks he will be able to make it home, so he continues. But with each passing second on the curving, hilly Rothesay Road framed by stately old trees and houses, Lewis takes another awkward step on his journey of private pain. It is Atlantic Canada and Lewis probably could get away with knocking on the door of one of the beautiful late nineteenth- or early twentieth-century homes and asking if he could use the bathroom. Or he could make up a story about needing to use the phone and sneak in a trip to the bathroom.

But he continues, adjusting his gait to a sort of fast creep where he tries to move his feet as far as he can while keeping them as close to the ground as possible so that he's putting the least amount of pressure on his bladder each time his foot comes down on the concrete sidewalk. His jaw and fists are clenched now, and he's breathing loudly through his nose. Tom and Maura's house is coming up, but he doesn't want to stop. Before he knows it he's past it. Until the final minute leading up his fateful decision, he thinks he will be able to get home safely. But when Rufus sees East Riverside-Kingshurst Park up ahead on the right, on the gently sloping banks of the Kennebecasis River, and pulls gently on his leash, Lewis quickly decides to lets Rufus lead him across the thankfully quiet road.

In following his dog, Lewis is not letting Rufus distract him from getting home as quickly as possible. In the heavy clumps of bushes and groups of trees — what one of his elderly British neighbours calls a copse — in the heart of the small park Lewis has recognized a solution to his predicament. Once across the road and inside the park, Lewis doesn't let Rufus stop, but pulls him along into the nearest group of bushes, drops the leash, and mercifully lets himself go. But the moment of relief is short-lived. In fact, it never really begins.

For as soon as Lewis unzips his khakis, puts his hand through the fly of his baby blue boxer shorts with their pattern of bright red ladybugs, reaches for his penis, and violently pulls it out, he knows his well-ordered life is about to unravel even further than it already has. He knows this unequivocally, even before his pent-up urine starts to gush in a fire hydrant burst and he begins to experience the intensely biological and sublime relief that comes from emptying a bladder that feels like it is about to rupture.

It is at that moment that Lewis first hears the high-pitched schoolgirl scream and elongation of vowels that is one of the verbal signatures of the current tribe of teenagers, along with the multitude of verbal fillers like "like," "you know," "um," and "sort of," all of which, in Lewis's eyes, denotes the vast distance from reality that overexposure to television and video games has inflicted on a whole generation. And then the dreaded words following the scream: "Oh my God, it's a pervert, he's exposing himself, ohhhhh-myyyyyygawwwwddddd!"

At this point Lewis forgets he has to pee. His loyal dog, Rufus, looks up at his master with concern, and asks him without being able to say a word whether Lewis wants to flee or fight. The way

Rufus's head is cocked and his body relaxed, ready for anything, seems to suggest to Lewis that his dog will support him and won't judge him regardless of what decision he makes.

Lewis isn't ashamed to admit he thinks about running for just an instant. He isn't in bad shape, and neither is Rufus. Although Lewis is forty, he doesn't doubt that with the aid of adrenalin and given his motivation to preserve his personal reputation and freedom he can easily outrun a gang of teenagers. Because in the split second that it takes Lewis to reach that conclusion he has turned his head and seen through a narrow vertical gap in the bushes in which he has chosen to relieve himself that it is indeed a gang of teenagers. Three boys and two girls. Girls always seem to have the upper hand when it comes to sexual supply and demand. They are sitting cross-legged on the grass, on the other side of the bushes in East Riverside-Kingshurst Park, smoking something and not really touching except for the knees of one couple.

Lewis is surprised, even in his physically and emotionally stressed condition, to observe that there is an almost complete absence of sexual tension among the group, which he takes to have an average age of about sixteen. Perhaps all those plastics with their hormone-mimicking chemicals really are doing their devil's work, and testosterone levels, average penis sizes, and the libidos of both sexes are indeed shrinking, if you believe some of the more alarming scientific studies that have made their way into the pages of Canada's national newspapers. It never occurs to Lewis that perhaps this new generation, with all their gadgets, their material comforts, their infinite and uninterrupted access to online information and porn, is just more at ease with themselves, more at peace in the universe than he has ever been.

Lewis is confident that if he runs and burns his blue boxers and khakis and doesn't walk Rufus anywhere in the Saint John suburb of Rothesay for the next three months, everything will blow over and he will be home free. He feels secure in his conviction that the teenagers' medium-term memories would be focused on the brief and likely blurred, and perhaps even disbelieved, glimpse of his penis and not on his face, making a positive identification difficult if not impossible.

But then, again in that split second that often decides so much, Lewis applies to his situation what basic understanding he has of criminal behaviour and how society judges guilty and innocent actions. Don't the guilty always run, because they have something to hide? Can't you go to jail for leaving the scene of a car accident? Only the guilty jump bail.

So in that split second, that atavistic fulcrum of fight or flee, the combination of Lewis's reptilian brain and his highly evolved, perhaps even over-evolved, cerebral cortex conspire to decide that Lewis isn't going to run. He isn't going to run because if he does he will be as much as admitting a deliberate intent to expose himself and will thereby compound an innocent error. And besides, isn't he a polite, upstanding member, no pun intended, of society? He is well spoken, and he is handsome enough in a nondescript, unthreatening way, despite the pronounced contrast of his brown eyes and blond hair.

Lewis decides he will simply return his penis to his pants, zip himself up with deliberation and with dignity, slowly walk over to the teenagers, and apologize for offending them. He will explain that he was walking back home from Tim Hortons — no, he will bring himself to say Tim's — with his dog after drinking a large cup of coffee and suddenly developed an overwhelming urge to relieve himself. He kept walking for ten minutes, hoping to be able to reach his home in time, but discovered in the last few minutes of teary-eyed agony that he simply couldn't. He entered the charming little East Riverside-Kingshurst Park nestled against the pebbly shores of the Kennebecasis River where it widened, deep in the heart of the quaint and charming Town of Rothesay. There Lewis found what he thought was a secluded spot, went into the bushes, started his private business, and unfortunately other, relatively young, human beings happened to have been sitting nearby on the grass and saw him in his moment of vulnerability. He simply wants to apologize. And then he will smile his most innocent smile.

Lewis begins to flawlessly execute the first part of his plan, and as he starts to walk over to the teenagers beyond the gap in the bushes, Rufus offers a low growl in friendly warning. Lewis tugs gently on the leash, and he could swear Rufus shakes his head from side to side, as if to indicate that after some careful canine reflection he now wholeheartedly disagrees with Lewis's intended course of action.

But undaunted, Lewis continues toward the group of three boys and two girls. He has just waved his hand in what he hopes is a friendly gesture of hello, the universal body language of greeting, surrender, and the declaration of a state of being unarmed. It takes Lewis about five physical steps for his mind, which he has been struggling to hold together for some weeks now, to comprehend that the boys and girls have gotten to their feet and are already backing away.

The taller of the two girls, the one who Lewis believes without any evidence is the one who screamed, is pointing at him with one hand, her fingers decorated with black nail polish. She has raised her other hand to her mouth like a surgical mask, in a gesture of disgust, as if trying to keep the scent of moral contagion from her mouth and nose. But even though her hand is in front of her mouth, and even though the logical processing part of Lewis's brain is in the midst of shutting down on him, Lewis can still clearly perceive her shouting, as if she were one of the disposable victims in a horror movie.

"Oh my gawdddd, I don't belieeeve it, he's coming toward us and shaking his hand at us, the hand that he was using to touch himself!" She turns to her companions with the set jaw, steady gaze, and mental certainty of a born leader. "Let's get out of here and call the police. Run. Let's go. Now."

As Lewis watches the girl and her followers run, he is in no state to conclude that the gang of teens chose that particular spot in East Riverside-Kingshurst Park to hang out at the particular teenager-unfriendly time of day — 10:00 a.m. — because they were probably playing hooky from school, or as Maritimers so much more evocatively, almost obscenely, called it, cuffing.

But Lewis does have enough shreds of presence of mind left to recognize he will have to return home to tell this story to his wife. His intelligent, beautiful, educated, kind, understanding wife. His better half. The missing piece of his soul. The woman who loves him so truly that like Cordelia she never flattered him to his face about any of his talents or accomplishments or pretended he was any better than he was. Not ever. Not once, even though it might have been welcome on occasion. The woman who is his smiling anchor in a sea of humanity and chaos, his beacon in an ever-shifting shadow land of bluster and broken promises. His Laura. So trusting is Lewis in the sincerity of words, including their absence, that he has never assumed or known that Laura, although she would never admit this to his face, thinks he is the best, smartest, most courageous, and best-looking man in the world and never passes a day without thinking to herself how lucky she is to be married to him.

The temptation to run, although Lewis hasn't run from anything in his life in over twenty years, reasserts itself after his youthful accusers run off. They expect him to follow, judging by how they keep turning around and urging each other on as they head for Rothesay Road. They must have thought he was a class A pervert. But Lewis just watches them disappear, his arms hanging at his sides, his hand barely holding on to Rufus's leash. Once the teenagers make their way up a cross street, Lewis turns around and runs faster than he has since high school. Ten minutes later he is home.

Laura is taking a break from her brilliant marketing and making a cup of coffee. She looks beautiful and trusting, and Lewis nearly doesn't tell her about his near-death experience in the park. But Lewis is hopelessly honest, and so he tells her.

He hasn't gotten very far, being just at the point when he was unzipping his pants behind the bushes, when Laura looks at him for the first time with an expression of disbelief mixed with disapproval and says, "You did what?"

Lewis is about to explain how he felt and how he had no choice but to relieve himself in the bushes, but Laura's reaction is no surprise to Lewis, he and Laura having discussed the topic of public urination on three previous occasions: Laura loves Lewis, but she thinks pissing in public at any age is a sign of a seriously anti-social personality. Lewis found this out once quite inadvertently. He was regaling Laura with stories of his wayward childhood in the wealthy City of Westmount, sprawled across the western slope of Mount Royal in the tight heart of inner-city Montreal, including the fact that he and his friends would sometimes pee between the Jaguars and Mercedes parked on the side of the road so they wouldn't have to run back to their houses while playing cops and robbers.

Lewis falters in his recounting for a moment before gamely carrying on, and he succeeds this time in getting as far as the girl screaming when Laura puts her hand over her mouth and says, disconcertingly, almost like the girl in the park, "Oh my God." Except when Laura says it she doesn't elongate the syllables and she doesn't sound as angry or youthful. Laura doesn't say anything else but sits down with her head in her hands. "Oh my God, Lewis. What happened then?"

When Lewis tells his darling, blond-haired, supportive Laura that he went after his accidental audience with an outstretched guilty hand to apologize and explain that he indeed was not an exhibitionist flashing them in the park but a respectable member of the community on the cusp of middle age out for a walk with his loyal dog, a hapless man who had held his bladder for as long as he could and who had found what he thought was a quiet spot in the bushes to privately relieve himself, Laura just stares at him and opens and closes her mouth without saying anything.

Lewis can't help thinking that his beautiful, perfect wife looks like a designer guppy genetically modified to possess certain human facial characteristics staring at him disconsolately from a tank in a very upscale pet store. And that is before Laura composes herself sufficiently to find her voice and tell him as she turns away, "You know, this wouldn't have happened if you had listened to me in the first place. You should have gone to the bathroom when and where you were supposed to."

And of course, there is nothing Lewis can think of in reply.

9

WHEN LEWIS RISES from his bed sometime between 5:30 and 6:00 a.m. the next day — he doesn't wake up because he never fell asleep the night before — and tiptoes downstairs to check the *Telegraph-Journal*, his near-worst fears are realized. He has to flip through to the third page of the City section before he finds it, but it is there, in black and white. It's not quite an article — it's in the Briefs section — but when it comes to this sort of thing, Lewis is convinced a brief is bad enough. So, the girl went to the police. Of course she did.

The small-print headline is brutal in its simplicity. Lewis has to acknowledge the headline writer felt little freedom to be witty. He has restricted himself to relating the bare facts of the incident. The piece itself will not win any literary awards. It reads as if written by an intern or co-op student.

Man exposes himself to Rothesay teens

By Richard Smith   **October 15, 2007**

Saint John, NB — Yesterday morning at 7:30 a.m. a man exposed himself to a small group of Rothesay teens at East Riverside-

Kingshurst Park in the heart of Rothesay on the Kennebecasis River.

"The victim did get a clear view of the perpetrator, and did provide a good likeness which was quickly captured by a police artist," confirms Detective William Blunt. "We are currently exploring a number of firm leads," he added.

The female victim cannot be named because she is a minor. Police authorities say she is in stable condition after receiving post-traumatic stress counselling at Saint John Regional Hospital.

The only thing missing from this article is his name: Lewis Morton. For one short, insanely irrational moment, Lewis thinks of changing his name. He wouldn't be the first one in his family to do so.

LEWIS'S PATERNAL GRANDFATHER, Shlomo, got off the ship from Romania in 1935, just a few lucky years ahead of the Holocaust and after successfully bribing Canadian immigration officials, who weren't welcoming many Jews with open arms. Shlomo landed in the New Country with a wife and three young children. The oldest, at five, was Mordecai. After giving away most of his meagre life savings to the corrupt immigration officials, Shlomo had nothing left in his threadbare pockets but twenty-two Canadian silver dollars. He had earned the coin of the realm and learned a handful of English words during the three-week transatlantic voyage, most of the words having to do with poker — like *ante*, *bet*, *raise*, and the idiomatic expression, "I'll see you" — which Mordecai would find hilarious for the rest of his life. After disembarking with his seasick children and disapproving wife in tow, Shlomo was asked his name by the thin, pale, preoccupied, and undoubtedly anti-Semitic immigration agent at Pier 21 in Halifax. His proud answer,

"Shlomo Mortinsky" in a heavy, throaty Eastern European accent, sounded almost Hebrew to the five-year-old Mordecai's ears.

The customs agent, whose name was Johnson, said aloud, "You're in Canada now," before handing back the Mortinsky patriarch an immigration card with the name "Samuel Morton" on it. Johnson had said in solemn and vaguely British tones, "Morton is a fine name that will do you in good stead in your new country, and it's a lot easier to pronounce. Welcome to Canada. God bless the King. Next." And so Mortinsky had morphed into Morton, and another new immigrant was efficiently processed into the stand-offish mosaic of Canada.

Lewis's *zayde* Shlomo (Mortinsky) Morton, who was the genetic source of Mordecai's sense of humour and Lewis's photographic memory, never forgot the name of the customs agent and never tired of rousing Lewis to great gales of laughter with his imitation of the man's clipped British accent. In Shlomo's version of the immigration story, invariably acted out with great dramatic talent — Lewis always thought his *zayde* should have been an actor, or at least a comic — "Mr. Johnson" was very cool and pseudo-British while processing the immigration papers until the moment when he handed Shlomo his new identity as Mr. Morton. Mr. Johnson suddenly became all smiles and put out his hand for Lewis's *zayde* to shake.

After Shlomo learned the English language, he could never control his laughter when he told anyone about Johnson's name. Years later, he would tell Lewis the story over and over again. "Can you picture this, he has a problem with 'Mortinsky,' meanwhile he's named after one of the stupid Canadian words for pecker. Can you imagine, going around being called Mr. Putz or Mr. Schmuck? What a crazy country!" And he and Lewis would laugh so hard tears would run down their cheeks.

Miranda liked Mordecai's original family name, and in the early years of their marriage she often urged him to change it back. Mordecai was sympathetic to her but didn't like changing names on principle, so even though Morton wasn't the real family name he wasn't going to change it at this point. Miranda decided she would do the next best thing, which was to sign all her paintings Miranda Mortinsky.

But as Lewis puts down the paper with the brief item about his transgression, the newsprint burning his hands, it's not his name he has to worry about. It's his unusual appearance. Many men are tall and thin. Very few have dark brown eyes and light blond hair. Lewis finds himself hoping the girl — he can't quite bring himself to call her "the victim" — is colour-blind.

10

THE NEXT DAY Lewis is so tired from being awake the previous night he falls asleep before the kids are put to bed. But his sleep is restless. The investigating detective's needlessly suggestive phrase "We are currently exploring a number of firm leads" has lodged itself in Lewis's receptive imagination. He wakes up seemingly every hour, and each time he fears every little sound outside the house is caused by the police coming to arrest him. And then what will his defence be? The police will never believe that he meant no harm, that it was all an innocent accident. Even if they did, so what? Lewis still committed an offence, intentional or not, whether or not the brief, almost subliminal sight of his flaccid penis held in his hands and extended unthreateningly to urinate will cause lasting psychological damage to a young, impressionable mind.

Lewis has trouble imagining a professional tomorrow now that Drescher is gone and he finds himself in legal limbo with an intellectual infringement lawsuit hanging over his head. But after the incident in the park he clearly sees his name being dragged viciously through the mud, through the dingy provincial courts of Saint John, "Lewis Morton" appearing in the papers beside the monikers of hardened but also hapless criminals.

For someone who grew up in Montreal with its storied Mafia and biker wars, Lewis has always found the criminals of Saint John to be particularly downtrodden and inept to the point of eliciting sympathy, as if they were never sufficiently loved or provided enough to eat when growing up. There is the recent case of the man who regularly stole trays of meat from the grocery store, or the twenty-year-old who, drunk on homemade wine, attempted to slash his sleeping roommate in one of the uptown's crumbling Victorian homes now subdivided into cramped apartments. The would-be murderer took up an eighteenth-century ceremonial samurai sword but passed out after hoisting the sword, barely grazing his still sleeping intended victim's leg as he hit the floor. Or there is the hapless, mysterious man "of no fixed address" who managed to hold up a convenience store with a water pistol, only to be apprehended by police two hours later because he dropped his wallet while fleeing the crime scene.

Once all the firm leads are fully explored and Lewis is apprehended by the police, as he increasingly assumes he will be, the "In the Courts" brief in the City section of the *Telegraph-Journal* will concisely record that Lewis Morton, resident of Rothesay, will be appearing in court on such and such a date to answer to charges of exposing himself in a public place. On the day the story runs, Laura — oh poor Laura — will die inwardly of shame, and Lewis's children will be teased mercilessly at school and return home with awkward questions that Lewis will have to make a semblance of answering. After a long and lurid trial, reported on in depth every day on the front pages, Lewis will be found guilty without a doubt. In his anxiety-driven state, Lewis is always found guilty in his imagination.

While Lewis will probably manage to get off with only community service and a suspended sentence — no hard time for the formerly respectable "Rothesay Flasher" — his once bright and assured future will be spectacularly ruined. His legal woes will converge because his conviction for indecent exposure will fatally taint his chances of emerging unscathed from Abercrom's legal action. Even if he somehow manages not to be convicted for stealing another architect's design, nobody will ever hire Lewis again based on the incident in the park alone. They will assume guilt, suppose the worst, in a best-case scenario believing that he isn't a sexual deviant but is simply cracking up over losing his mentor and any clients.

Lewis can already hear the oblique comments dropped into conversations in the Quispamsis Tim Hortons by people who know him as a colleague, architect, or acquaintance: "He always seemed so nice." Spoken incredulously, with just a hint of *schadenfreude*. Or "Losing his partner and all his commissions must have really got to him." And others will nod wisely as they sip their double-doubles, uttering with conviction as they roll down the rim, "You know, you always have to watch the quiet ones. They come across as so gentle, so calm, but usually that kind of facade hides a lot." Lewis will never find another job, having to settle for sporadic work as an inexpert real estate agent or car salesman.

Lewis decides he will never go back to little East Riverside-Kingshurst Park with its smattering of trees and pebbly beach. Instead he will grow a beard and cut his hair in a buzz cut. He once read a James Bond book in which the villain, putting to work former Nazi scientists in his plot du jour to take over the world, confides that the best way to disguise a man is to have him shave his head and grow a beard. Even his own mother won't recognize him.

For several days, Lewis refuses to leave the house, even to walk Judah and Alexandra down the hill to the bus or pick them up or take Rufus for a walk. Lewis declines even to go to the front door if the doorbell rings or to walk past the front windows in case he is being surreptitiously observed. He cuts his hair and grows his scraggly blond beard — Lewis has never been able to grow a real one where you can't see through the hair to his cheeks and chin — and he waits every day for the loud knock at the door. Lewis's worry doesn't prevent him from reflecting on the irony that it is walking, a habit he took up after Drescher's death and his own subsequent ostracism within the firm, that is partly responsible for the second potential legal predicament in which he now finds himself.

When Lewis does again work up the courage to walk his two older children down to the bus, after four days, he puts on a sports jacket to preserve a sense of normalcy. He makes an effort to wave cheerily to his mostly elderly and retired neighbours if he sees them — happily for them, they no longer have to worry about work — kisses Judah and Alexandra on their foreheads, and waves them off as they get on the bus.

Luckily for Lewis, his neighbours are governed by an innate Atlantic Canadian reticence and politeness. They might talk about him in the privacy of their parlours, but outwardly they respect his newfound appearance in the neighbourhood at times when he should be at work. If they see him on the street as he walks back up the hill to his home, they never once ask him why he is around so much. They say hello and keep on walking. They don't spy on him from behind the curtains of their houses like Lewis's childhood neighbour Mrs. Staunton staying abreast of Miranda's unplanned visits to and from the hospital.

DURING HER STAYS in the psychiatric ward after each of her over-doses, Miranda would manage to escape every few weeks, improb-ably eluding security, somehow getting to the ground floor of the hospital and walking out the main doors in her hospital clothes, her middle-aged buttocks visible through the untied blue hospital gown. Sometimes she was clever enough to wear a coat or house-coat, but not always.

Once outside, Miranda would hail a cab. Most of the time the driver would take Miranda home to her Victorian brick house on Arlington Avenue just up the steep hill from Sherbrooke Street, where she would ring the bell. If he were home, Mordecai would answer and take her in his arms; while he was paying the taxi fare, Miranda would be unsteadily climbing the stairs and collapsing into bed, usually falling straight asleep, sometimes with the benefit of overdosing again on sleeping pills.

If Miranda was not overdosing, Mordecai would have to call the police to take her back to hospital, and she would scream Mordecai's name and ask how he could do this to her as the officers took her away. If Miranda had overdosed, it was the ambulance that came, and the paramedics would pump her stomach. When Miranda regained consciousness the following day, Lewis and Mordecai would be there to hold her hand and feed her Jell-O and tell her it was okay as she cried and apologized for worrying them. And even though he loved Miranda, Lewis couldn't help feeling embarrassed when the police cars or the ambulances arrived and all the neighbours pretended not to look through their pulled-back curtains at the scene unfolding before them.

Once Lewis happened to glimpse the well-dressed Mrs. Staunton, who lived across the street, peeking through her lace curtains as an unconscious Miranda was wheeled out of the house on a stretcher and lifted into an ambulance. Lewis wasn't sure, but he almost thought he could see a slight smile on Mrs. Staunton's face through the century-old glass of her living room window. Mrs. Staunton was the proud widow of Joe Staunton, a Westmount born and bred boy who played rugby regularly at Westmount Park and went on to become "one of Montreal's most prominent and philanthropic orthopedic surgeons," as the *Montreal Star*'s society columnist always referred to him when he was still alive. Mrs. Staunton never said more than "Hello" or "Nice weather we're having, isn't it?" to Miranda or Lewis while passing on the street, but she was a regular at Chez Nick, and Lewis always suspected that Mrs. Staunton was one of Miranda's reluctant models, as well as one of her harshest, if always silent, critics.

ON THE FIFTH day after the incident in the park, after Lewis drops off the kids at the bus stop and returns to the safety of his house, he paces from one end to the other, from the dining room through the spacious entrance hall through the living room into the family room. And back again. And back again, twenty times. As he walks he checks his phone, and two minutes later he checks it again, hoping in vain for an email from somebody, anybody, hoping for some question he could apply his mind to, ideally a complex architectural issue about light or space that will force him to think logically.

When Lewis's phone mercifully rings somewhere between his living room and his dining room, it isn't anyone calling to commiserate or to offer him a job. It's Miriam. Drescher's widow. To Lewis's overly sensitive ears, Miriam sounds remarkably upbeat for a woman who has unexpectedly lost a husband in the prime of his life. Lewis last saw her when she was sitting shiva. Laura prepared a vegetarian dish and a cake, and she and Lewis took it over to the 1890s mansion on Mount Pleasant.

Drescher could have afforded to live well in any city in the world. Having chosen to build an architectural firm in Saint John, New Brunswick, he easily might have lived fifteen kilometres out in the little quaint suburb of Rothesay. He could have bought a large property right on the river. Lewis never understood why Drescher chose the tiny enclave of Mount Pleasant at the top of the hill that overlooked a heavily industrial part of the city: nothing but train yards and marine terminals and mills and the refinery. Worst of all, Mount Pleasant, like most of Saint John, was situated firmly in the heavy fog belt that settled over the city on most days outside of winter. But Drescher loved the spacious late Victorian mansion with its high-quality interior art deco features that had been added during a major renovation in the early 1920s.

"Lewis, would you be able to come over today? There is something of Leon's I would like you to have."

Lewis looks at his watch. It's 8:45 a.m. He has nowhere to be, no people to see. "Sure, Miriam. What time were you thinking?"

"Let us say three. We can have tea."

WHEN MIRIAM ANSWERS the door, she isn't dressed head to toe in black as she was when Lewis last saw her. He is pleased to see she is wearing a very colourful, very expensive-looking dress. The tea is ready in minutes, and she serves it burning hot in fine china.

From all indications, Drescher's and Miriam's marriage was a happy one. Maybe this is why Miriam doesn't feel the need to overdo the mourning-wife role. She looks relaxed. At peace. And she asks Lewis how he is doing before he ever has a chance to ask how she is coping.

"Not bad," Lewis says. Judging from Miriam's smile, she knows he is lying. She and Laura speak regularly. "And you?"

"I'm doing okay. I would have liked more time with him, but

you take what you can get. And we had almost thirty great years."

Lewis nods. He doesn't know what to say. He seems to be having more trouble with Drescher's death than Miriam is.

"He really liked you, you know. As both a friend and a partner." Miriam takes a long sip of tea. The teacup looks even finer in her unlined hand. "He wasn't old enough to be your father, but he thought of you as a younger brother." She smiles again. "If his younger brother had been an architect." Lewis remembers something about Drescher's younger brother making a fortune in scrap metal.

They drink tea and made small talk about the weather and what Miriam might do now that Drescher is gone. It's clear that Miriam neither desires nor deserves any pity. When she says, "I have children to visit, and we have our house in Oxford," Lewis assumes he's misheard. And of course, he doesn't know how to hide his surprise.

Drescher never told him anything about a house in Oxford. Lewis doesn't want Miriam to notice his sense of shock, but he is already turning red, and although he doesn't make eye contact, he knows from the expression on Miriam's face that she realizes she has let something slip that Drescher never did.

As if to spare his feelings she adds, "It's just a small indulgence, bought not too long ago on a whim." Miriam is kind and not a very good liar, and Lewis is torn between gratefulness that she is lying to him and disappointment that she can't tell him the truth he imagines behind her words. After a moment of awkward silence, they resume their conversation as though they have both agreed that the last few minutes have not happened.

As the two of them are finishing their tea, Miriam explains why she invited Lewis over. "I'd like you to have Leon's suits, Lewis." She looks him over quickly with an appraising eye. "You're almost exactly the same size. Tall and thin."

Despite himself, Lewis finds himself smiling.

"He would have wanted you to have them." It is exactly the kind of thing a widow might do for the younger brother of her dead husband. And exactly the kind of thing she would say.

And so it is that Lewis finds himself the proud owner of fifteen bespoke Harry Rosen suits that each fit him like a glove. Miriam makes him try them all on quickly before she puts them neatly in garment bags for him. He doesn't have to alter a single one. The jackets fit him snugly across the shoulders and chest. The pants hang against his stomach and hip bones without being too tight or requiring a belt. All he has to do now is find clients and commissions so he has a reason to wear them.

11

LEWIS HAS BEEN in professional and legal limbo for nearly three weeks when he gets his first call from Tom Graham. If Lewis had a best friend, it would be Tom. Tom is married to Maura, who has been Laura's real best friend since they met in high school in Oakville. When the two women went off to different universities they didn't see each other often. But when Laura moved to Saint John with Lewis for his job with Drescher & Drescher, her best friend was already waiting. A year earlier, Maura had moved to Saint John to marry her university sweetheart, Tom. Lewis and Tom were quickly introduced.

Tom is as outgoing as Lewis is not, and from their first encounter the extrovert adopted the introvert as part of his social circle, almost like a mascot. Tom is tall and blond — and, unlike Lewis, blue-eyed — and looks good in outdoorsy clothes. He is good at being friends and has lots of them. He is also good at making money in his job as a senior stockbroker and investment adviser, and consequently has lots of that too. Lewis has reflected more than once that the combination of making money and making friends is one that suits Tom well. Lewis doesn't make friends easily or particularly well, but he always appreciates Tom's interest and enthusiasm.

"Hi, Lewie, how are you doing?"

Lewis has never had the heart to tell Tom that he hates being called Lewie. If he has ever had any excuse to tell Tom the truth — after being exiled from his firm — now would be the time. But Lewis knows that Tom will be offended, so he says, "I'm fine."

"Hmm." It is clear from Tom's unusually ruminative silence that he doesn't believe Lewis. Tom and Lewis have not yet had a conversation about Lewis's precarious position at the firm and the looming legal action. But Lewis knows Tom would already have the scoop from Maura, who would have gotten it from Laura. The day Lewis came home early with the news that Montcalm was taking him off all client work, the two women were on the phone. Lewis wasn't sure if Laura called Maura or Maura called Laura. Maura always seemed to have a sixth sense about anything going on in other people's lives. Laura was speaking in semi-hushed tones up in the spare room they called their study, but Lewis overheard isolated snippets of conversation from his supine place on the living room couch. "He could go in if he wants to, but he's not allowed to do any work ... yes, he was close to Drescher ... has some irons in the fire ... we'll be fine, but thank you ... let's definitely have coffee tomorrow ..."

Thankfully, Tom didn't call Lewis immediately to express either condolences or congratulations. Like a good male friend, he left Lewis alone for a recognizable amount of time to see if he would figure things out on his own. But now he is calling. Laura must have told Maura that Lewis is moping around the house.

"Well, you certainly sound fine." That is the essence of Tom's philosophy in dealing with any problem he encounters: pretend something is fine hard enough and long enough and eventually it becomes so. Lewis knows — from everything that Maura has regularly confided to Laura and the small bits that Tom has deliberately let slip over the years — that this approach has worked for him his whole determinedly charmed life. Through his first year at university when his football talent that got him through high school was no longer good enough to get him on the school team and through his boring business classes taught by professors who weren't impressed by him. Through his first few miserable years following in his father's footsteps as an investment adviser when most of the time he didn't know what he was doing with other people's money and the rest of the time he didn't care.

His determination that everything was always fine even worked in his favour miraculously when just a few years into their marriage he and Maura "experienced some problems," which was Tom's way of explaining to Lewis that he had been having an affair and Maura found out about it. Tom pretended everything was okay then, or at least that it would be okay, and somehow it turned out that way.

Tom's confidence and enthusiasm are infectious. But Lewis knows his friend's attitude to everything hasn't always been as easy and effortless as it appears, whether Tom is sweet-talking a new client into signing with him or making yet another friend on the sloping greens of the Riverside Country Club, a stone's throw from his house. But it is at Tom and Maura's cocktail parties that Lewis's friend's stellar sociability is on full display. And it is to the promised social tonic of one of these get-togethers that Tom turns this evening.

Once the opening pleasantries are out of the way, Tom jumps to the purpose of his call. "Maura and I are having a few people over for a cocktail party this Friday. Why don't you and Laura swing by?" Lewis hates cocktail parties, but he doesn't have anywhere better to be and he doesn't want to be rude to Tom, who means well. Besides, he knows that Maura probably already invited Laura, who probably already accepted on their behalf.

"That would be great. Thanks, Tom."

"No problem. Would be great to see you. Eight p.m. Take care now, Lewie, and call me if you want to talk about anything before then."

TOM AND MAURA'S house is only a ten-minute walk away, but Laura doesn't want to totter over on her high heels. As Lewis pulls into their friends' long driveway at five minutes past eight, he shouldn't be surprised by how close their Rothesay Road house is to East Riverside-Kingshurst Park, but he is. The distance cannot be more than five hundred metres across Rothesay Road. On that morning when he had to pee so badly, why didn't he just walk over and ask to use his friend's bathroom? Tom would probably have been at work for hours by then, but it was likely that Maura at least would have been at home.

The driveway is full of cars, and Lewis and Laura have to walk nearly a hundred metres to the door. As Laura balances on the high heels she rarely wears, she reaches for Lewis's hand, gives it an encouraging squeeze, and whispers quickly, "It won't be so bad. Relax. Enjoy yourself." Lewis musters a smile for her benefit and holds his facial muscles in place as Laura rings the doorbell.

Lewis is wearing one of Drescher's Harry Rosen suits. Solid pattern, black Italian weave. It's a bit formal for the occasion, but it is a cocktail party at Tom's house, after all, and the suit fits him well, like a lightweight coat of mail. When Lewis puts it on and fastens the top button, he feels the material against his rib cage, and his increasing tendency toward low-intensity hyperventilation is arrested, at least temporarily. Since he no longer has any work,

Lewis has started eating poorly. He drinks Cokes and eats chips at least once a day. But with all the walking and worrying, he's still burning calories efficiently and his waistline has not expanded — at least not yet.

When Tom opens the door, he is wearing a fitted black velvet sports jacket, designer jeans, and a big smile. He is dressed more appropriately than Lewis, and he looks as fit and happy as ever. He kisses Laura enthusiastically on the cheeks and grabs Lewis's hand. In what seems like one fluid motion he closes the door, ushers them in, introduces them to three couples on the way to the kitchen, and hands them each a glass of wine: red for Laura and white for Lewis. Within minutes of arriving in the kitchen, which has just been renovated for the second time in five years and which is bigger than Lewis's and Laura's living room, the Mortons have been smoothly separated according to gender.

Laura is whisked off by Maura. Lewis finds himself part of a circle with Tom and two other men standing where the grey slate tiles of the kitchen meet the polished birch of the dining room floor. The kitchen light hanging from the ceiling is unusually bright, and Lewis stands almost without thinking so that his back is to it. Tom introduced him on arriving, but Lewis is already unsure about the other two men's names. He thinks the taller, outdoorsy-looking one is Bob Fielding and the chubbier, paler one is Fred Landry. And in this, Lewis is in fact right.

Bob Fielding is dressed expensively. Fred Landry, less so. The entire downstairs is teeming with people. Judging from the high volume of cheerful animated conversation, every other guest is productively and perhaps even happily employed. Lewis is very much not, and he can't escape that fact, not even amidst the expensive white wine and canapés and the hired cook and server that Lewis clearly is not able to comfortably afford.

Lewis has never enjoyed cocktail parties, but at least before Drescher's death he never feared conversation. He actually felt proud when someone approached him with the human version of the dog-to-dog anus-sniffing routine, the question "So, what do you do?" But now Lewis feels insecure, inferior, at a loss, adrift on a sea of social perceptions. He always downplayed the magnitude of his role as a senior partner at Drescher & Drescher, answering the question of what he did for living with something vague like, "I work at an architectural firm." Only if asked which one would he volunteer that the firm in question was indeed Drescher & Drescher.

If the person asking him knew anything about architecture, Lewis would see the lights of respect going on in their eyes, and their next question became the deferential "And what do you do there?"

"Oh, I'm a partner," uttered in barely a murmur. And Lewis's exalted position established, the conversation could then move on without regret to books, movies, the state of the economy, or, God forbid, sports. Which, as Lewis fights to concentrate on the words being spoken with great animation less than two feet away from him, he determines is the exact subject of the current conversation. A topic about which, needless to say, Lewis knows less than nothing. Mordecai has always been lean and strong, so he must have lifted or pushed something somewhere between his work and home, but unlike most men in Montreal he never watched or talked about hockey or baseball, let alone played either sport with Lewis.

Lewis knows that the biggest sin at a cocktail party is to be boring, and tonight he feels even more boring than usual. Unlike the other men he is speaking with, or more accurately listening to, Lewis doesn't play any sports. Worse, he has never developed any real hobbies or interests other than drawing or painting when he was young. And he gave up art years ago. Lewis doesn't do any hands-on woodworking or esoteric model shipbuilding or daredevil go-kart racing. No dedicated golfing or immature video gaming or macho hunting. No hearty poker and wing nights with "the boys." (Lewis has no "boys." He has no "posse.") Two years earlier, one of the other partners invited Lewis over to a "boys' night." There were two other fathers there, one of whom Lewis knew slightly from Judah's basketball games. They drank beer, ate chips, and played poker with good cheer. One of the men made semi-risqué remarks about "hot" actresses while munching on Miss Vickie's salt and vinegar chips. All the while, Lewis couldn't help thinking that he'd rather be home in bed reading. Or in bed with Laura. Or both. He left early at 9:30 p.m., pleading fatigue, and felt guilty for somehow letting down the masculine side. He was never invited back.

Lewis has no other interests outside architecture and his family. Laura is his complete opposite in this respect, and Lewis has always been quietly envious of her catholic tastes. Laura's wide range of interests both complements and expands her professional interest in marketing, beginning with a passion for decorating magazines, cooking, fashion, and art. Laura loves gardening, flowers, herbs, and exotic grasses that she collects and grows outside in their garden and in pots in the house. She enjoys jazz, CBC Radio, movies, children's clothes, antiques, sculpture, mystery novels, renovation TV shows, Internet shopping, and shopping in general, which Lewis finds to be at best an unpleasant chore and at his grumpy worst a sign of the decline of the American empire. Laura loves her friends, socializing, Persian carpets, restored antique furniture, particularly Empire period furniture, but also spool beds and antique light fixtures as well as stainless steel German-engineered dishwashers that purr while they run, not to mention finding bargains on eBay, buying and selling things on Kijiji, celebrating holidays, putting up Christmas decorations, discovering household and garden tools manufactured by companies with a flair for design, and on the list goes.

Tom and Bob have been reliving the seniors' league hockey game they both played in last night, which went into overtime and didn't finish until 1:30 a.m. As the talk among Lewis's little cocktail party circle glides from recreational hockey to the promising prospects of the Sea Dogs — the Saint John minor league hockey team is on an early-season winning streak — Lewis hears Laura's laugh. He turns his head and is surprised by how intense a feeling of happiness comes over him just from seeing her a few short feet behind him. She is standing in the kitchen, holding a large glass of red wine and laughing shamelessly at something Maura has apparently said.

"I also thought it was a terrible book, unbelievably stupid," Laura says as her laughter subsides. "But have you read Alice Munro's latest?"

"I just finished it and I loved it," Maura says as she clinks glasses with Laura. Lewis reflects that the two women aren't good friends for nothing.

"I'm sure this is isn't politically correct, but the older I get, the more I think that only women can write about themselves. Male writers hardly ever do their female characters justice. "

"You certainly get the feeling that they're trying a little too hard!" And the two of them burst out laughing together.

Like most men, Lewis doesn't read much fiction, but he is now deliberately trying to eavesdrop on the women when the talk among the men pivots somehow from hockey to hunting and their voices seem to get deeper and louder.

"I just got my deer hunting licence," says the one Lewis thinks is called Bob.

"Me too," says Tom as if it is somehow a strange coincidence. Lewis doesn't know how to respond so he just nods. Tom notices that Lewis hasn't said anything to anyone since he introduced him. "Lewis, have you ever hunted?" At least Tom doesn't call him Lewie when it's more than just the two of them.

"No." The closest Lewis has ever come to hunting is seeing the act depicted — albeit in Miranda's wonderfully idiosyncratic fashion — in one of his mother's most famous paintings: *Deer Family*.

WHEN MIRANDA MADE her first suicide attempt, she was in the midst of painting Lewis, Mordecai, and herself. But she wasn't painting them sitting in their living room or garden. That would have been too predictable. Instead, she painted the three of them in a forest. Miranda was running, Mordecai was peeking out from behind a tree. And Lewis was playing in the dirt in a small clearing in the foreground.

They were each clearly recognizable: by their clothes, the shape of their bodies, the way they held themselves as they played or ran or hid. But Miranda changed their heads. She gave each of them the head of deer, or a baby deer, or in Mordecai's case a stag with big, shaggy antlers. As the critic who later wrote about the painting noted, Miranda did a reverse Frida Kahlo. But in Miranda's case she chose the harder task: it was easier to paint your own head on a deer's body as Kahlo had done. It was another thing to capture the essence of a human face through the head of a deer. But somehow she did it. Her own deer's head was pale, with big, watchful eyes taking in the whole landscape of the painting, even as she was running. Lewis's face was innocent and intent. He wasn't paying attention to his surroundings. And Mordecai's stag face underneath his dark antlers was grinning and managing to wink in the direction of Miranda running toward him while at the same time keeping one protective eye on Lewis digging in the dirt.

At first, progress on the painting was steady, and Lewis was pleased, as he always was, to see the painting emerge from the blank canvas with Miranda's usual command of colour, texture, and composition. Each evening, with the arrival of dusk, Lewis would sit with Miranda as she studied the results of her work from that day. She would make mental notes for her work the following day and explain to Lewis what she had done and why. Why she was using certain colours, why the brushstrokes were long or short, focusing not only on the details and technique but on what she was trying to communicate to the viewer.

But after three weeks, Lewis noticed Miranda wasn't saying much at night. Instead, she was just staring at her work, and sometimes her eyes would glaze over, like the milky third eyelid on a cat's eye, and Lewis noticed that less and less progress was being made each day. In the fourth week of working on the painting, Miranda lost her patience for the sittings in which she had posed Mordecai and Lewis in their garden. She would get frustrated if the light was not quite right or if Mordecai moved his arm to scratch himself, and she accused Lewis of smiling just to annoy her. By the fifth week, Miranda abandoned the painting. Two weeks later she overdosed for the first time.

"NEVER HUNTED?" SAYS Bob as if he can't believe a man has never killed another living creature in the woods. "Hell, you should join us this season. We always head out the third weekend in November." Bob doesn't know Lewis, but he has Tom's confidence that everyone he has just met is dying to become his friend.

"That would be great," says Tom, without missing a beat. "Bob,

Fred, and I do an annual hunting trip," he says to Lewis. Lewis just nods again, as politely but noncommittally as he can. "Bob owns a nice piece of land out by the Belleisle. The deer love it."

Bob has been doing most of the talking, but the other man, the one Lewis thinks is named Fred, says, "We always have a great time. Though last year was tough on Tom! Ha, ha."

Tom smiles weakly. "Certainly messed up my hunting." He turns to Lewis. "Had an upset stomach. Never get one, but for some reason I couldn't stop going to the bathroom."

"Which was in the great outdoors!" says the one possibly called Fred. Ha, ha. "Speaking of which," says Fred, "did you guys hear about the idiot who exposed himself to a bunch of girls just across the street? Just last week. Right here," and he points violently out the window toward the river. "At East Riverside. Made the paper."

Lewis's shoulders tighten and raise slightly of their own accord within the suddenly less reassuring confines of Drescher's suit. His large feet have shifted position during the last few minutes, and he edges back a couple of feet so he's standing right in front of the kitchen light.

"Really?" says Tom noncommittally to Fred.

In his heightened state, a well-dressed prey animal, Lewis notices Bob glancing down and around. Lewis has never met him before, but the way he is pursing his lips and moving his head seems somehow uncharacteristic. He is looking for all intents and purposes like someone hoping for a quick change of conversation topic, not like the self-satisfied, well-off lawyer that Lewis has taken him for since he met him less than twenty minutes ago. Lewis has never prided himself on hiding his feelings but hopes he's not looking as uncomfortable as Bob.

"Yeah," Fred continues, taking Tom's laconic question for genuine interest. "I can't believe this is happening in Rothesay. You'd expect it in uptown Saint John, with all the homeless, maybe even in King Square where they hang out, but not here." Fred glances at the three other men, looking for confirmation that the sleepy suburb of Rothesay should be immune from indecent exposure.

"Maybe he just had to really go to the bathroom," Tom suggests helpfully. Good old practical Tom. Beneath his designer clothes and killer social graces lurks a tolerant man. If everybody were like Tom, Lewis would have nothing to worry about it.

At this, Bob lifts his head and looks directly at his host. His physical unease has been replaced by an urgent resolve to speak. "Not a fucking chance." Bob clearly has the floor now. The other men don't have to wait long for more. "This was *not* some homeless guy out taking a leak."

"Really?" Tom says.

"Really." Bob is grim. "Definitely not homeless. Psychotic, maybe." He takes a noisy sip of wine and swallows. It's clear from how he's tensing his jaw that he's willing himself to continue. He looks down when he says, "Elspeth was involved," but from the way his jaw slackens a little, the sentence is cathartic.

"What?" says Fred.

"Elspeth is his daughter," Tom says helpfully for Lewis's benefit.

Bob nods at this, as if to confirm Tom is telling the truth. "I'm probably not supposed to be telling you this — Elspeth's identity is not being revealed because she's a minor — but if you can't talk to your friends, who can you talk to? You won't believe it when I tell you. I still can't believe it. Hell, I find it hard to even talk about it. But if my story helps you protect your own daughters, it will be worth it." Even in his nervous state of anticipation, Lewis can't help observing that fathers put a lot more effort into protecting their daughters than their sons. Bob takes a big sip of wine as if he needs to fortify himself again.

Bob doesn't have what might be called a sensitive face, but he looks like he is about to cry. "Believe it or not, some fucker ... flashed her. Flashed my Elspeth." Bob's eyes widen in pain and disbelief. "As Fred said, it happened just across the street from here, at the park." Bob is pointing out the darkened window in the direction of the river and glaring at Tom as if the proximity of the crime to his home is somehow his fault. "And there were boys too, not just girls," he adds as if the presence of both genders somehow makes it even worse. Bob, ever the lawyer, has a deep-seated compulsion for factual accuracy.

"You're not serious," says Tom, but despite himself he can't stop smiling just a little at the mental picture of Bob's teenage daughter coming across a flasher. Luckily for their friendship, Bob has been drinking all evening and doesn't notice.

"Totally. She was with friends walking by the park on the way to catch the bus when some maniac jumped out of the bushes grabbing his cock! He mumbled something about having to take a pee, but he was holding himself and shaking it at her!" He turns to Fred as if to reprimand him and says, "This was not some homeless guy who had nowhere to go! This is someone who has deep issues with women." Said, perhaps inadvertently, with the quiet confidence that comes from first-hand knowledge. And then quickly returning his attention to Tom and Lewis: "Can you believe this happened here in Rothesay? I used to take Elspeth to play in the park when she was a little girl." He takes another gulp of wine. Looks again like he might be about to cry.

Lewis fears a real bout of hyperventilation coming on, and he notices the guilty hand in question, which now just happens to be holding his wine glass, is shaking. He pulls his suddenly large, evil-looking hand toward him so he's holding the glass tightly against his chest. His young persecutor has a lovely name: Elspeth Fielding.

"Oh my God," says Tom. "How is Elspeth doing?" For some reason Lewis is relieved that Tom finally has his crazy smiling under control.

"As good as can be expected. Poor girl. It shouldn't happen to anyone." Another thirsty sip. "Luckily she got a good description."

Lewis involuntarily looks down at the floor before realizing what he's doing and lifts his chin so quickly he is afraid he has given himself a mild case of whiplash. He is still standing with his back to the bright kitchen light, but now he moves slightly to his left so the light is directly behind him. He hopes the effect on his face is somewhat like an eclipse.

"I took her down to the police station after school. She made a report and sat down with the police sketch artist to describe the flasher." Now that Bob is into the details he is calming down, sounding almost reflective. "Strange-looking fucker from what she told me. Tall, good dresser, not bad-looking. But weird: blond and brown-eyed. Had a dog with him, too. I didn't see the drawing myself, but Elspeth says it's pretty accurate. Elspeth did her part, of course. She has excellent eyesight — which is part of the reason she's so good at sports — and is good at describing things. But the artist who does the drawing is one of the best in the business. Simon Turner. My wife, Jacqueline, knows him from her work on the Beaverbrook's Board of Governors. Apparently he paints on the side. He's supposed to be quite good at that as well."

Lewis hopes the man is a closet Picasso with ambition to burn. Anything but the type of talented mediocre painter whom the birth of photography forever consigned to oblivion: someone compelled to record everything he sees without sufficient imagination or desire to alter it in the slightest. The kind of artist who produces work that people who don't know anything about art think is great — in short, the kind of artist Miranda would have hated.

Bob pauses as if in thought. "Normally they would have passed Elspeth onto one of the street cops and the whole thing would have gone nowhere. But I put in a quiet word with the chief. He assigned one of his top detectives: our own Billy Blunt." Fred and Tom nod.

"We all know him from hockey," Tom says to Lewis.

"Good guy," says Bob, as if agreeing with Tom. "He told me he was going to stake out the park himself for the next couple of weeks."

Lewis finds himself hunching over, slouching his shoulders. He can't help running his free hand through his hair, trying to brush it away from his forehead, even though he's already cut it short to avoid being recognized by the police. He is pleased to find it feeling more than a little greasy. Since he stopped going into the office he has stopped showering and washing his hair every day. If he skips a day, his hair appears darker by a couple of shades. But Bob isn't paying him the slightest attention. Neither is Tom or Fred. Fucking flashers don't attend Tom and Maura's cocktail parties.

"Lucky you're a lawyer and know the system," says Tom, probably still thinking of Elspeth.

At this point Lewis determines his own precarious luck is just about to run out. He swallows the rest of his expensive wine, mumbles a few words of sympathy to Bob, mutters the good-to-meet-you platitude to Fred, and excuses himself to Tom. He says something about going to refill his glass and clumsily backs away from the group while remaining firmly ensconced in the shadow of the bright kitchen light.

12

AFTER THEY RETURN from Tom's and Maura's, as they are lying together in bed, Laura sleepily askes Lewis to tell her something. But Lewis is out of stories. No humorous anecdotes about Randall. No witty "Drescherisms." No mini epics of design dragons that have to be slain. Aside from helping Laura make organic lunches for the children and pacing the house, almost nothing has happened to Lewis in recent memory. Nothing except the incident in the park. Or was it an episode? Lewis is not sure which word is more appropriate. Maybe what happened has no word: maybe it is so ineffable it is defined solely by its location: "the park." No matter the word, it is the only thing worth talking about, but neither Lewis nor Laura are prepared to bring it up. Lewis is hoping that if he doesn't talk about it it will, at least on some level, cease to exist. Since *the park*, Lewis has not even been able to walk Rufus because he doesn't want to be recognized publicly in the presence of his dog.

Rufus is irrevocably loyal to Lewis, and if he is disappointed, he doesn't show it. But he must feel something. After Lewis stopped going into the office he took Rufus for two to three walks a day. Indeed, the only living creature in the Morton household for whom

Lewis having no work was a boon — at least initially — was Rufus. With all the walks Lewis took in vain attempts to calm his nerves prior to the episode in the park, Rufus is in better shape than when he was a puppy.

Instead of listening to Lewis tell her a funny or suspenseful story of life at Drescher & Drescher, Laura is falling asleep on his shoulder in silence. Lewis is conscious of his shallow breathing, the feeling of unease in his stomach, the random worries that are starting to afflict him for the first time in years as soon as he is alone with his thoughts, which is now happening almost all the time. Without the respectable, and therefore manageable, pressures, dramas, and risks of work to deal with — will he get such and such a client, will the client like the proposed design, will the client be able to afford the design, will the design meet the client and Lewis's expectations, will the design win any awards — Lewis starts worrying again about everything else.

The day before, Alexandra came down with a very painful ear infection. Laura took her to the doctor and she's now on antibiotics. But Lewis wonders if the infection will clear up or prove resistant because of all the antibiotics everyone is ingesting in their milk and chicken thanks to unscrupulous farmers who are trying to keep their animals alive long enough to slaughter them. Will the ear infection therefore worsen, and will Alexandra's little eardrum burst? And if that happens, will it really heal on its own as the doctor assured them, or will little darling Alexandra suffer irreversible hearing damage?

But while worrying about Alexandra, why stop there? Will baby Skye ever learn to walk? Will kinetic Samuel, who has developed an infatuation with Spider-Man, crack his head open when he jumps on and off the living room couch pretending he is scaling buildings? Will Lewis's underemployed status affect Judah's emotional development? Will the little dog Laura has fallen in love with at the animal shelter and is threatening to bring home as a companion to both her and Rufus end up peeing regularly on the floor? Will Lewis ever win out against the weeds that threaten to overrun their garden because Laura refuses to use herbicides or pesticides? Will the oceans continue to be polluted with mercury, and will commercial fisheries push every fish to extinction? Will the cute mole on Laura's back change colour one day and turn to cancer?

Lewis's anxiety is not mitigated or bound by any real sense of probability: the only boundary is possibility. If something is possible then it is worth fearing. This is why even the occasion of the birth of their first son was fraught with such mixed emotions. When Judah was born, what should have been an unadulterated occasion of bliss for Lewis became a new source of intense anxiety. The worry actually started several months before the birth.

At eighteen weeks, Laura had her first ultrasound, and she and Lewis found out they were having a boy. Judah would not be technically Jewish according to the strict religious law stipulating that Judaism was passed down through the mother — the exception being liberal Reform Judaism, in which a child could be Jewish as long as one parent was. However, it had always been Lewis's and Laura's intent to raise all their children as at least half Jewish and, with the boys anyway, to have them circumcised.

But in the months leading up to Judah's birth, Lewis happened to encounter several articles about the cruelties of circumcision, including the pain involved and the lesser enjoyment of sex it apparently inflicted. The prevailing current wisdom seemed to be that circumcision was a barbaric custom held over from the Old Testament and was certainly unfit for modern society. Considering that most boys were circumcised as infants, it was hard to compare sexual pleasure before and after, but Lewis came across the story of an African man who had grown up with his foreskin, only to be circumcised in adulthood due to some complication with said foreskin, which occasionally happened if it was too tight. This man claimed that his ability to enjoy sex had been greatly lessened by the operation. The fear and sense of guilt that perhaps Lewis was condemning his son to a lifetime of sexual unfulfillment and incompleteness would normally have been sufficient to give Lewis a minor panic attack.

But Lewis was sent off the edge into a whole new world of apprehension when he happened to read a two-page spread in the national newspaper about the strange 1950s case of a boy whose circumcision was botched and who as a result was subsequently turned into a girl. Apparently the circumcision itself had gone well, but when a relatively new medical tool designed to cauterize the wound had malfunctioned, burning off most of the innocent little penis, the stricken parents had made the battlefield decision to amputate what was left of the injured member and the little day-old testicles and to create a vagina. Years later, the woman, who never felt fully comfortable as a female, found out what had happened. It was like rediscovering a lost part of her (him) self, and she went in for gender re-reassignment surgery to build a hanging piece of flesh to return her to some semblance of maleness. Lewis could sort of understand the process of starting off as a man and becoming a woman, going from the presence of something to the absence of something. Although when Lewis did think about this, he often found himself wondering whether there were any cases of men wanting to become women, going through with the operation, and then waking up the next day sans penis and balls and regretting their decision. But while worrying on the overall subject, Lewis could never figure out how the new man-made male genitalia worked, or *if* they did, and what they used to stand in for testicles.

All Lewis could think of as his little boy Judah came out with a long-looking, foreskinned penis that was so perfect was why his forefathers had come up with such a brutal and child-unfriendly custom to mark their boys as chosen. Why couldn't they have come up with a special tattoo? Or a traditionally shaped earring? Or a bracelet? Or long hair like the Sikhs? Although in Judaism the ritual operation was supposed to happen at eight days, and while Lewis knew the sooner the better, he put it off until Judah was three weeks old. Finally, he and Laura brought Judah back to the hospital to have it done.

Lewis couldn't bear to look but stayed in another room while the doctor strapped his baby boy, flesh of his flesh, onto the piece of plastic board with the straps for his hands and feet and bound tight those little wrists and ankles. As the doctor began to cut the foreskin — so different from the mohel in the synagogue who cut while the parents held the baby in the centre of a crowd of relatives and friends who sang and swayed and celebrated a new Jewish baby being ushered into the tribe with a blade — Lewis worried that the doctor might have a sudden paroxysm or fainting fit and would accidentally slice off the tip of Judah's baby-sized penis. In Saint John, with its infinitesimal Jewish population, there was no mohel, and they had to settle for a skilled and empathetic pediatrician.

When they brought Judah home, his little penis was black and blue from base to sawed-off tip, and it seemed so much smaller than before. It looked like a bloody stump, and Lewis couldn't bear to change him. Although it was his religion that was being honoured with the snipping of the flesh, Lewis delegated to Laura the smearing of the Vaseline that had to be applied several times a day so the wounded little penis didn't stick to the diaper. When it still did occasionally, Lewis was never so sick with grief and guilt and regret.

Weeks later, when the horror receded and Judah's penis looked to be fine and appeared to act that way through the welcome manifestation of multiple newborn erections, Lewis's guilt shifted to having caused his first-born to look different in a region of the country where circumcision wasn't as popular as it was in the major urban centres. Lewis could only hope that Judah would never develop an interest in team sports and would never have to disrobe in the locker room.

Once something terrible, like a botched circumcision, is suggested to Lewis, he cannot ever get it out of his mind. Worse, he feels compelled to imagine what it would be like to experience it. Not only does Lewis have to fully imagine the horrible situation, he has to mentally assure himself that if it did happen to him he would be able to deal with it. But despite all his best efforts, Lewis has never been able to figure out how he would cope with the loss of a filial penis.

BECAUSE LEWIS IS living with increasing levels of anxiety, for the sake of his dwindling sense of sanity he seeks safe ground where he can live up to some standard of masculinity, courage, and self-respect. He must find a small place to channel his irrationality into courage, not fear, into productive action, not passivity. And because he is not working he has to find this special place, this state of mind, at home. Specifically, in household chores. Now that Lewis is home, he is expected to help out more around the house. Changing diapers, making lunches, cleaning up the kitchen. Not that Lewis doesn't appreciate the opportunity to contribute more. But it soon becomes apparent that he and his soulmate, Laura, have different attitudes to the basic building blocks of domestic life.

The morning after the cocktail party, Laura is making lunches and directing Lewis to put every completed element in the children's lunch containers. Lewis reaches for the plastic wrap and is halfway to wrapping Judah's veggie ham sandwich — the wrap is sticking in all the wrong places — when Laura pauses her organic carrot peeling and turns to Lewis. "What are you doing?"

Lewis is now uncertain. "Wrapping lunches?"

"It might be fine for you — you're a grown man — but we don't use plastic for the kids." Lewis looks blank for a moment, so Laura reminds him, "It's a proven hormone disrupter," before returning to her carrot peeling. "Please use the stainless steel containers." Laura adds, "They're over there," pointing to one of the kitchen drawers that Lewis is not overly familiar with.

Lewis has heard all the facts before about estrogen-mimicking hormones in some plastics that are causing ever-decreasing levels of testosterone in males, shorter average penis sizes for male newborns, and the metamorphosis of male frogs into female ones around major city sewage outlets as a result of the birth control residue that millions of women urinate into the toilet multiple times a day. Lewis isn't sure whether the water and soap used to clean the containers each day is much better for the environment, but for Laura the answer is crystal clear.

Lewis complies with Laura's directive, but he so resents the constant pressure to be environmentally virtuous within the new limitations of his domestic responsibilities that he resolves to rebel that evening. When clearing off the plates after supper, while nobody is looking, he will sweep clearly compostable materials into the garbage container under the kitchen sink, thereby thumbing his nose at the world of do-gooders and political correctness and channeling his inner rebel without a cause. Laura must sense that Lewis has not fully bought in to her philosophy because she says, without bothering to look up from the carrots she is now assiduously rinsing, "Maybe you don't care about your own health or the environment, but I'm sure you do care about the health of our children and the health of our children's future children."

Lewis concedes the point with a nod that Laura can't see. But inside he is still a rebel. Because now that Lewis no longer has any architectural work to live for, he is learning he likes to live danger-ously. This is paradoxical to him because he is also increasingly anxious. In the short respites between his panic attacks, it occurs to Lewis that perhaps anxiety begets a wild, reckless courage, as if he were fictional Francis Macomber about to conquer his fear of lions in Hemingway's short story. While Laura is still occupied with rinsing, Lewis quickly wraps himself a snack in tinfoil because he has two coffee meetings with two architects he barely knows to suss out professional opportunities.

As Lewis and Laura argue over packaging, Samuel is refusing to eat his small helping of organic oatmeal with equally organic maple syrup. Instead he is carefully filling in a page in his favourite colouring book: *Superhero Friends*. A week earlier he saw the book on TV, and Laura had to visit four stores to find it. Then Samuel made her buy three packs of crayons before he could find one with the exact right red for Spider-Man's costume. Today he is colouring Superman's blue tights. He is intent and content, but Lewis, despite a seemingly safe distance of nearly thirty years separating him from his childhood, can't suppress a feeling of uneasiness as he watches Samuel colour between the lines.

MIRANDA WOULD REGULARLY encourage Lewis to capture, interpret, and reinvent the world around him, and she used every occasion — birthdays, annual grade school graduations, and holidays — to reward and motivate him with gifts of art supplies. Sketchbooks of fine paper, coloured and black pencils in assorted degrees of hardness and softness, oil pastels, charcoals, soft white German erasers and finely engineered steel pencil sharpeners, watercolour paints in a variety of quaintly decorated tins. By the age of ten, Lewis had — by far — the best collection of pastels and drawing charcoal of anyone in his school.

When other elementary school-aged children were happy to receive as gifts colouring books and markers or books of con-nect-the-dot exercises that brought to life cartoons of Mickey Mouse or other Disney icons, Miranda was buying Lewis art books with images he never forgot. Fat naked people lolling around; people being burned, flayed alive, stabbed, bayoneted; people holding their ears and screaming on bridges; people dying on battlefields, in beds, in each other's arms, hanging dead from trees, sitting alive with their ears cut off. Not once in her life did Miranda ever buy Lewis a simple colouring book: she thought they were the most unimaginative and heinous things in the world, an insult to the creativity inside every child. If Lewis received a colouring book as a gift from an ignorant relative or the parents of a friend, Miranda would throw it in the garbage before the end of the day. It was a lesson that Lewis internalized and never forgot.

WHEN HE GREW up and he and Laura began to have children, Lewis never bought any of them a colouring book. And when Lewis sees any of his beloved children colouring at the kitchen table — because Laura has none of Miranda's artistic qualms — he can't pass by without a nervous feeling in his stomach. But he refuses to ever say anything about it to any of his children or to Laura, so today, as he encourages Samuel to eat his oatmeal, he also compliments him on his colouring. Samuel doesn't look up, but his "Thanks, Dad," is filled with pride.

The vegetables are finally scrubbed to Laura's satisfaction, but her small sense of accomplishment turns to frustration when she sees Lewis guiltily shoving his own snack into a plastic grocery bag with the store receipt still in it. Because it's his health at stake and not that of their progeny, Laura doesn't bother with words and instead settles for a dramatic eye roll. Lewis finds the expression strangely attractive, and perhaps this spurs him to take the verbal risk of defending the indefensible: "Laura, I know environmental studies link exposure to aluminum foil to Alzheimer's. I want to get early Alzheimer's so I don't notice and feel depressed about the shrinking size of my penis and my plummeting testosterone levels from my lunches on the other days when I wrap everything in plastic." Lewis says this with a smile and a joking tone, but Laura doesn't laugh. She harrumphs and walks out of the room. But before she does, she stops at the kitchen door and leaves him with something to ponder.

"You can laugh, but you should know the paper used to print store receipts is coated in bisphenol A. It gets on your skin and from there it can get into your bloodstream. It's a known hormone disruptor: it mimics estrogen. And in case you've forgotten, estrogen is good for women, to a point. But less good for men." And Laura looks pointedly down at his groin with an oh-well shake of her head and shrug of her shoulders. Then she's gone.

After this, Lewis's rebellious stance flags just a little. As vigorously, but also as quietly, as he can, he washes his hands in soapy water. To demonstrate his newfound courage in the face of adversity and to combat his increasing anxiety levels, Lewis is now able to joke bravely about the emasculating effects of everyday chemicals on his penis and testicles. But he is not quite ready to give up on his genitalia entirely.

AS SOON AS the children get on their respective buses with their paper bag lunches containing only organic ingredients, and after Lewis watches each bus turn the corner on the way to school without having veered off the road into the river, he rushes back up the hill and jumps in his car. He gave Laura the impression that he was in a rush, but his first networking meeting is not for another two hours. He just wants to drive by the scene of the crime, to stake out the stakeout, if there really is one underway. When he reaches Rothesay Road at the bottom of the steep hill, he turns right. Up ahead he can already see the small parking lot at East Riverside-Kingshurst Park. It is empty except for a suspicious-looking dark blue Taurus that Lewis assumes belongs to Detective Blunt.

Lewis's car is now barely moving as he slows down to take in the scene. He illogically assumes that Blunt — if the detective glances toward the road and not the bushes while he waits for the Rothesay Flasher to put in another appearance — will interpret Lewis's slow speed as the natural overreaction to any police car on the road, especially an unmoving and unmarked one. As Lewis cruises by the park he is able to just make out the outline of the detective in the driver's seat of his car. From what Lewis can see of Blunt's body language, he is unusually observant. He is bringing a cup of Tim Hortons to his lips and clearly pretending to be on a coffee break. But his head is turned and he's scanning the park, especially the areas with bushes. On the dashboard he has a piece of paper. Lewis can't make it out in detail, but it looks like a drawing. It must be the police artist's drawing of him. And Blunt has a partner with him. Except this man sitting in the passenger seat doesn't look anything like a police officer, not even one in plain clothes like Blunt. He is thin and pale, and his hair is too long. Maybe he's an informant or another witness.

And then Lewis is past the parked car.

Lewis hasn't thought regularly about Mordecai in years. But as he drives away from the park and tries to decide where he will kill time before his first networking coffee of the day, he wonders briefly and only half consciously what Mordecai would think about his grown son's panicky thoughts. Mordecai wouldn't waste a precious second of his life worrying about a police officer of any rank. He would have everything firmly under control.

PART TWO

What would Drescher do?

— LEWIS MORTON

13

AS LEWIS'S LEGAL limbo and exile from Drescher & Drescher stretches past a month, he begins to regret not having pursued more hobbies over the course of his life. And as his increasing inability to concentrate and enjoy anything lowers the probability of him being able to take up any new hobbies, he is both amazed and horrified to discover how brutish and unsupported life is on the "outside."

While nestled securely within Drescher & Drescher's protective cocoon, Lewis was able to focus his entire mind and soul on designing beautiful buildings. He never had to worry about infinitely unimportant telecommunications or IT or photocopiers or mail or even booking rooms or appointments. His saintly sixty-year-old assistant, Elizabeth, made everything happen like an effective Wizard of Oz. Lewis just had to buzz her once on the office intercom and she would appear. She never complained about being interrupted or not being able to accomplish the daily litany of tasks that Lewis threw at her without any sense of the limitation of the laws of physics. Elizabeth would take notes, smile, perhaps ask a question or two, and then disappear. And everything in Lewis's world that needed to occur for him to devote himself to designing buildings would happen.

When Lewis stops going into the office he has no idea how to do anything that everyone else takes for granted, like remembering his password for voicemail. When Lewis can't figure out how to sum a column in Excel, he is about to reach for the phone when he realizes he no longer has access to any IT support. Figuring out how to use Laura's three-in-one laser printer, fax machine, and photocopier seems beyond his grasp. When it comes to anything outside of architecture, Lewis is helpless. At Drescher & Drescher he knew how to get things done, how to delegate, and, more importantly, what needed to be done. But the last time he did any-thing himself other than think big thoughts and put pen to paper, he was in university. And the world has changed a lot in nearly twenty years.

Lewis, who never worried about his writing, including his fine spelling and highly honed ability to avoid stupid grammatical mis-takes, now becomes paralyzed by the thought and act of writing an email. He who formerly led a team of younger architects and fired off emails — questions, directions, exhortations, fragments of thoughts spilling out of his brain about light, space, materials, and clients faster than his fingers could keep up on the keyboard at all hours of the day, when just waking up or before going to bed, while on the toilet, eating, or walking — without ever worrying about whether he was writing in complete sentences or repeating words or missing words, as long as the sense came across, now frets whenever he finds himself at a keyboard.

Lewis has read that piece on the Internet that shows that even if most of the letters in a word are jumbled, as long as the first and last letters remain unchanged people can still amazingly and easily read them. But now, as Lewis looks for a new position outside

Drescher & Drescher that will lift him out of the limbo in which Montcalm has placed him, Lewis has to prove himself again each time, and the slightest error can disqualify him. So he pores over the resume that he tailors for each job and over every cover letter he writes. He rereads them aloud multiple times and begins to sweat as he hears himself give voice to his words.

Lewis is no longer providing direction, expressing appreciation, offering wisdom, surfacing hidden meaning, or laying down an irresistible challenge to his team or peers: now Lewis is engaged in that most unromantic, unheroic, overrated, over-examined, borderline suicidal writing of the modern age: the composition of the Cover Letter. When it comes to the Cover Letter, Lewis never knows where to end or, compounding his problems, where to begin. With himself? With the job? How much to tell about himself? How much to brag?

He googles cover letter templates on the Internet, and they all look fine, if a little generic and over the top, like he will be making himself out to be the archetypal executive, which he is not. He is an architect. And so he agonizes over every word and writes every cover letter from scratch. Over time, as the non-replies mount — Lewis has an imaginary stack of rejection letters on his desk — he becomes a little more self-promotional. But still he lingers over every word and is tentative with his thoughts, which increasingly seem to him like a building that will not stand, and he reads and rereads his work several times before he presses "send." It's as if he has forgotten how to spell. Lewis blames his ever-weakening nerves.

ONE MORNING, LEWIS feels more confident than usual. He is applying for a job with a firm that specializes in designing public buildings and spaces. Lewis has worked on some major projects with Drescher and knows that his experience and projects stand out in the region. So he loads his cover letter with a few key examples — public squares, corporate buildings, museum renovations — and he finishes with what he has no doubt is a marketing tour de force: "In summary, I feel confident that my experience with public architecture is unparalleled in the region."

Although Lewis is feeling unusually positive about his credentials, his cover letter, his experience, his chances, he rereads his email three times, one of those times backwards because he has learned that technique on the Internet. On his third read he catches one missing word, an *and*, and types it in. He confirms that he has correctly spelled it (twice) and triple-checks the spelling of his name, because he knows that sometimes when he is in a rush, instead of spelling "Lewis" his finger slides over a little to the left and "Lewis" will come out as "Lewia" on the screen. Happily, this time he has it right. And with a strangely buoyant feeling, Lewis hits "send."

Just as Lewis presses the button, he recognizes he has made only one small error in his email cover letter. He has left out just one little letter, an "l." But his fingers are no match for his brain, and like a president who presses launch on the missile system only to realize at that split second that there is a glitch in his defence system, that indeed no missiles have been launched against him but it is too late to do anything about it, Lewis watches as his email is sent to its destination. Only in this case the missile is pointed at him.

Normally the mistake would have merely frustrated and embarrassed Lewis. But this time it unhinges him. For on either side of where the "l" should have been, like a line solidly defining the border between success and failure, between Lewis the sane and Lewis the insane, Lewis the cool and collected and Lewis the incapable, is a "b" and an "i."

In the writing nightmare scenario of public relations people everywhere with reference to spelling out the name of their profession, Lewis meant to write "public" as in "public architecture," but he has inadvertently — or perhaps it was a Freudian slip, who knows these days — just emailed a cover letter for a job having included the immortal phrase "pubic architecture." As in Lewis has the most familiarity of any architect in the region with "pubic architecture."

THE EPISODE WITH the cover letter unsettles Lewis, and he wonders again if he should turn himself in to the police. Ever since he was first made aware of it, the threat of Maurits Abercrom's lawsuit has been stalking Lewis's professional future like an unseen lion. Lewis can hear its distant roar: deep and formidable yet somehow unreal in sleepy Rothesay. But for weeks after the incident in East Riverside-Kingshurst Park, as Lewis is waking up, falling asleep, taking the older children to or from the school bus, cleaning the house, pretending to read but really staring blindly out the window, Lewis has been beset by acute anxiety and an immediate sense of indecision.

Should he should give himself up? Drive over to police headquarters and make a full confession? Throw himself completely on the mercy of the court? On the mercy of his teenage prosecutor, who now has a name? Elspeth. Elspeth Fielding. Elspeth, daughter of Bob. Lewis has to concede the girl who could single-handedly put him in jail has a beautiful name. Ever since he was a child and learned that his family name was once Mortinsky, Lewis has had a particular interest in names. He googles the name Elspeth and is not surprised when the Internet tells him the name means "God is perfection." Or "God is my oath." Now that the girl in the park has a name, Lewis's fears become even more defined.

If Elspeth decides to press charges, and if Lewis is convicted, which he is sure he will be — intent is only a mitigating factor in murder cases — his life is finished. Nobody will ever hire him again. He will lose his house. The children will be ridiculed or shunned at school. The bullying will get to them, and they will grow up psychologically broken. People will pass Lewis on the street with a knowing smile or a smirk. He will become the prurient topic of conversation at dinner parties, like the local doctor who slept with her patients or the upstanding CEO of the local high-profile, do-gooding not-for-profit who was found in the closet with his secretary. Or the teenage boy from a good family in Rothesay who one lovely summer evening took out the family Cadillac Escalade and exposed himself over the course of an hour to three separate parties of middle-aged women out for walks. Based on the stories Lewis has heard over the years, it is a rite of passage for liberated twentieth- and twenty-first-century women to be unwillingly exposed in their lives to the sight of at least one penis, usually glimpsed from or in a moving car.

At least the teenager was able to mount a defence with a straight face that he had been smoking up for most of the day leading up to his rampage. The boy's father, who happened to be a former wild, hard-drinking bagman for the provincial Conservatives but who had become a grey-haired and sober judge counting down the days to his retirement after twenty-five years of suffering through the legal profession that he hated, was embarrassed when the police officer came to the door and asked him a lot of questions about his vehicle and his whereabouts the evening before. But the accused was still a teenager and "boys will be boys," and his father's handpicked lawyer with a Gaelic gift of the gab, a Hollywood smile, and an infinite web of political connections spun the joyride as just another freshman dare gone a little awry and got his youthful client off with a suspended sentence and a warning.

But what excuse does Lewis have? He is a grown man, years beyond his early twenties, sober father of four, devoted husband, technically still employed as an architect with a leading regional firm. He has never smoked dope in his life. Always drank extremely moderately, although now he is starting to regret his previous borderline teetotalling ways, his absolute reasonableness in every social situation. Lewis has never drunk himself into a stupor or fallen down dead drunk at anyone's feet, never made inappropriate remarks while holding onto a handrail, never drunkenly proclaimed his love for a sports team or a religion or a vanished way of life to a cheering audience composed of close friends and complete strangers.

Lewis can easily see how the prosecution will approach his case. They will paint the picture of a quiet, inoffensive man who has never done anything out of the ordinary but who was suddenly and very firmly pushed over the edge by losing the anchor of his cherished and prestigious professional position. Lewis will be framed by the prosecutor as the latest poster boy for the middle-aged man — he is almost that — who lost his professional identify and his self-respect. As a result, he regressed to an adolescent who couldn't distinguish right from wrong and who, with too much time on his hands — the devil makes work for idle hands, no pun intended — began to derive his jollies from severely immature but nonetheless highly dangerous and socially deviant behaviour.

Everyone knows what starts as a simple case of indecent exposure in a park will quickly escalate if left unchecked into far worse crimes that Lewis can't bring himself to contemplate. And doesn't he have a habit of walking around the house with his fly unzipped, as Laura never ceases to remind him? She sees it as a sign both of absent-mindedness and lasciviousness, wondering if he conducts himself at work that way. Each time Laura looks down disapprovingly at his un-gated nether regions and Lewis reaches for his zipper he has to remind her that no, no, and no, he never walks around that way at work, it is only at home when he is relaxed.

In his increasing disquiet, Lewis finds he is asking himself another of the great questions of his life. The first significant question of Lewis's late childhood and early adolescence, before he began to wonder what he should become and how he might keep himself sane, was about his parents. What should Mordecai have done to keep Miranda out of hospital? The current existential question eternally on Lewis's mind is the abbreviated WWDD? As in, What Would Drescher Do?, after those thought-provoking licence plates reminding you to ask yourself WWJD?, as in, What Would Jesus Do?

It is after the "pubic architecture" typo, when Lewis is asking himself whether Drescher would have let it go or followed up quickly with an apology and a correction, that Lewis tries on one of Drescher's suits he received from Miriam, a dark blue pin-stripe. This is the second time Lewis has worn one of the suits. The first time he had Tom's cocktail party to attend. This time there is no social occasion, no outward purpose. Lewis is dressing in the suit solely for himself. He puts it on slowly, contemplatively, almost religiously, as if hoping Drescher's aura will rub off on him, as though Drescher's spirit can somehow speak to Lewis through the fine Italian wool that once touched his skin. The suit feels good on his body, and a nervous habit is immediately formed. If Lewis is feeling particularly anxious about a course of action, from now on he will try on one of Drescher's suits for solace and wisdom. But each time the suits, as finely tailored as they are, remain silent.

Whenever Lewis asks himself WWDD with respect to *the park* — which is now multiple times a day — he torments himself each time with the answer. He knows that if Drescher, being the steadfast and courageous straight shooter he was, no pun intended, had ever found himself in Lewis's public-urination-interrupted situation, he would have wasted no time in marching on down to the police station with clear eyes, a set jaw, and an un-furrowed forehead bordered by closely cropped but impeccably coiffed silver hair. Drescher would have declared himself, and with those über-civilized, well-enunciated, almost European-sounding tones immediately cleared up the misunderstanding beyond a shadow of a doubt.

Lewis knows that all the police officers on duty, both senior and junior, would have believed Drescher and would have come away convinced that the episode in the park was what it was, a misunderstanding. How could anyone doubt Drescher's silver-haired assurance, his benign, confident, steady grey-eyed gaze, his tanned skin that he acquired each winter in the Caribbean and that never deserted him, not even in Saint John's rainy, foggy moistness, his sense of poise, the impression he created without ever trying that everything that came out of his mouth was unassailable and indisputable, like the pharaoh in the MGM blockbuster *The Ten Commandments*, played by some famous Hollywood bald guy, who finished every sentence with "So let it be written. So let it be done." Only Drescher never even had to say it, it just was. Drescher never spoke loudly, but he always gave off the impression — like a whiff of testosterone — that he was in command and was impervious to pressure or panic. This quality, which Lewis so admired because he saw so little of it in himself, was evident in Drescher's devotion to his craft in the face of sometimes overbearing client demands.

It was Randall at Drescher & Drescher who always said that one of the traps that even good architects sometimes fell into was giving clients what they wanted rather than what they needed and so absolving themselves of responsibility for a litany of architectural monstrosities, like a sequence of rooms that was one non sequitur after another or windows of varying size with no unifying theme or a mishmash of materials that screamed nothing. Drescher was fanatical about avoiding this failing. He was a flexible man in many respects, but he would sooner fire a client than do what the client wanted if what the client wanted clashed with Drescher & Drescher's vision of architectural beauty, the marriage of form and function where function was the master and form was the mistress of the house.

And Drescher fired clients on more than one celebrated occasion, storming out in a huff when a famous Hollywood actor demanded a house that was the result of the repeated hallucinations of his wife, an actress with no architectural sense. The ink drawings she handed off to Drescher on silk napkins were a dizzying cocktail of art nouveau, Spanish colonial, Bauhaus, and neo-colonial styles. When the actor stood in front of Drescher and melodramatically shouted that he absolutely would not allow Drescher to leave until he designed his house, as if he were reciting lines in a bad action movie, and put his big hands menacingly on Drescher's shoulders, Drescher felt he was being physically intimidated. He punched the actor in the mouth, breaking one of his capped white teeth, and said, "Fuck you," only he drew out the second word for several seconds. The actor wanted to sue, but his agent eventually talked him out of it. He convinced him that the publicity surrounding being on the wrong end of a fight with his skinny, fashionable, older architect had the potential to seriously and permanently tarnish his well-cultivated image as an action hero.

But whenever Lewis lapses into these unproductive masochistic fantasies, in which what Drescher does is invariably braver, more sensible, and more successful than anything he himself is doing or not doing, Lewis always reaches the same inevitable conclusion: Drescher never would have found himself in the same position in the first place. He wouldn't have walked so far that he got ahead of his bladder, and if he had he would have had enough mental and physical discipline to walk back home before relieving himself in public, never putting himself in the weak and indefensible position of being exposed and spied upon by a marauding party of barbaric adolescents.

14

THE MORTON CLAN is enjoying that transitional time after supper and before bed when the day is slowly unwinding. Judah is working on his homework at the dining room table. He doesn't look stressed or hurried. He has a book open on the table and is completing some English homework on his laptop. At least Lewis assumes it is English because from the kitchen where he is loading the dishwasher he can make out several distinct paragraphs. It looks suspiciously like a well-thought-out essay. Lewis can't see the title of Judah's book from where he's standing, but he is secretly pleased that his son still reads old-fashioned print books and that his public school still assigns old-fashioned essays.

Lewis is secretly pleased with many things about Judah, as he is with all his children. Lewis watches as his first-born son types away. Judah stops occasionally to think — which is good, in Lewis's eyes — but when he is in the midst of typing, his strokes are regular and deliberate. He knows what he wants to say. He doesn't hesitate, doesn't search for words or phrases. This is the way Judah approaches all his subjects, and he excels at every single one, whether English, math, or gym. No right brain, left brain confusion going on in Judah's well-screwed-on twelve-year-old head.

He has also done well in art when it has been offered in school, but so far Judah has shown no unnatural interest in the discipline or in anything remotely approaching architecture, which also secretly pleases Lewis. As Lewis loads the last of the dishes, places the environmentally friendly dish detergent tab in its small compartment, and shuts the dishwasher door, which starts the expensive German machine humming, Lewis finds himself silently hoping. Hoping that Judah will be one of those sons who, without managing to think too much about it, perhaps without even being conscious of his thought processes, chooses to study a discipline that has nothing to do with his father's profession. He hopes Judah's decision about his career will come easy to him.

LEWIS HAD NO idea what he wanted to study in CEGEP, the two-year college intermezzo between a truncated high school and an abbreviated university in unique Quebec where students were able to choose their own courses and set their own schedules, and where teachers and students spent a typically uninspiring fifteen hours a week together in the classroom. During his first year at Dawson College, Lewis took a bit of everything, but especially art, because he was good at it and because with Miranda as his mother he never assumed he would study anything else.

The man who taught "Introduction to Painting" at Dawson College was a little over five and a half feet tall, a perfectly bilingual and bicultural Toulouse-Lautrec who was famous in the incestuous Montreal art world for the tonality and psychological power of his abstracted and distracted nudes and for the profanity of his temper tantrums, which he visited liberally on his friends, lovers of alternating genders, art dealers, critics, and patrons.

Nobody was immune from André Jones's wrath or his desire to

paint them, standing, crouching, lying, crawling, running, alone on the canvas or together, completely naked, with not just their bodies but also their minds completely exposed to his gaze. Jones's models' bodies and minds came in various states of health and repair, age, and commitment, and it was rare to find a model who didn't reveal some innate or at least camouflaged inner despair once at the mercy of his brush.

When Lewis had him as a teacher, Jones was just entering his prime, becoming widely known across Canada. The days when Jones's paintings would sell for over $100,000 and a New York art critic would first compare him to the great Lucian Freud were just a few years away, but he was beginning to taste the sweet fruits of fame and starting to think he might — just might — become one of the great late twentieth-century North American painters.

André Jones also happened to be the Morton family friend who only a few years earlier had painted Miranda at forty — naturally naked — the results of which were already hanging proudly in the permanent collection of the Museé national des beaux-arts du Québec. The painting was completed just a few months before Miranda's second nervous breakdown. André Jones had immortalized Miranda standing in the doorway of her bedroom, one hand leaning on the doorjamb.

The critics had a field day with Miranda's ambiguous stance. From the way Jones had painted her, the viewer couldn't tell if Miranda was supposed to be entering or leaving the room: she was both blocking the doorway with her body and trying to emerge from it at the same time, as if she couldn't make up her own mind. One of Miranda's three beloved cats, the striped brown tabby, Ninotchka, curled around her right foot. Not a stitch of clothing or jewelry adorned Miranda's nakedness except for a large silver pendant with a red stone hanging from her neck. Her blond hair, which she was no longer bothering to dye to hide the increasing traces of grey, fell across her shoulders, uncombed, her pale blue eyes seeing both too much and not enough.

Lewis never saw Jones in the same mood twice. Some days he was manic; others taciturn, almost depressed; often exhibiting various degrees of anger; even once or twice close to tears. He delivered some lectures in such a speedy monologue that his students had to strain to follow; others were confined to slow, barely uttered monosyllables, just above grunts. Although Jones knew Lewis, he always made a point of treating him like any other student in his class.

For the first five classes of the semester, Jones made everyone paint each other's faces, and then their own, in little mirrors that were slightly distorting. At the sixth class, Jones brought in a nude model who looked like a fellow student, only more distant and uncommitted, as if his only experience with higher education had been holding a naked pose in art school. At the start of class, the model was wearing a robe, but as he was about to take it off, Jones stopped him. "*Attend*. Wait." Jones turned to face the students.

"Today you are about to embark on a lifelong adventure: to capture the essence of what it means to be human." Jones shook his head. "*Non*, not the face, not the eyes, which can sometimes, and often do, lie. *Le corps*. The human body. The vessel for our soul. To be human means to carry the weight of our mortality, on our backs, on our legs, in our skin, our muscles, our tendons, our shell of flesh and bone, the fact of our corporality. The study of the human body obsessed men like Michelangelo and Leonardo da Vinci their entire lives. It was an activity, a quest, which never, ever bored them, because it never ends, *ce n'est jamais fini*, whether you're searching for the human form hidden in a block of marble or trying to recreate it on canvas with a liquid." Jones paused.

"But, and it's a big but, you can never truly capture the essence of another human being without first capturing the essence of yourself. *Vous ne pouvez pas.* You cannot graduate to painting another's naked body until you have first painted your own. You cannot expect to be mature enough to ask someone else to take off their clothes for the sake of truth and art until you have proven you are ready to take off yours. Until you are willing to remove all your disguises, your defences, your masks that you use to shield yourself from the world, until you have the courage to see yourself completely exposed without any adornment, you are not ready to be an artist. *Alors.* I want each of you to take off your clothes now and find a space in the room in front of one of the tall mirrors. You can sit, you can stand, you can crouch, you can stand on your head — but the assignment is to paint yourself nude." The room was silent.

Jones laughed. "Don't worry, this is not sexual harassment. If anyone is under eighteen, please leave. If anyone is uncomfortable, please feel free to leave. You can do another assignment for credit. It will be worth just as much. But just don't expect to ever become an artist." Jones turned back to the model and said, "Take the day off. You'll still get paid, but these students need to do this first."

Lewis glanced around the room and saw one or two students start to take off their clothes. Others looked unsure. After what seemed like a long time, Lewis bent down and untied and removed his shoes. He slowly took off his socks. His feet appeared pale and red at the same time on the grey-tiled floor. He unbuckled his belt and began to unzip his khakis. But he didn't let his pants drop. Lewis held them up with one hand while he stared at the floor. The whole room went quiet for him. He didn't hear a group of twenty people wriggling out of their clothes. Lewis stayed like this for minutes, like an artist's model holding a painful, half-articulated pose, half dressed, half undressed.

Finally, without looking at anyone else, Lewis bent down and put his socks and shoes back on and zipped up his pants. He quietly picked up his paints and paintbrushes and walked slowly out of the room without making eye contact with anyone. A week later, after Lewis officially withdrew from the course, he learned he had failed what the students who remained all came to know as the "Nakedness Test."

As Lewis was leaving the classroom, and as he was thinking to himself that Miranda would have had no qualms about taking off her clothes in the service of art, Miranda was making another suicide attempt. Miranda attempted suicide four times. The first three attempts were ambivalent, half-hearted, as if she couldn't quite make up her mind. The fourth was definitive.

15

THE MORNINGS ARE the worst. They start in darkness. It is November now, and the winter solstice is approaching. Each morning Lewis wakes up early and depressed in his warmly blanketed antique bed that Laura picked up for a good price at one of the city's many fine estate auctions. But today Lewis is having a nightmare. The nightmare is about his childhood home.

Even though Lewis grew up in Westmount, the miniature mountain city nestled within the city of Montreal, home to some of the most beautiful residential buildings in Canada, and even though he went on to become an architect, for most of his life Lewis never understood the multi-generational affection that some families have for their homes. Lewis recognized the obsession with house and land from TV dramatizations of canonical British novels written in the nineteenth or early twentieth centuries, but the attachment to a particular place enclosed by walls always struck Lewis as foreign, most often Anglo-Saxon, definitely un-Jewish, situated firmly in the realm of history books and the insensitive custom of primogeniture.

Jews could never afford the luxury of forming attachments to places, let alone buildings, their history being one of continuous movement and exile, the destruction of not one temple but two burned into their collective consciousness. Lewis has always conceived of Jewish architecture as portable. It is the imaginary and longed-for architecture of the suitcase stored under the bed, into which, thanks to the tip of a friendly gentile neighbour or well-placed civil servant friend, the family silver, jewels, and books can be stuffed and whisked away just hours ahead of the pogrom, train shipment, or border closing. The Jewish collective experience with architecture is irrevocably coloured by its destruction.

Lewis's inability to understand the attachment to place and home changed abruptly in 1997 when he and Laura found their dream house. Built originally in 1903 to serve as a summer cottage for a young Saint John pulp mill owner when Rothesay was a train ride away from downtown Saint John, the Dutch neo-colonial style house is neither too large nor too small. It is a modest house and, in many ways, out of sync with modern ideas of beauty and expectations. But this is partly why Lewis loves it.

The house perches itself on a sloping acre, about one quarter of the way up the hill on its lot. Lewis doesn't mind how he and Laura and the children have to squeeze themselves into the small, old-fashioned kitchen, antithetical to the dreams of young wives and mothers eager to have a wood, chrome, and stone palace in which to cook up delights for their friends and young children and enlist the help of their liberated husbands.

Like a well-designed castle built for defence, the house towers over anybody who approaches from the front, not because it is big but because of the ten feet of elevation from the dead-end street and the stone steps that have to be climbed to reach the door. The natural flagstones in the path are beautiful even though the cement between some of them is crumbling, and the path from the stone steps to the wood steps of the porch slants upwards in a way that is unsafe in winter, when ice and frost pool in the cracks between the stones and make them slippery like the surface of a frozen pond.

The wide white steps of the wooden front porch are majestic even though some are rotting beneath the layers of paint that have to be applied each summer. Lewis never tires of seeing the two wooden columns on the porch landing that suggest the portico of a Doric temple, each pillar tapering to perfection; if he looks closely he can see past the illusion of a solid column, how each pillar is formed of several vertical wooden boards, glued together to form a cylinder. The century-old windows with their bubbles and waves in the glass panes remind him of windows in a church. Even though, as he knows from his own eyes and skin and the energy audit Laura had them do five years earlier, the windows are terribly inefficient, Lewis will never replace them with modern glass.

Every time he walks upon the floors made of thick but narrow planks of light maple, with their blond wave and weave, Lewis is reminded of how each board's impractical and inefficient narrowness is so un-modern, paler and more refined than oak, like Laura's skin, the skin of a woman who doesn't court the sun but who is the genetic carrier of pure skin that needs no adorning tan.

Growing up in Westmount, Lewis was visually spoiled, and by the time he started to notice the architectural history around him it was too late for his childhood. He didn't appreciate the soaring brick beauty of his middle Victorian home until he went to architectural school. But from an early age, Lewis feared the loss of his home, and his greatest childhood nightmare was about this fear. Lewis first experienced the nightmare soon after Miranda's first suicide attempt, and the dream didn't stop recurring until after her third. It was Lewis's worst childhood nightmare. The dream was so terrifying that it finally challenged Lewis's slender and civilized ego to take control and dominate his dark, muscular, illiterate id. It was also Lewis's first architectural dream. The nightmare was about both architecture and its absence. But really the dream was about everything else.

Lewis hasn't had the dream for over twenty years, and he has forgotten how he learned to cope with it. In the dream this morning, as always, the action starts in mid-afternoon, in school with the final bell. Lewis gets his knapsack and his coat because today it's cold in Montreal, says goodbye to his friends, and begins walking the five blocks from Selwyn House up Cote St. Antoine to his house near the top of Arlington. This part of the dream, as always, is foreshortened in the relative time dimension of all dreams. Lewis is not so much doing all these things as knowing he has done them just as his dream is beginning, the walk home uneventful. In fact, the dream is completely normal and unremarkable until Lewis reaches his street, turns left, and begins walking down the hill to his house. As he reaches his house and is about to turn left onto his walkway, he looks up. And when Lewis looks up, his house is not there.

It's not that his house has disappeared, leaving a blank space like a gap in someone's teeth, or burned down or been bombed into a mess of rubble. Lewis's childhood house and the houses on either side of it have never existed. The dream's instant and unassailable logic offers three differing but simultaneous explanations. All the houses, including his own, are older, as if Lewis has travelled back in time. Yet somehow all the houses are also newer, part of a futuristic neighbourhood that resembles a science fiction cityscape with a highway running overhead and the descendants of cars zooming by in a blur, as if Lewis has time-travelled forward.

And of course, all the houses are neither older nor newer but just different.

Lewis now walks up and down what is his street, thinking maybe he has turned down the wrong one. He walks along the driveway to the back of his house to see if perhaps the garden is still there (it never is), and he goes up to the front door to ring the bell. A stranger comes to the door and says no, he has never heard of the Mortons or any of their neighbours. The dream is always the same. And then Lewis wakes up.

As an adult, Lewis has become a good amateur interpreter of his and Laura's dreams, but between the ages of eleven and sixteen Lewis dreamed without any ability or attempt to impose an explanation, a rational order on the unconscious spinning of his mind. Yet as a child and adolescent he was always old enough to fully experience and feel the dream, and sometimes when he was awake and not dreaming and was coming home from school he would feel a quiet sense of relief, of destiny cheated, when he would turn onto his street and everything was the same as he had left it when he had gone to school in the morning.

In those non-dreaming moments, Lewis would walk up to the solid oak front door of his house and go inside. And without being conscious of it, each time Lewis entered his house he would touch the front door with his hand to reassure himself that it was indeed real. He would cross the threshold into his real house that existed perfectly in the present and that hadn't been replaced by another house imagined into some alternate reality by his sleeping brain. But then one night Lewis's dreaming changed.

HE WAS SIXTEEN, and Miranda was just starting to come home for short periods following her hospitalization after her third suicide attempt. Lewis was regularly dreaming the dream in which he couldn't find his house. But one night in his dream Lewis overheard himself telling himself that he was only dreaming, that it wasn't real, and therefore his disappeared house wasn't anything to be afraid of. And he woke up.

From then on, until Drescher died and Lewis stopped going into the office and his subconscious began to reassert itself, Lewis's nightmares had no hold over him. He would go to sleep and wake up calm, no matter what he dreamed. Through sheer willpower he learned how to be self-aware even in his dreams. The presence of Lewis's conscious mind in his dreams carried on into adulthood, with the result that he was the same person, with the same thoughts and morals, when he was dreaming as when he was awake. As a result, Lewis was faithful to Laura not only in real life but in his dreams, turning down imaginary women who wanted to sleep with him time and time again.

Years later, over smoked meat sandwiches at the Union Deli in Saint John, Drescher told Lewis about a dream he'd had the night before. "It was about a skyscraper I'd designed for the Old Port of Montreal." The fact the building was art deco seemed important to Drescher, and he spent some time describing the building's symmetry, geometry, and bright colours. "The funny part of the dream, which woke me up, happened at the moment of the ribbon cutting. All of Montreal was there, and I was making my speech, but everyone in the audience had trouble paying attention. They kept looking skyward behind me. Needless to say, I found this fucking rude. Finally, I decided to stop talking and see for myself what the hell was so distracting. When I turned around I saw something amazing: my building wasn't finished. It kept growing and growing!"

Dresher and Lewis both had a good laugh at the blatant Freudian psychology. The dream reminded them of the game they played whenever they travelled to a real city, like Toronto or New York. In between meetings they would walk through the man-made canyons of steel and glass skyscrapers, and one of them would look up and say, "Now." This meant each of them had three seconds to look up at the building they were walking past and guess its number of storeys, not based on having time to count rows of windows but relying on their architectural instincts and their eyes. Only after they had shared their guesses would the two of them stop and count the floors, or if they were in a rush they would go inside to the elevator banks or ask at the reception desk.

After listening to the story of Drescher's incredibly growing skyscraper dream, Lewis felt comfortable enough to tell Drescher the story of how as a teenager he had suddenly discovered the ability to be conscious in his dreams. To Lewis's surprise, Drescher looked alarmed. "Fuck, Lewis, God knows an architect can't afford the crazy freedom of the artist," Drescher said just before he used his napkin to vigorously wipe away juice from the smoked meat dribbling down his clean-shaven chin. "Our buildings have to stand. They have to have a purpose. But are you ever in trouble if you end up being self-conscious in your dreams! Do you know what it means when you can turn your dreams off and on, when you are the master of them?"

Lewis didn't but knew he wasn't going to like the answer.

"It means you've gone and put your imagination in prison."

16

IT HAS BEEN exactly two weeks since Tom's cocktail party. Lewis still doesn't know if he's going to be charged for indecent exposure or forced completely out of Drescher & Drescher because of the Abercrom legal action. Lewis is mulling the possibility of both when Tom phones.

"Lewie, how are things?

"Fine."

The male catechism of inquiring after another's male's presumably non-existent feelings and receiving a lie in return having been dispensed with, Tom gets down to business. "I have a few guest passes to GoodLife. I'm going to work out tomorrow morning, and I thought it might be nice if you came with me." Tom is not asking. He is suggesting. Lewis has always assumed this is how Tom advises all his financial clients.

Lewis hasn't stepped foot in a gym since adolescence, but he figures it can't hurt. Lewis was a skinny kid — you could see his ribs up until the age of seventeen. He was what the old-fashioned books about body types would have called an endomorph, with a thin torso and long, skinny arms. The only natural and visible attributes Lewis had going for him as a teenager were his height — six foot two — and his half-decent shoulders and relatively muscular legs. The latter probably weren't great to look at on their own but were covered by a half-inch of fat, so they appeared more substantial at first glance. But with his passable shoulders, natural skinniness, and an acute sense of anxiety that only increased with each of Miranda's successive suicide attempts, Lewis had the basic building blocks for a successful teenage gym experience. Add in newly evolving societal ideas about what it meant to be and look like a man and there was no way a young Lewis could escape the gym.

Like most adolescent boys in the 1980s, Lewis felt compelled to take up weightlifting to live up to the new ideal of masculinity that was burning through men's fragile egos thanks to the Napoleon-obsessed weightlifting evangelist from Montreal, Joe Weider, and the equal gender opportunity ideals of Hollywood where more and more leading men were disobeying Michael Caine's personal dictum of preserving some mystery about his physical person. Eventually Caine would break his own rule in his eighties, but until then he made a point of never taking off his shirt in any film. However, the new leading men were taking theirs off with wild abandon, like fame-obsessed starlets trying to impress the director.

Because of the exposure to art that Miranda had seen fit to impose on him as a child, not only did the teenage Lewis have Hollywood stars to measure himself against, but he had also internalized a need to live up to classical ideas of male beauty as captured in marble so many years ago. So, Lewis went to the gym with his friends and lifted weights until his muscles burned and his mind and stomach churned with emptiness because he wasn't keeping up with enough calorie consumption to replace what he was losing. After every workout, Lewis checked himself in the mirror to see how his chest was coming along, and his naturally long and skinny biceps, and whether the major vein in the middle of his left bicep was pushing out and remaining visible not just immediately following his workout but also the day afterward.

Lewis even started doing sit-ups and was on his way toward having a somewhat washboard stomach when he entered architecture school and fell in love with Laura. He became tired of being tired and irritable from the long workouts and looking at his body. He realized he would rather look at his architecture books and Laura's body, so he eased up and took up moderate cycling and did the occasional set of push-ups and sit-ups at home.

When Lewis began working with Drescher and the children came and he was up sometimes in the night with Laura and filling every hour outside of Drescher's with helping or playing with the kids, even those bike rides and minimalist home workouts fell by the wayside. As he moved through his thirties, Lewis ate chocolate bars at the office when he was agonizing over a design and began to carry a bit of a gut. Thankfully, it was not a huge one because his metabolism was still efficient. But his ribs were no longer visible, and Lewis realized he no longer cared whether he had any muscles.

However, now that he no longer has any work to occupy his mind, Lewis is adrift again and open to suggestions about his body. As Lewis says, "Sure, I'll come," he reflects that in inviting him to the cocktail party and now to the gym, Tom is prescribing the two great modern cures for depression: socializing with people and working up a sweat.

Luckily, Tom hasn't advised Lewis to take up dancing lessons, and for good reason. To begin with, Lewis has a phobia of dancing lessons. His dread starts with a core principle: dancing is not something you do in public. Lewis doesn't like the idea of bouncing around to the sound of music in a room full of strangers. Why would you want to hold your wife in public through her clothes? The fact of the matter is that Lewis often can't help getting an erection if he is pressed against Laura, much to her ongoing annoyance and chagrin, when much of the time all she wants is just a hug, and perhaps to smell Lewis and hold him tightly. Every time Laura gives Lewis a hug and he becomes aroused, Lewis feels he is letting her down.

From the principle flows the fear. Early in Lewis's and Laura's marriage, one of Laura's friends couldn't stop raving about the salsa lessons she and her husband had taken up. She encouraged Laura to bring Lewis and join them on Saturday nights. Laura had been caught up in the moment, and when she asked Lewis if he was interested, he sputtered, "You know, at these dancing lessons you don't just get to dance with your spouse or partner. They actually make you dance with other people." When Laura asked Lewis how he knew, he said he just did. And that was that.

If pressed, Lewis would have replied that dancing with other people was too intimate and led invariably to other things. It was like the old joke: Why don't Baptists have sex standing up? Because it might lead to dancing. And Laura, who thought Lewis ridiculous, developed a newfound respect for his illogical wisdom about dancing when six months later Maura came to her in shock, announcing that Tom had been having an affair with a woman he had met at salsa lessons. Their marriage survived. But the dancing lessons did not.

TRUE TO HIS word, Tom picks up Lewis at 9:55 on Saturday morning. He is at the wheel of a navy blue BMW that smells of leather and new car, and Lewis compliments Tom on it because he knows his cars mean a lot to him.

"Thanks, Lewie."

In the changing room, Lewis is amused to see Tom carefully pull on a tank top and what look like uncomfortably tight shorts. Lewis throws on a loose T-shirt and some old cargo shorts. Conscientious about maintaining his public disguise, Lewis puts on a baseball hat over his crew cut. Tom is excited about taking Lewis out to pump iron, but first they have to work up a sweat.

"Cardio, Lewie. A good workout always starts with cardio."

Lewis has his choice of bike, treadmill, Stairmaster, or a machine that looks like a combination of hiking and skiing with a bit of jazz dancing thrown in. Lewis chooses the bike. He knows he will find biking boring, so he picks up a magazine from the rack. Lewis has never been a magazine reader except for *Architectural Digest*. Needless to say, no architectural magazines are on display. There are no current affairs magazines, either. For the first time in his life, Lewis picks up *Men's Fitness*.

Lewis starts biking leisurely and flipping through the magazine. It is full of photos of smiling muscular men and a few of smiling, semi-undressed women. The pages with more words than pictures offer up tip after helpful tip on how to be strong and lean and even sexy. As in most magazines, wisdom is offered confidently and confidentially and somewhat breathlessly, as if nobody has ever heard the secret before and the writer can't wait to share it with the reader. The general tone is knowing, authoritative, quasi-biblical with just a trace of irony and self-awareness.

As Lewis flips the pages, he glances up to look for Tom. He is one row ahead and six machines over to Lewis's right. They are both only two minutes into the cardio part of their workout, but Tom is already running full tilt on a treadmill. When Lewis returns his attention to *Men's Fitness*, the magazine is open to the first page of an article that appears to be about war injuries. Surprisingly there are no pictures, no text boxes containing any tips. Lewis picks up the pace of his peddling just a little and starts reading.

The story opens with the simple, almost Hemingway-esque premise, non-threatening and informative, that every war has its particular injury. As befitting its dual name, the First World War or Great War had two signature injuries, one physical and the other mental: burned-out lungs from the mustard gas the Kaiser's scientists pioneered, and shell shock from witnessing or participating in what happened on the battlefield.

The U.S. Civil War's typical injury was missing arms or legs. Almost every bullet wound that didn't affect the torso resulted in a shredded limb that had to be amputated on the field to prevent death by blood loss or infection. The fact that death often resulted from the operation didn't make the injury any less valid.

The Second World War's distinguishing injury didn't stand out for Lewis in his nervous skimming, but according to the author the Second Gulf War's trademark injury is straight out of *The Sun Also Rises*. This was the war of the improvised land mine, the IED. So it is fitting that the characteristic casualty is blown-off genitals. Lewis's right foot slips off the pedal, and he nearly falls out of his seat.

Lewis can't help himself: he starts weeping silently when he reads about the eighteen-year-old from Louisiana who lost both his legs and complete set of genitalia to a crude Revolutionary Guard land mine on the sandy outskirts of Baghdad. Lewis is crying not only in sadness and sympathy but also in ashamed admiration for the interviewee. Compared to despondent and desperately anxious Lewis, the poor ball-less American bugger is the epitome of positive thinking and living testimony to the comforting power of religion. He tells the interviewer that he thanks God every day that his life was spared. And this brave Cajun admits without rancour that while it sometimes gets him down that he no longer has a penis and testicles, he tries not to dwell too deeply on their loss. "You have to go on. What else can you do?" the former private asks rhetorically and stoically. The interviewer has no satisfactory response or commentary. Like any good writer, he lets the story tell itself.

Some of the men who suffered this grotesque insult and injury while earning low pay in a desert thousands of miles and worlds away from Oklahoma or New York or Corpus Christi were married before they went overseas — Lewis can't help wondering how any single ones might fare in the open marriage market sans cock and balls — and the writer delicately hints at the lengths to which these relatively newlywed husbands will go to please their wives. One saintly young wife gamely giggles while speaking about how lovemaking is better than ever before because her husband is now so much more attentive to her needs. Lewis is amazed at how the mutilated men experience mental erections that last for hours like a wet dream in a Viagra ad, the intense penile equivalent of phantom limb pain, except these ghost feelings are pleasurable.

As Lewis finishes the story, his eyes fill with tears. He feels eminently grateful for his penis and thanks God for giving him one that has loyally done its part to keep at bay the anxiety that has lately been on the cusp of overrunning him like a coalition of the willing surging across the Iraqi desert. Ever since Lewis can remember, he has been mildly and benignly obsessed with his penis, with its size, its length and girth, with the way it hangs, always a little to the left. Lewis is obsessed with the way his penis's skin shrivels up when it just hangs there, with how it dangles. But mostly Lewis is obsessed with keeping his penis and not losing it. Luckily, he is not a soldier and doesn't plan on enlisting anytime soon, even if he is still having trouble finding meaningful work.

So, his worries are more mundane and peaceful, mostly involving disease. Lewis worries about testicular cancer. Or he worries about prostate cancer and becoming impotent as result of treatment. Lewis often thinks that if he gets prostate cancer he will refuse medical care and hope for the best. Lewis can't conceive of the value of living life without a working penis.

Lewis has been so worried about his penis that he hasn't noticed the dark-haired man start peddling on the bicycle beside him. The man is around forty, like Lewis, but he is compact and lean, without an ounce of fat on him. He isn't reading or looking at the TV or even listening to an iPod. Instead he is closely watching everyone exercise. After a very short warm-up, just like Tom on his treadmill the man is going full throttle on his machine. But he isn't even breaking a sweat. He seems to be drawing energy from observing the rows of bikes and treadmills with his wide-apart green eyes, from studying the people at various levels of strength and skill sweating around him.

Fifteen minutes later, Lewis sees Tom slow down and after what seems like only a one-minute cool-down hop off the treadmill while it is still slowly moving and start walking over. But on his way Tom stops, like a local politician, to smile and exchange pleasantries with no less than three people. Tom is fully engaged in the masculine camaraderie of the gym, where all the usual social and economic differences are temporarily suspended, like wars during the ancient Olympics. Men take off their suits or coveralls and put on the same uniform of T-shirt, shorts, and running shoes, and lawyers and truck drivers exchange warm witticisms and mingle on an equal footing. The neighbourhood you live in or the car you drive or whether you dropped out of high school or finished a graduate degree doesn't matter while you're in the gym. Just as he is about to reach Lewis, Tom stops by the green-eyed man on the bike.

"Hi, Billy, how's it going? All set for hockey?"

"Things are good, Tom. And yeah, just getting my legs in shape." The man speaks as if he were standing still, without any attempt to catch his breath.

Lewis is admiring Tom's easy way with people when his friend looks over and seems to notice Lewis for the first time. "Billy, I'd like you to meet my friend Lewis. Lewis, Billy." The two bikes are too far away for them to shake hands, so Billy lifts up his hand in a friendly, upbeat gym wave. Lewis follows suit as best he can and can't help noticing the man with the wide apart and calm green eyes still isn't sweating. The perspiration gathering on Lewis's shiny forehead is starting to sting his eyes.

"Well, I'm done with my warm-up," Tom said. "Meet you over by the weights."

Grateful for the excuse, Lewis says he too is done. After a quick, half-hearted cool-down he wanders over to the free weights, where, under Tom's tutelage and his own fragmented memories of his adolescent marathon workouts, he proceeds to pull almost every muscle in his upper body.

Later, on the short drive home, Tom looks thoughtful. As they approach the East Riverside-Kingshurst Park, Tom says, as if he has been deeply pondering it, "I still can't believe what happened to Elspeth. Poor girl."

Lewis can only manage a brief, "Mmm," which he hopes sounded sufficiently sympathetic.

"By the way, I was speaking with Bob yesterday. The hunting trip is happening the Sunday after next."

Lewis has never hunted nor had any desire to hunt in his life. But men who take the lives of other living creatures probably possess a great degree of mental toughness. A level of resilience on par with that demonstrated by the soldiers in the *Men's Fitness* article who have had their genitalia blown off but who just keep on living their lives and pleasing their wives. Maybe if Lewis goes along on a hunting trip some of that unbeatable courage will rub off on him. So, without thinking too much about it, he says, "Yeah. I'll come."

"Excellent." As Tom slows down in preparation for turning up Lewis's street he says, "You know, I sure wouldn't want to be in that flasher's shoes. Billy Blunt is as good a detective as he is a hockey player. And he's a fine hockey player. Despite his size."

17

EXERCISE IS SUPPOSED to release endorphins and lift your mental mood, but it's not working for Lewis. Around the time that Lewis's sleeping hours become filled again with the recurring dream of his youth, he is only mildly surprised that his waking hours have imperceptibly grown to include thoughts of suicide.

These reflections, when they glide across the uneven surface of Lewis's brain, are not acute or even worrying. His suicidal thoughts are strangely peaceful, almost comforting, like a form of meditation. Lewis has not stepped foot in the office for nearly two months now and has almost convinced himself he will never be employed again. Even more troubling, as Detective Blunt diligently searches for someone who matches the unusual description given by Elspeth Fielding, and as Abercrom's lawsuit winds its way through the courts, Lewis has the threat of arrest and possible jail time looming over him for indecent exposure, and possibly worse for intellectual property theft. Even if Lewis manages to escape going to jail for the incident in the park, just being charged will cause him to be publicly humiliated as a pervert. And if he loses the lawsuit, he will be ostracized by his profession. He will never work again. At best, he will get to design the occasional twelve-hundred-foot bungalow for clients who never follow the news.

Lewis hasn't been sleeping regularly since Drescher's death, and like a conniving friend, suicide is beginning to helpfully suggest itself as an easy way out of his present predicament. With every new sleepless night, Lewis sees suicide increasingly as an antidote to feeling guilty and anxious. Guilty of needlessly exposing himself in a public park. Guilty of not coping nobly and courageously with not being allowed to do any work. Anxious about going to prison for either indecent exposure or intellectual property theft. Or both. With his luck, the prison sentences will probably be consecutive. Lewis also sees suicide as an answer to the fear that he will never find another job after he finally emerges from prison, by this time having been firmly pushed out of Drescher & Drescher, which means he won't be able to support Laura and their children in the manner they have become accustomed to and he has become accustomed to providing. Suicide is a way of escaping public humiliation, professional ignominy, and perpetual poverty.

So in between worrying about all these possible outcomes and doing household chores to distract himself and get into Laura's good graces, Lewis not only contemplates suicide in great detail, he goes so far as to rank the various available methods. This he does according to the obvious criteria: level of pain, speed, probability of mistakes and incompletion, messiness, and flair or drama. In this very well thought out ranking, a gunshot to the head ranks high for pain, high for speed, and somewhat in the middle of the road for potential for mistakes (Lewis has read the stories of people — well, usually men — who accidently shot off their faces but missed their brains and lived). And it is definitely the winner on drama.

Hanging seems more painful and definitely slower. Chances of incompletion lie in the possibility that someone finds you and cuts you down before you die but after you have permanently brain damaged yourself due to lack of oxygen. In terms of messiness, hanging doesn't rank nearly as high as a self-inflicted gunshot wound with blood splattered all over your suicide note. However, Lewis isn't fond of the accounts of hanging in which the victim always seems to void his bladder and bowels in a paroxysm upon expiring. This will ruin Lewis's fine Tilford pants with their expert tailoring and quality weave.

As images of suicide skate gracefully over the thin layer of Lewis's psyche, he finds himself wondering if this was how it was with Miranda. The unhurried falling apart, piece by piece. A slow, almost imperceptible acceptance of a terrible outcome as perfectly logical and understandable. But Miranda seemed distraught and distant, frustrated with her inability to concentrate on her painting when she lapsed into the depression that preceded each suicide attempt. Lewis feels calm. Rational even, which makes Lewis feels proud. He seriously doubts that Miranda would have ranked the various suicide options in as dispassionate manner as he has. But he knows she would have instinctively avoided any method that would have disfigured her face and body. Even in her depressed state, Miranda would have thought clearly and far enough ahead to consider how she would appear in her open coffin.

LEWIS HAS NEVER been sure if Miranda really wanted to succeed on her final suicide attempt or if it just turned out that way. The circumstances in which it happened would suggest it was another plea for attention.

On the morning of the day Lewis was failing Jones's "Naked-ness Test," Miranda called Mordecai at the office. Later Mordecai would recollect that she sounded fine, calmer even than usual. Miranda asked Mordecai when he would be home and he said in the early afternoon. The coroner concluded Miranda took the pills just before noon, within an hour of getting off the phone with Mordecai. For all intents and purposes, she expected Mordecai to find her, call the ambulance, and be there after the paramedics pumped her stomach and she woke up in Intensive Care crying and apologetic.

But on that particular day, family patriarch and client-among-clients Mr. Massimo Messana cornered Mordecai just as he was heading out of the office and asked him to go to lunch at Moshe's with him and a potential business partner. The thick, expensive steaks were flawlessly grilled and the wine perfectly paired. The elderly male waiters served and poured with unobtrusive dignity as lunch stretched on, relationships were formed, and a deal was struck. But by the time Mordecai stumbled home close to 4:00 p.m., Miranda had slipped into a deep coma.

Luckily for Lewis, it was Mordecai and not he who found her. Miranda still cared enough about Lewis to make what became her final suicide attempt when she knew he would be in class, just like she had done every other time. Mordecai found her naked in bed, lying neatly on her side as if waiting for him to arrive, the empty bottle of antidepressants held tightly in her hand, the glass of water spilled and smashed on the floor beside the night table. The ambulance came within minutes, but this time Mordecai knew he was too late. Lewis might have been home around the same time as Mordecai, but he had stopped at Westmount Park on the way. He had sat down on a bench by the water, watched the ducks, and tried not to think about art class.

When Mordecai came home that evening and told Lewis that Miranda had died on the way to the hospital, Lewis didn't say anything. It seemed unbelievable, almost anticlimactic, after all the other suicide attempts. When Mordecai explained, without any sense of self-pity and in a numb, almost disbelieving voice, that he had intended to be home earlier that day but had spent most of the afternoon at Moshe's, Lewis didn't respond. He left Mordecai alone and went up to his room.

Lewis locked his door, turned on his radio, and began to methodically take down from the wall every single painting and drawing he had done since he was a child. Miranda had enthusiastically praised each work and framed them at the expensive shop down the hill on Sherbrooke. Lewis's bedroom had always looked like a miniature art gallery, with drawings and paintings hanging on the wall from waist height almost to the ceiling. Miranda had only been dead for a few hours, but Lewis smashed every frame, shredded every piece of sketch paper with his hands, and slashed every canvas with his Swiss Army knife.

Lewis had always assumed he would use his art as his portfolio to gain admittance to Concordia University's highly regarded Fine Arts program. Lewis had fifty framed pieces in all: mostly drawings and paintings of Mordecai and Miranda. Some of the portraits were of himself, but in different poses and with different expressions so if you didn't know you couldn't tell: Lewis as a businessman, smirking in a tie and suit; a caveman screaming with his mouth wide open and eyes dilated after committing his first homicide; smiling like a Roman senator as the republic slipped bloodily into empire, eyes leaking arrogance above a cruelly curved mouth; a stunned adolescent staring into the future with everything in front of him still a mystery. Lewis had never taken formal art lessons, but he had learned a lot from listening to and watching Miranda, and the raw power of his lines, strokes, and colour was indisputable.

Lewis's favourite painting was his one of Mordecai staring out with challenging eyes at the viewer, any sense of lawyerly diffidence banished from his expression, almost taunting the viewer to take a swing at him so he could knock him down. Lewis had painted Mordecai only in shades of red, his long black hair almost purple, slicked back above his forehead as always and curling above his ears like miniature ram's horns. The monochromatic colour scheme had never been a conscious decision, but the result had been a portrait that no viewer could easily turn away from. That night, Lewis cut the painting into twenty-five strips of canvas.

When Lewis next saw Miranda it was at Paperman's Funeral Home. She was wrapped in her favourite dress, the blue one adorned with ravens. Her blond hair, now noticeably streaked with grey, was swept back off her forehead, her lips redder than they should have been. Her eyes, of course, were closed, but Lewis imagined Miranda waking up, slowly opening her eyes, pale blue, in wide surprise at everyone who had come to mourn, including André Jones and at least three other famous Montreal artists. Even Mrs. Staunton was there, wearing what looked like a black Victorian dress, and Lewis could have sworn she looked upset.

As Miranda lay there in her open coffin and as Lewis refused to cry, his eighteen-year-old mind had a blasphemous thought. He imagined Miranda wanting to paint herself as she lay there dead in the expensive coffin that Mordecai had chosen, not naked this time as she usually was in her paintings but clothed in the dress that Mordecai had selected because he knew it was Miranda's favourite. In his mind, Lewis heard Miranda speaking to him like she always did when she was painting. This time, as she executed the self-portrait of her dead body, she was explaining to Lewis why she was choosing certain colours and how she was going to capture her waxy grey complexion, her sunken face with the skin stretched across her high cheekbones, the sense of incongruously welcome repose. And Lewis, who should have been crying, had to suppress a quiet hysterical laugh at his vision of Miranda refusing to stop painting herself even when she was dead.

After Miranda was buried at the family plot on Mount Royal, Mordecai and Lewis sat shiva for the customary eight days. Mordecai was not religious, but he insisted they wear only black, cover all Miranda's beloved mirrors, ritually rip their favourite ties, and refrain from shaving. The heavy front door to their beautiful Westmount home remained unlocked, and relatives and friends came by at all hours of the day and night with plates of food, cold cuts, soup, and desserts so Mordecai and Lewis would never be alone with their grief. *Bubbe* Rivke and *Zayde* Saul were there every day from early afternoon to early evening, holding court in their understated mourning. The Messanas sent boxes of fresh pasta and pastries from their personal chef each day at noon.

During the whole shiva, when Lewis hoped nobody was looking, he would wrestle with his ripped Hermès tie that had been a gift from Mordecai on his sixteenth birthday. The one with little pale blue dogs leaping through a field of green. Sometimes the knot was too tight. Sometimes it was too loose. The tie never seemed to hang straight but was always askew to the left or the right. Several times a day, Lewis would excuse himself from whatever conversation he was having with his relatives or family friends and head upstairs to the bathroom where he would undo and re-knot and fiddle with the tie. At least one of his aunts was convinced he was suffering from a bladder infection or diarrhea.

For eight days, Mordecai and Lewis were never alone and never had to do anything for themselves except shower and get dressed. One late afternoon, halfway through the ritual period of mourning, Lewis was surprised to see Mordecai laughing through what already appeared to be a heavy beard. He was speaking with a colleague, another middle-aged lawyer. The man probably hadn't meant to make Mordecai laugh so hard, but Lewis quietly withdrew and went to his room.

On the ninth day, when shiva was over, Lewis shaved. As he shaved, he accidentally cut himself, and as his blood ran more quickly down his chin than he had expected and as he observed that his blood was redder than he had remembered or imagined, Lewis studied his face in the mirror. He saw both Mordecai and Miranda in his features, in his dark brown eyes and his hair that had stubbornly remained light blond beyond childhood. If Lewis's parents were represented in contrast in his eyes and hair, they had blended in his skin. Lewis's skin was lighter than Mordecai's and darker than Miranda's. It was more olive than pale but still it burned easily in the sun. The mirrors in the house had been covered for eight days, and Lewis looked vaguely unfamiliar to himself. He appeared paler than he remembered, as if his skin were paying its respects to Miranda. But his eyes were as dark as ever.

For the first time in his life, Lewis felt no urge to draw or paint himself standing in front of a mirror. He wasn't interested in the texture of his skin, the contours of his face, the way the strands of his hair fell over his forehead. When Lewis finally turned away from the mirror and walked away, he was surprised by how easy it was.

OVERDOSING ON PILLS, Miranda's MO of choice, seems so civilized, the modern equivalent of the aristocratic Roman quietly slitting his wrists and leaning back in the marble tub to run out the hourglass of his life after having suffered the temporary insanity of writing an insulting letter to the emperor. Putting one's head in the oven with the gas on like Sylvia Plath appears attractive and peaceful, with its intimations of warm, cosy kitchens and Friday night meals of chicken and roast potatoes. But who has a gas stove in Atlantic Canada?

Despite himself, and not knowing quite why, Lewis keeps returning to the idea of a self-inflicted gunshot. Maybe it will not be as painful as it might first appear. It will be most likely fatal if he goes about it properly. It is certainly the manly way to go out. Good enough for Hemingway …

With the barely functioning, still semi-rational part of his brain, Lewis knows this kind of thinking isn't healthy, but he can't help himself. Thinking about suicide is like eating too much rich chocolate. The more Lewis knows that he should stop, the more he wants to indulge. If Lewis were to die, then Laura could collect on his very generous life insurance policy. Each month when he pays the hefty premium Lewis is reminded that his life insurance policy is substantial.

But even the payment is just another source of worry for Lewis as he slices and dices his monthly budget and tries to figure out how to reduce unnecessary expenses so he can afford to take the lower paying positions that appear to be the best possible options now that he is being squeezed out of Drescher & Drescher. Lewis can't stop himself from thinking that he is worth far more to Laura dead than alive because then she will be able to collect and live off the insurance money rather than live on the embarrassing salary that he is sure will be lower than the partner income he used to earn at Drescher & Drescher when he finally does move on.

But Lewis also knows in his more lucid moments that if he were to end his life by suicide, then Laura wouldn't collect any insurance money. Lewis doesn't know a lot about life insurance, but he knows that if the cause of death is determined to be self-inflicted then the insurance companies won't have to pay a cent. And

Lewis knows this because one of his great-uncles on Mordecai's side of the family died of carbon monoxide poisoning while sitting in his car in his garage. Lewis doesn't know how anybody dies this way without it being suicide, but Mordecai always insisted it had been an accident, that his uncle was depressed and distracted by a long period of unsuccessful business dealings and forgot that he left his motor running with the garage door closed while he sat and worried himself to death in his 1952 Chevrolet. Mordecai's most compelling piece of evidence for his point of view was that the insurance company agreed because they paid up.

So naturally Lewis begins to think about how he can stage a credible accident that won't look like suicide. He can drive off the road, over a cliff, with a coffee dumped on his lap so the insurance company investigators will assume he accidentally spilled it, perhaps burned himself, and became distracted, realizing seconds too late that he has lost control and driven over the edge. He can drive too fast and off the road and into the river like Drescher. Lewis often indulges this particular fantasy while driving, but never with any children or Laura in the car.

The positive side of contemplating suicide, often and regularly, and for long periods of time, is that death is no longer a primary or even a secondary concern. Lewis no longer cares if he lives or dies. Whereas before Lewis feared cancer of the prostate because it would probably result in impotence, or any other cancer, had in fact worried before every routine visit to the doctor when he was a boy because it might turn up a brain tumour; dreaded flying because the plane might crash; steered clear of any boating because the boat might sink — now Lewis no longer has any fear of death. Death would be a welcome respite from life. It is life that Lewis now fears, plain and simple. More specifically, it is the fear of not being able to replicate the life he has somehow

THE ART OF BEING LEWIS ◆ 167

accidentally fallen into, at work, with Laura, the charmed life that he never thought possible when he was growing up. Instead, death has become a pleasant and welcome daydream for Lewis, like winning the lottery.

Losing the fear of death, like suddenly realizing you aren't ticklish when your dad comes to tickle you, is liberating. Now that Lewis has conquered his fear of death, he becomes reasonably reckless with his life, but not like young, despondent men in 1960s America who volunteered to be helicopter gunners in Vietnam, or men who deal or take crack, or drink vodka until they fall down, or race their cars too fast. Instead Lewis carries his iPhone in his pocket close to his testes, no longer worrying about testicular cancer, previously a minor recurring motif in both his sleeping and waking nightmares. Much to Laura's chagrin, Lewis now delights in buying non-organic pears or plums or apples and biting into their pesticide-laden skins without assiduous pre-washing.

In his new mode, Lewis courts death every hour of the day. But even in this death-defying period of his life, he is still measured and conscientious. In any risk Lewis takes, the potential harm is directed only at himself, not at others. So, for instance, Lewis never drives above the speed limit, or when he does, it is only by five or at most ten kilometres. He never does the risky race car manoeuvres that young drivers attempt on the highways, weaving in and out of traffic like wannabe Formula One drivers. Instead, Lewis drives short distances around town, to get gas, or to go to the supermarket, or on the first few blocks of a longer trip, without bothering to buckle up his seat belt. He listens for the warning sound, feeling the bold nakedness of his shoulder without the strap, flouting the rules and feeling comfortingly a little like Drescher, who had nothing but contempt for seat belts when he was alive. Drescher's indifference to his personal safety made Lewis even more nervous on the occasions when he was driving. Lewis always turned to Drescher before shifting into drive, asking him to please put on his seat belt.

PART THREE

Become who you are.
— FRIEDRICH NIETZSCHE

18

IN BETWEEN WORRYING about going to jail, gently contemplating suicide, and lying awake on one of the dark early mornings after one of his recurring nightmares about his disappearing childhood house, Lewis gets religion. Or more accurately, he decides to get it, or makes up his mind to get it as much as he ever can. After living with increasing levels of anxiety since his last conversation with Montcalm nearly two months ago, Lewis's mind and soul have been sufficiently softened up for him to think of putting himself in God's hands. "Gaining perspective," as Laura approvingly puts it when he tells her what he is thinking. "It's a good idea," she adds as if patting him on the head.

Getting to this point is no small feat for Lewis. He is a highly moral man who if he comes across an insect in the house refuses to kill it, instead trapping it one of Laura's thousand Tupperware containers and gently carrying it outside to freedom rather than death. But Lewis has always distrusted organized religion for the hierarchy it sets up between believers and heathens, the perceptual dichotomy of "us" and "them," and the arrogant but inescapable belief held by each religion that its particular acolytes are in possession of the one true path to God. Lewis is not sure whether his conviction about his lack of religious conviction is innate or genetically inherited from Mordecai, but Lewis has never forgotten overhearing his father telling Miranda one day while they were having cocktails on the patio in their garden, "Either one religion is right and the others are all wrong, or all are wrong, or all are right in their own ways."

Mordecai never deliberately set out to influence Lewis's attitude to religion, but nonetheless the father's skepticism shaped the son's religious view. This is why Lewis never developed the desire to spend every Saturday morning in synagogue, serving time in organized religion, which, no matter what the stripe or logo — star, cross, crescent — always seemed to Lewis to find ways to justify every injustice committed in its name. Lewis always felt that the Jews were lucky in a way that Hitler had persecuted them, because if he had chosen to persecute others, say left-handed people, then the Nazis probably would have numbered Jews among them.

All the talk about Jews being a "light unto the gentiles" never ceased to embarrass Lewis as he was growing up, and this only got worse when he learned about Mordecai's secret professional life. Christianity appeared as an evolution to the adolescent Lewis, with its self-contained "Do unto others as you would have others do unto you" axiom that he found so pragmatic and appealing, and which he endeavoured to follow every minute of his waking existence. An evolution of justice into love, a positive "Do this" rather than the gigantic looming negative of "Thou shalt not." A Canadian Jewish bad-boy poet whose name Lewis has forgotten once provocatively called Christianity "Judaism with a nose job," and Lewis has always felt that was about right.

Truth be told, it is hard not to admire the early Christians' project management skills in the phenomenally successful growth of their faith: their deliberate decision to graft the new religion onto the trunk of the older pagan rituals, their political astuteness in moving Jesus's birth to December to blur with Saturnalia, their deliberate cultivation of converts — unlike the Jews who disdained them and made it difficult to join the very exclusive circumcised circle of trust — and their politician's love of kissing babies and wooing voters.

Best of all is Christianity's doing away with the messy and painful ceremony of circumcision. What sane adult man would want to go through that just to change his lineup of personal gods? Lewis even finds Christianity's attitude to art more mature and cosmopolitan, unlike Judaism, which in its early insecure years forbade all graven images. And the music is certainly better: those beautiful hymns that evoke the mysterious Middle Ages, a whole cartload of monks — with a few eager castratos thrown in — singing about love, Jesus, and eternal life.

On the other hand, the Jewish lack of clarity about an afterlife is a provocative, almost modernist, certainly mentally tough, and perversely appealing notion. Lewis never tires of gently shocking his mother-in-law, Rose, with the notion that the afterlife doesn't figure nearly as heavily in Judaism as it does in Christianity, and that the emphasis on doing good and being rewarded or punished is much more on the here and now. In Judaism, if you follow God and are well-behaved, you will be granted the good fortune to conquer your enemies, harvest their foreskins, and take their women — if you believe the Old Testament examples — and write psalms and worship God, all in this mysterious, beautiful, frightening lifetime.

Conversely, if you offend God and He is in the midst of one of His murderous wanting-to-teach-his-chosen-people-a-lesson fits, you will see your cities smashed and burned and your women thrown over the hairy shoulders of others and whisked off to Babylon to serve out the rest of their lives in this valley of tears as concubines. If you are lucky enough to escape with your life, you will be sold into slavery, where you can write sad songs while you sit disconsolate by foreign rivers, again all in this short, brutal, wonderful life.

The bottom line is that there is a clear and quick line to consequence. You know where you stand, there is no misunderstanding, no confusing time lapse between act and reward or punishment, which, as every good psychologist, teacher, parent, or dog trainer knows, is the most important factor in shaping productive behaviours. Christianity is all about the future and endurance, trading present-day suffering for the promise of future reward, a lifetime of misery and slavery for an eternity of whiteness, Harlequin card angels, and sitting by Jesus's knee.

At heart, Lewis is ambivalent about the two religions that are represented in his home. When he is feeling particularly chauvinistic and uncharitable or uncensored, he will call Christianity a slave religion in Laura's presence, and she will play her typecast role with aplomb and politely turn the other cheek. But despite all this skepticism, this sense that religion is something you practise the night before you go into battle, a situational and opportunistic piety designed to protect oneself and hinder one's enemies in a particular time of risk and fear, Lewis finds himself increasingly unfit to cope with his current situation and therefore more and more inclined to place himself in the comforting hand of a higher power.

He wants to transfer his burden of guilt and fear somewhere else, to believe that yes, indeed, everything does happen for a reason; that he is suffering for some higher purpose; and that in the end, although hopefully in his lifetime and not the next, he will be rewarded. Lewis even tries praying once or twice, when nobody in the house is looking. The experience strikes him as mildly blasphemous and a bit emotionally awkward and tentative, like someone with a low sex drive deciding one evening to commit the esoteric biblical sin of onanism.

Lewis's decision to get religion is driven in part by his hope that if he goes to synagogue he might find it easier to pray. But Lewis certainly is not Jewish in any formally religious sense of the term, and if any blame for that is to be assigned then Mordecai has to bear at least part of it. Mordecai and Miranda didn't attend synagogue regularly or even irregularly. In fact, before Lewis married Laura and she expressed an interest in learning about Judaism, Lewis had only been in a synagogue for reasons other than attending a bar mitzvah, bat mitzvah, or wedding once in his life. And he is embarrassed he can't remember the occasion.

Lewis had a bar mitzvah, but probably it would not have been recognized as such because it took place at home outside on his parents' back patio. Lewis read his Biblical portion and delivered his speech in English, and there was no rabbi. In fact, Mordecai in his paternal wisdom played rabbi, studying the Old Testament with Lewis every evening over the course of the year. As a result of his unusual bar mitzvah training, Lewis never learned to speak any Hebrew.

Still, Lewis considers himself to be a Jew by heritage, by history, by blood, by culture, and perhaps by world view. And Lewis is fiercely, if quietly, proud to be a Jew, the way someone else might be proud to be a backup player on a winning football team. Not that the Jews have ever won much in the traditional sporting or militaristic sense, at least not since the glory days of King David and then not until recently with the birth of Israel. But Lewis is

proud that the Jews have won out in an anthropological survival
or genetic sense, winning more than their share of Nobel prizes,
producing disproportionately more doctors and lawyers and, if
you believe the anti-Semitic propaganda, more than their share
of Hollywood moguls and media magnates. But despite this
chauvinistic pride, Lewis has always had trouble refuting Mordecai's arguments about how Christianity beat out the Jews in the
conversion game.

"When it comes right down to it," Mordecai would regularly
declaim during Lewis's year of bar mitzvah lessons, "Jews are not
so good at PR. The Christians pay attention to perceptions; the
Jews ignore them at their peril."

But Lewis feels most conflicted between his and Laura's religions as an architect, and never more so than when comparing
churches and synagogues. Whenever Lewis enters an old-fashioned
church — he won't step foot in a modern one — he can feel his very
breath being snatched away, as if God is grabbing him around the
chest with his fist and squeezing. Lewis's eyes, mind, and heart are
swiftly drawn inward and upward, to the high sweeping ceilings,
the naves, the soaring buttresses mimicking a heaven that floats
above him, the columns leading up from the ground to remind
him of the potential of his better nature. Whenever Lewis enters
a church he can't help thinking about God.

Whereas in a synagogue, Lewis could be in any other building:
a dentist's office, a school, a union hall. When Lewis tries to think
about God in a synagogue his mind wanders. There is little sense
of physical beauty, of creating a place where you can be close
to God. If you trust the descriptions in the Old Testament, Jews
once knew how to build such beautiful places, and Lewis has
visited some of the old European synagogues, but generally he
feels ashamed of his religion when he brings his family to a North

American synagogue on the high holidays and there is no sense of wonder created by the use of materials and space.

"Just what I've always told you," Mordecai would say when the thirteen-year-old Lewis first brought up this comparison. "As undeniably smart as we are, our people have no sense of stagecraft, of event management. We might be the accountants to the rock stars, but I bet none of us are working to develop their light shows."

Luckily for Lewis, the Shaarei Zedek Synagogue, which caters to the ever-dwindling local Jewish community, is still located in a deconsecrated yellow brick church. While certainly not ancient, the building at least conforms to Lewis's idea of what a place of worship should be. So, one warm Saturday in mid-November Lewis finds himself walking through the doors of the Shaarei Zedek Synagogue in the uptown, just a couple of blocks away and up the hill from the Trans-Canada Highway, which cuts shamelessly through the middle of the city. The former church's steeple has been sawed off, and the bell has been taken away. Lewis loves the sound of church bells and can't help thinking of the former church as a person who has lost her voice.

As he enters the sanctuary, Lewis grabs a prayer book from the shelf. He has arrived only a few minutes early, but the crowd is still sparse. The Saint John Jewish community might still claim Louis B. Mayer of MGM fame as one of their own over a century after he left the city, but today in the early years of the twenty-first century they can barely muster a *minyan*. Lewis sits as far back as he can without appearing standoffish and begins to prepare himself for the service by meditating. He doesn't know much about meditation but knows at least that he is supposed to focus on his breathing.

Although he isn't a regular attendee, being inside the synagogue is not a completely novel experience for Lewis. Soon after moving to Saint John, he and Laura started attending synagogue twice a year: in dark December on the first night of Hanukkah for the public menorah lighting presided over by the mayor and in bright spring for the annual Holocaust memorial service. Each year a survivor would be brought in to speak and Lewis would feel Jewish for a second time in six months. For Lewis is also a Holocaust Jew, defining himself in unspoken ways like many others by that almost indescribable event, to which he is at least once removed. But many relatives whom he never met, great-aunts and uncles and second cousins, died in the Shoah, and ever since Lewis first heard about the cataclysm as a boy he has been struggling to comprehend. As an adolescent Lewis concluded that either God didn't exist or else He stood by and let it happen. And both, for Lewis, amount to the same thing.

But today at synagogue is an ordinary Sabbath. No candles are being lit. No six million are being remembered. Lewis has been to synagogue so few times in his life that he expects the service to take an hour. He has mentally prepared himself for that amount of time. It is the length of time with which he associates a church service. The Sabbath service starts off slowly with a lot of chanting in Hebrew and much standing, almost milling, around. The rabbi's rambling talk — it can't be called a sermon because it is far too discursive and intellectual — is the opposite of memorable, and Lewis has trouble paying attention. In fact, there is no rabbi. The Saint John congregation is so small it can't afford one. In place of a rabbi, a few of the older members of the congregation have been trained to lead services. On high holidays, a rabbi from Toronto or New York is flown in to officiate. Due to his delinquent Jewish upbringing, Lewis can't follow the Hebrew, and his mind easily begins to stray. Instead of paying attention to the Torah, Lewis remembers Mordecai's cutting words on the vernacular in liturgy: "The first rule of public relations is to speak the language of your audience. The Protestants figured this out a long time ago when they ditched Latin for English, but we still persist with Hebrew."

From the bare English translations on the left-hand side of the page — Lewis has forgotten that Hebrew is written and read from right to left — the prayers all appear to be about praising God for being the best and thanking Him for delivering the Hebrews from their enemies. "That's the other major difference, Lewis," Mordecai would say. "It's the classic case of extroverts versus introverts. We Jews, we worship God so He will deliver us from our enemies. We're externally focused. The introverted Christians, they worship God to deliver them from themselves. When you're Christian it doesn't matter if your life is miserable and you're always being thrown to the lions — you've got paradise coming if you only just hang on to the faith, if you ask for forgiveness from your sins. We *meshugenah* Jews, on the other hand, we just have one life to live." It sounded like a pop song. When Mordecai spoke like that, Lewis felt more like a Christian. He likes the hymns. Although he finds it nearly impossible to do in practice, some part of Lewis likes the idea of placing his fate in a higher power. He loves the beauty of churches. But still he finds it hard to be a fan of organized religion.

Maybe it was his quasi meditation before the service had started, but as his mind wanders back to memories of Mordecai, Lewis finds that he is able to pray. Yet he is deliberately vague at first, not being so presumptuous as to ask God for a way out of his present double predicament. Instead, he asks God for the courage to get through the next few months, as this is what he remembers reading about how Christians pray. Asking for the strength and grace to endure God-given adversity rather than having the chutzpah to ask God to end it is the polite, respectful, and non-pushy way to beg. Lewis also prays to be forgiven for putting Laura through the uncertainty arising from the incident in the park.

But Lewis, despite his ambivalent feelings toward his faith and his determination not to be importunate, can't help tapping into thousands of years of collective spiritual memory. Before he knows it, he finds himself bargaining like Jacob with the God of his fathers. When God appeared to Jacob in the desert, the patriarch's opening position was that if God protected Jacob and enabled him to return safely to his home then Jacob would deign to worship this God who proved Himself to be so useful. In Lewis's case he bargains with his invisible and silent God that if He sees fit to deliver Lewis from indecent exposure charges and the intellectual infringement lawsuit, then Lewis will start going to synagogue regularly, as a way of saying thanks and paying more respect to God going forward.

Lewis's opening meditation and foray into prayer carries him through the first hour of reading, and more praying, and bowing his head, and standing up. But the quickly emerging problem is that Lewis's natural tolerance for a religious service extends only to one hour. After that he reaches his psychological breaking point. He can no longer sit still. This is just one more reason why he prefers churches and the Christian liturgy. Christians have it all figured out, with their one-hour services. At exactly five minutes past the one-hour mark, when Lewis realizes the service is nowhere near being over, he finds himself looking up at the ceiling. But unfortunately, because he isn't in a church he isn't thinking about God. Lewis has the good manners to at least feel guilty that now of all times he wishes he were at church, ideally at one of the Christmas Eve services he usually attends with Laura.

THE ART OF BEING LEWIS ♦ 181

AS A BOY, Lewis was a foreigner when it came to Christmas. He was an outsider for the obvious reasons: when the wealthy and secular part of the world went mad once a year and worshipped the birth of their Lord with an orgy of shopping, eating, decorating, and music, Lewis was the poor boy looking in on the Ogilvy's Christmas display from the coldness and cheapness of Saint Catherine Street in winter. As a child, Lewis felt utterly left out on Christmas Eve when all his friends went to bed barely able to sleep amidst their pure anticipation of Santa Claus's imminent visit and the proof of his presence: presents under the tree.

Hanukkah was so boring and quiet in comparison, with very few gifts and no surrounding suspense. Of course, Lewis didn't let on to his friends. When they all assumed he received a gift every day for eight days he just smiled and nodded as if he were the luckiest kid in the world. One year he convinced Mordecai and Miranda to borrow a small artificial tree from some family friends and he put his Hanukkah gifts under the tree, happily relinquishing the Jewish emphasis on the here and now through the instant gratification of receiving presents the night before in exchange for the more painful Christian pleasure of postponing the reward by going to bed, waking up early, rushing downstairs, turning on the tree lights, and opening up his presents at dawn.

But outsider status had its cheap consolations. Because Lewis grew up with no illusions, he intuitively knew himself at the age of five to be a complete non-victim of the great conspiracy of Santa Claus's existence. Lewis felt wise, and deliciously cynical, when his friends would talk for weeks about Santa Claus while he was inwardly confident, absolutely certain without a shred of agnostic doubt that Santa Claus didn't exist, that he was a figment of benevolent parents' desires to control and amuse their children.

Yet as Lewis got older and married Laura, and as the children started coming with startling regularity, and with Christmas first at Laura's parents then on their own, Lewis began to unquestioningly enjoy the semi-pagan ritual of having a tree inside the house without the accompanying sense of guilt that he was somehow letting down his side, disrespecting the memory of his thousands of forbears who had so stubbornly risked or given up their lives so they didn't have to worship at the altar of false gods. Lewis even started to attend church services on Christmas Eve with his growing family.

Lewis began to enjoy Christmas as much as anyone else: not just the turkey and the glorious unwrapping of presents but also the late nights leading up to the great night that were spent hidden away in the basement assembling the Santa gifts for the children that Lewis learned were usually left unwrapped because Santa didn't wrap gifts, at least not the big ones. When it came to Christmas, Lewis had evolved in the short space of twenty-odd years from skeptical child outsider secure in his superior knowledge about the non-existence of Santa to enthusiastic adult acolyte as he married Laura and became an honorary member of the Christian tribe.

However, as Lewis hit his late thirties and perhaps because he felt he now had the legitimacy of an insider and therefore had earned the right to criticize, he began to inwardly compare and contrast Christmas with the Jewish holidays. Out of loyalty to Laura and respect for her heritage, and as a result of a highly developed superego, Lewis tried his best not to even think these sacrilegious thoughts. But, despite his efforts, Lewis found it almost morbidly fascinating how defanged the Christian holidays had become, how completely centred on children.

Christmas was, after all, at the winter solstice, the still pagan-infused celebration of the birth of a god. Easter occurred at the pagan-tempered spring equinox, mourning the death of a god and celebrating his ultimate rebirth year after year. Both holidays, therefore, should have been freighted with awe, terror, and wild celebration, but instead they had become festivals for children, with a cola-inspired Santa and his cornucopia of presents, the harmless mythology of a jolly fat man slipping down a chimney, the easy magic of commercialism and presents, the innocuous Easter egg hunts instead of hunting for your lost soul.

The Jewish holidays, on the other hand, although they also catered to children and the future — with dreidels, fried foods, and hiding of the matzo — were grown-up holidays, celebrating in the case of not just Hanukkah but also Passover and Purim the bloody and costly escape from brutality, deception, arrogance, and slavery. This endless replay of standing up to evil and earning freedom had led to the recurring Jewish holiday dinner joke that Mordecai never missed a chance to tell at each celebration: "Why are we here today? There was a war, we won, let's eat." It was Mordecai who set the stage for the Morton family obsession with the interplay between Christianity and Judaism.

Mordecai allowed a Christmas tree into the Morton family home to slake Lewis's curiosity and perhaps address his own personal need to break taboos. But when it came to Christianity, Mordecai was impressed with only one thing: the bloody single-mindedness that Christians had brought to conversion, their God-given fervour for spreading the gospel that Jews, despite their best efforts, could never seem to muster. In fact, Jews worked hard to dissuade anyone wanting to join their small, serious band. Mordecai had to give the Christians credit for their superior political instincts and insight into human nature: what sane red-blooded male over the age of eight days would willingly choose the painfully acquired taste for circumcision over the simple pleasures of rum-laced eggnog around a sweet-smelling Christmas tree?

But despite his natural bias toward Judaism over Christianity, Mordecai wasn't a fan of religious conversion in either direction. Mordecai never raised any concerns that his grandchildren were being raised as half Christians and half Jews or gave any indication that he thought Laura should have converted. Through an empathy engrained in his Jewish genes that had evolved over three thousand years of religious persecution and forced conversions, Mordecai considered any conversion, whether by the sword or domestic blackmail or nagging, to be an unfair expectation.

But when the young Lewis was feeling somehow left out in the cold while most of his friends were celebrating Christmas, Mordecai found opportunities to build up his Jewish pride. One December, Mordecai came upon the ten-year-old Lewis sitting at the kitchen table listening intently to "Frosty the Snowman" on the radio. Mordecai stopped and sat down with Lewis. "Did you know half your modern Christmas songs were written either by or secretly about Jews?"

Mordecai assumed the answer was no and continued. "Take 'Rudolph the Red-Nosed Reindeer.' Lyrics written by a Jew, one Robert May. His brother-in-law, Johnny Marks, also a Jew, wrote the music. Okay, so far so good, Jewish enough. But it's also a secret Jewish allegory. Bobby May based it on his lonely childhood. Rudolph is obviously Jewish. He is being discriminated against by the other reindeer *because* he is Jewish. 'Left out of their reindeer games' — get it? He might as well have written 'gentile games.' And Rudolph's probably a communist too — many Jews were, at least in the beginning — with that red nose of his. The red nose, in case you missed it, is also a symbol of being chosen, of being special, of having talents and gifts that others are jealous of. See, on one level it's a simple Christmas carol; on the other it's a complex song about exclusion, about difference, about anti-Semitism. It is a song about being proud of who you are."

Later, when Lewis grew up and met Laura and they had children, Hanukkah would blend into Christmas and back again. When they gave Jewish books to their children for Christmas and played Christian games at Hanukkah, when the menorah and the Christmas lights dazzled throughout the house and nobody knew which holiday was which, Laura would question whether they were doing the right thing, raising their children without a strong sense of one identity or the other. She wondered whether the two religions would cancel each other out and the children would grow up in a spiritual no man's land.

Whenever they were having this conversation, Lewis would put his hand on Laura's shoulders and draw her closer to him. He would lean down the five inches that he had on her and nuzzle her hair, inhale her smell, and they would hold each other like two animals. Lewis would shake his head and say no, they weren't doing anything wrong, this was the way God had meant it to be, for all the religions to blur their truths together. It didn't matter whether the truth was justice — proscribing what could not or should not be done — or love — telling humans how they should treat each other — or spiritual surrender, or being part of the larger world, with animals, plants, and stones together making a larger truth. Religions weren't supposed to be like a loud league of sports teams elbowing each other out of the way, trying to smash in each other's skulls and staking claim to being the sole winner.

Laura would say of course Lewis was right, and she would nuzzle him back, and the children would go on playing, screaming, and fighting their way through the kaleidoscope of holidays. When Lewis was feeling irreverent he would call their children *mischlings*, his beautiful blond, blue-eyed *mischlings*, his half and halfs, his flesh and blood, flesh of his bone, his beautiful growing beings who were the partial bearers of his crazy genes: diluting them, repairing them, making them stronger, and carrying them forward into the future on their sturdy legs and with their bright eyes that were not wary or watchful but brave, trusting, and hawk sharp.

YET TODAY IN synagogue, after Lewis bows and prays and stands up and sits down for what seems like forever, after the rabbi and the congregation praise God for the umpteenth time, Lewis experiences a strange sensation. The hairs on the back of his neck rise. He thinks perhaps he is becoming lightheaded from all the getting up and getting down. Possibly his repeatedly bowed head is putting pressure on the arteries in his neck and restricting blood flow to his brain. He has the distinct feeling he is being watched. Maybe this is what it feels like to have a religious experience. Perhaps God is reaching down to grab him by the neck as a violent preamble to addressing him directly. Lewis can't shake the feeling that he is the object of special attention, and after some deliberation he quickly turns around to see. But God is nowhere in sight.

Instead Lewis finds himself staring almost point-blank into the smirking face of Michael Milkman in the row behind him. Milkman's red *kippah* and strange resemblance to Al Pacino make him look more like a worldly medieval Italian cardinal than a twenty-first-century Jewish litigator specializing in intellectual property cases. Milkman makes no effort to hide the fact he has been watching Lewis. He nods in greeting and grins so widely that Lewis can see most of his teeth.

With the sight of those very white and very sharp teeth — a pointed reminder of the pending lawsuit — any restorative effect that Lewis might have taken from the Sabbath service deserts him.

His mood is altered as quickly as Moses's elation was dashed when, after traipsing down Mount Sinai with tablets in hand, he glimpsed his people gyrating in adoration of the golden calf.

19

IT IS 8:00 p.m. at the Morton household. Judah is about half an hour away from finishing his homework, after which he will play video games across the Internet with friends until he goes to bed an hour later. But Alexandra and Samuel are going in and out of the bathroom, putting on pyjamas and brushing small white teeth that are, astonishingly to Lewis, still free of cavities. Lewis is waiting until they are in bed so he can tuck them in.

Lewis never has to work late anymore now that he no longer has any work to do, at least not for the foreseeable future. But he is finding it hard to enjoy the paternal joy of helping to put his children to bed every night. Alexandra will read in bed for fifteen minutes, but Samuel still likes to be read to before bed. He is only four, but he's developed a keen taste for the Horrible Histories books, marketed as "History with the horrible bits left in." Lewis has read the whole series with Judah, but he is reliving *The Rotten Romans* with Samuel. Afterward Lewis will kiss his two children goodnight.

When he was building his career and working late more often than not, the first thing Lewis did when he got home was to look in on all of his sleeping children. He would stand silently in the dark in the centre of their rooms like a thief as he watched their little chests rise and fall. When he worked up the courage he would walk softly over to their beds and kiss them lightly on the top of their heads, afraid to wake them. But his greatest fear was that something would happen to them and they wouldn't turn out perfectly. After they were born, and after Lewis could see with his own eyes that each of them was healthy and strong, Lewis worried about what might happen to them as they grew.

Lewis works hard not to be a nervous parent in front of Judah, Alexandra, Samuel, and even the baby, Skye. But he has been worrying about his children long before they were born. Even before he met Laura, Lewis was already pondering the great calamities that could irrevocably be set in motion for his future children. And being someone who prized reason, he began to reasonably plan how to lower the risks. Lewis did all this between attending classes in architecture and learning how to restrict the infinite possibilities of space. While his classmates were enjoying the new-found freedom and joys of being university students, Lewis was planning how to avoid fathering children with mental illness.

MCGILL UNIVERSITY SCHOOL of Architecture was filled with students who weren't sure where they belonged and were surprised and disappointed by where they found themselves. Half the incoming class were engineers at heart who thought architecture school was too artsy, formless, and undisciplined. The other half considered themselves artists and found architecture studies overly scientific and mathematical. They couldn't cope with the limits imposed by the physical world on their dreaming.

But following the death of Miranda, the mathematical and scientific discipline applied to art was precisely why Lewis chose the math and science courses in his second year of CEGEP so he could get accepted into architecture school. Lewis had the competitive advantage of having artistic talent, which he knew intuitively he shouldn't waste. But it was in architecture that his artistic impulse could be safely channeled and contained. And architecture studies didn't disappoint.

As a student at McGill, Lewis didn't just embrace what it meant to be an architect, to have an architect's soul, to observe through an architect's eyes, to see the world as a vast space waiting to be enclosed, to channel light, the eye, and movement to find the balance between beauty and function. Lewis began to cultivate a style of living and appearance and dress that suited his conception of what was to become his profession. He would carry this sense of style while at university and down the years throughout his time at Drescher & Drescher.

After growing his blond hair long in adolescence, Lewis began to wear it shorter but not so short that it was noticeable. And with every dollar that Lewis earned working part-time at Chez Nick's, he began to buy expensive clothes that didn't look expensive. He eschewed the architect-as-black-enveloped-rock-star look, choosing instead fine wool pants that were tan, blue, or grey, white dress shirts, and tailored dark blue wool blazers. He went to bed before ten-thirty each night and generally slept well.

Lewis's only private nod to his still colourful and unpredictable but increasingly hidden inner self was his underwear. Beneath his toned-down Samuelsohn pants that fell across his nondescript Cole Haan shoes, Lewis would wear the brightest coloured boxer shorts. But despite their wild colour, Lewis imposed one aesthetic rule on his underwear: each pair had to have a pattern of animals in a brilliant colour set against an equally vivid but contrasting background. When Lewis and Laura first slept together, on their third date, Laura's first glimpse of those boxer shorts made her smile. Lewis was wearing boxers with fluorescent green iguanas sunning themselves a sunset backdrop of orange and pink.

In his second and final year at Dawson College, when Lewis was taking calculus and physics and drawing the beautiful houses of Westmount to build a new portfolio, he also took an American history course. It was there that Lewis first encountered the sociological phenomenon of those African Americans who, in the years following emancipation and into the twentieth century, were determined that their descendants would "pass" from black to white.

So that their sons, grandsons, daughters, and granddaughters would never have to deal with the consequences of being black in an intolerant white continent, these determined men and women searched for light-skinned black brides and bridegrooms, and then encouraged the same for their progeny, so that within two generations their descendants' skin was white enough that they began to pass, like ghosts, into the safe and unaware white majority.

Like these men and women who wanted to bleach the vestiges of their identity in subsequent generations, Lewis was determined his children and grandchildren would have healthier genes and minds. It wasn't just Miranda's descent into mental illness and eventual suicide that Lewis was concerned about inheriting and passing on. He felt like a genetic case of double jeopardy. Mordecai's side of the family was not immune. Mordecai's slightly older cousin Anya, despite her wealth, beauty, brains, and talent, suffered silently from depression. She committed suicide at the age of forty-eight by taking a stiff gin and tonic to her marble bath tub and slitting her slender wrists in two feet of warm, bubbly water. She also happened to have been the only member of her immediate family to survive the Holocaust. But to the young, judgmental Lewis, those childhood circumstances were insufficiently extenuating.

Less dramatically, Lewis had always wondered about his uncle Yossel and his wife, Frida. Yossel was outgoing but permanently quiet around Frida, almost to the point of depression. And Frida, who was high-strung at the best of times, seemed tenser around her husband. It was as if the two of them, normal around other members of the family, formed one complete manic-depressive when put together. Lewis was convinced he had to thin out his family blood.

So, starting in university, after his acceptance to McGill's prestigious School of Architecture, and when he began to date with some regularity and focus, Lewis carefully and diplomatically investigated any serious girlfriends for the slightest hints of mental illness in them or in their immediate families. He was suspicious, and a harsh judge, of any mood swings, sadness, or signs of obsession or jealousy that he was in a position to observe and that went beyond the normal university boyfriend/girlfriend fixation. But like the Nazi race experts who reached back to grandparents to determine degrees of Jewishness, Lewis also combed through two generations in his search for mental purity.

If a potential mate revealed hints of serious mental illness — including but not limited to manic-depression and schizophrenia — among their brothers, sisters, parents, or grandparents, she found herself swiftly discarded, without explanation, sometimes overnight. Lewis would often just stop calling. Just one instance of suicide, or even an attempt, anywhere in her family disqualified someone from eventually becoming Mrs. Lewis Morton, as did the hospitalization of any family member for any mental health issues. Even one visit to a psychiatrist made someone damaged goods in Lewis's eyes, as if he were a senator and trusted friend of

194 ♦ DANIEL GOODWIN

the American president-elect vetting candidates for vice-president.

In his second year of university, Lewis went one step further. Having already assumed a positive correlation between artistic tendencies and mental illness, Lewis began to weed out girlfriends who had the misfortune to come from families of artists, writers, musicians, or actors. One woman he met in class, Nora, who turned out to be a good conversationalist on two dates, was revealed on the third, which was proceeding well toward its logical conclusion, to be a case of double jeopardy: both her parents were actors at Stratford.

When Nora unwittingly revealed this seemingly innocuous fact after the two of them had amazed each other with the revelation that they both shared the same choice of favourite dessert, Lewis mumbled some disjointed monologue about the future that seemed incoherent even as he was delivering it and left Nora completely startled and abandoned at the restaurant table while they were waiting for their double order of crème brûlée.

Then there was Anna, the daughter of a famous Toronto novelist, whom, despite the artistic connection, Lewis was inclined to give the benefit of the doubt. But she had to be ruled out after Lewis researched her father and discovered he had written a memoir, after a five-year drought of writing novels, about his lifelong battle with depression. Anna didn't take Lewis's rejection well and slapped him so hard across the face she gave him a hairline fracture of his right cheekbone and a ringing sensation in his ears that lasted for two weeks.

Quasi-incestuous marriages in the family — i.e. between first cousins — although not uncommon in some of the Eastern European *shtetls* where both Mordecai's and Miranda's families hailed from, were also a big no-no.

When Lewis met Laura, a second-year marketing student,

over drinks with friends at the Peel Pub a few blocks south of the McGill campus, and when he subsequently met her for dinner and a movie, and then repeated the sequence one week later, he was so taken with her that for reasons he never quite understood he procrastinated for six weeks in initiating his usual and not always so subtle interrogation on the matter of the mental health and artistic proclivities of her and her family. Laura ended up having a solitary black mark against her, but by the time Lewis got around to discovering it he was so smitten that he made a once-in-a-lifetime exception.

On the positive side of the ledger, Laura had no artistic members of her family to speak of. They were all exemplars of late twentieth-century Upper Canadian upper-crust Protestant society: Oakville-bred accomplished professionals, businesspeople, bankers, community volunteers, executives of the Rotary Club. Taken as a collective they possessed a preponderance of blond hair, blue eyes, and natural tans derived from jogging and boating and skiing and appeared to have no unnatural interests. No open marriages. No extroverted extramarital affairs. No messy divorces. No unreasonable career dreams: no wannabe painters or novelists who dreamed of chucking in their healthy six-figure salaries for a life in a garret capturing or reinventing reality. Laura's uncles and male cousins possessed good healthy drinking habits but nothing approaching substance abuse. As far as Lewis could tell, nobody in Laura's family bought original art or even went to the theatre. They liked music, which was forgivable as long as they didn't create any of their own on the side, which thankfully they didn't.

But Lewis eventually, and accidentally, did discover one black sheep in Laura's blessedly near-perfect family. Great-uncle Alistair Mackenzie was a retired high school English teacher living in Kingston. He was also mildly schizophrenic. Most days Great-Uncle

Mackenzie behaved more or less normally — at least for an English teacher — reciting Tennyson to his two Maine Coon cats in his Black Watch tartan pajamas, but on others he was firmly convinced he was the reincarnation of William the Conqueror.

On these magnificent days Alistair would shuffle around his small apartment in the Queen's University student ghetto speaking what Lewis thought was a surprisingly credible Norman-sounding French and complaining about the time it was taking either to run Harold to ground or complete the Domesday Book. But by the time Lewis first experienced Great-Uncle Mackenzie in full flight it was too late. Six weeks in, Lewis was inescapably in love and willing to take a risk on Laura's genes.

But it wasn't until years later, after Lewis and Laura had their first-born Judah, and a few years later Alexandra followed Judah, and Samuel quickly followed Alexandra, to be followed without negative incident by Skye, who turned one just before Drescher drove his car into the Kennebecasis River, that Lewis felt he could breathe a sigh of relief. As each child in turn grew miraculously into a boy or girl who was not afraid of the dark, or monsters, or getting cancer and dying, or their parents getting cancer and dying or being killed in a car accident when they went out to a neighbourhood party, or their house disappearing, or another Holocaust, or their pets getting run over, or getting beat up at school, or failing to catch the lazy fly ball that was floating up into the sky, all things that kept Lewis awake at night when he was a boy, Lewis finally allowed himself the luxury of thinking that maybe, just maybe, his family's genetic predilection for mental illness had somehow bypassed his children.

TONIGHT, AFTER READING about the horrible origin of gladiator fights — as a way to honour the dead at Roman funerals — Samuel is sleepy and his eyes are already closing as Lewis pulls the covers up over his small straight shoulders and kisses him on his blond head. Lewis looks in on Alexandra engrossed in a book. She raises her eyes to him and says, "Goodnight, Dad," and Lewis kisses her on her nose, which is a miniature version of Laura's.

20

IT IS TOM who uncharacteristically calls Lewis to tell him the news. It's not news to Lewis, but now it's news to the rest of the world. Lewis has just dropped the older children off at the bus stop and is settling down at his laptop to search the Internet for mirage jobs.

"Lewie, you okay? I just read the paper."

"What paper?" Lewis isn't really paying attention to Tom.

"The *T-J.* You're front-page news."

Lewis stops breathing, and the room starts spinning. Everything is happening as he has feared. He is being exposed in the pages of the local paper as a pervert. In the space of no more than five seconds Lewis imagines little Alexandra coming home from school at the end of the day.

"Dad, what's a pervert?" She is looking up at him in the cinema of Lewis's mind. Despite the seriousness of the question, there is the hint of a smile on her face. Lewis experiences an initial sense of panic at the sight of his daughter smiling at his predicament, but Alexandra's face is so earnest and playful at the same time he is certain she has already figured it all out. She knows the word, she knows what is being said about him, but she also knows, in her big, constant heart, even at the wisp of the age of six, that it is all false. That her father is not a pervert. It is this certainty that allows Lewis to keep his voice level as he replies to her in his imagination.

"A pervert is someone who does bad things. Why do you ask?"

Alexandra doesn't wait to decide how to answer. "A kid at school said you were a pervert." Again, that beginning of a smile doesn't leave her face, as if she and Lewis are two adults smirking at the stupidity of the world around them. As if there is always some scrap of humour to be found in any situation, no matter how upsetting, no matter how bleak. Her look of confidence in Lewis's imagined version of the near future is so infectious that it lightens Lewis's mood despite himself and he chuckles in his daydream.

"Lewie, you all right? Are you laughing?"

Lewis is brought back to the present. "Sorry, I'm fine." He is lying, but he is feeling a bit better than he was a minute ago.

"Hmm. You never told me about the lawsuit," Tom says as if Lewis has been holding out on him.

Lewis starts breathing again. The room stops moving. It is certainly not good, but a story about something he most certainly hasn't done isn't quite as bad as being charged with indecent exposure. "I haven't seen the story yet."

"If you need anything, I just want you to know I have your back." Lewis assumes Maura saw the article and advised Tom to call Lewis right away to offer his moral support. Left to his own devices, Tom would have waited for Lewis to bring it up.

When Lewis says he has to get off the phone to read the story, Tom sounds relieved. "Okay, Lewie. And don't forget hunting on Sunday. We'll pick you up at eight a.m." Lewis forgot he agreed to go hunting. Laura supported Lewis going to synagogue, and she was neutral about him working out. But of hunting she does not approve. It runs counter to everything she holds dear.

Lewis runs to the front door and picks up the *Telegraph-Journal* that was thrown on the porch and is still rolled in its clear plastic bag. Lewis could have looked for the article on the web, but he still prefers paper when it's available. He assumes newspapers will only be printed for ten more years, at the outside.

Although it begins on the front page, the story is far below the fold and doesn't feature a photo of Lewis. Instead, there is a photo of a man who looks to be in his early fifties, with thick white hair combed straight back from his forehead, black designer glasses, and a neck that disappears into a black turtleneck. Maurits Abercrom, rock star architect. The story itself is two columns wide:

Local architectural firm facing legal action

Dave Demmings   **November 28, 2007**

Saint John, NB — Award-winning Saint John-based architectural firm Drescher & Drescher finds itself embroiled in controversy only a few months after the dramatic death of its founder, Leon Drescher.

The *Telegraph-Journal* has learned Drescher & Drescher is facing legal action in an alleged case of copyright infringement. Earlier this year lawyers for celebrated U.S. architect Maurits Abercrom filed in a Bermuda court alleging that Mr. Drescher misappropriated one of his designs and used it for the recently opened Macdonald Arts and Culture Building on the Halifax waterfront.

Shortly following Mr. Drescher's death, caused when he drove his car at excessive speed down Fox Farm Road into the Kennebecasis River, his eponymous firm was sold to a U.K.-based global architectural holding company. According to a source familiar with the case, who spoke only on condition of anonymity, this recent change in ownership and the fact that one of the architects named in the lawsuit is no longer alive will have little bearing on the outcome.

"If the court finds that the copyright for the design was indeed infringed upon, then the firm itself and any of the architects involved will still be liable for damages." According to this source, in designing the $100-million Macdonald Arts and Culture Building, Mr. Drescher followed his usual practice of working closely with his long-time partner Lewis Morton. "The two were inseparable. They worked on everything together."

Reached for comment, newly installed Drescher & Drescher managing partner Edward Montcalm said, "As I am sure you can appreciate, I cannot comment on this matter as it is still before the courts. However, I can confirm that Mr. Morton, the other architect named in the legal action, has been removed from all client files and is essentially suspended with pay."

Mr. Abercrom has designed over sixty-five major office buildings and private luxury homes around the world. He is a two-time recipient of the American Institute of Architects Gold Medal and was the 2002 winner of the Pritzker Architecture Prize, widely considered to be the Nobel Prize of the architectural profession.

Mordecai calls thirty minutes later.

"Lew, are you okay?"

"Why wouldn't I be?"

"Well, it's not every day you're named in a copyright infringement lawsuit and suspended with pay and then have all your neighbours read about it." Lewis appreciates that Mordecai hasn't become any less direct as he's aged.

He also realizes he hasn't even told Mordecai that he is no longer doing any work at Drescher & Drescher. Lewis usually sees his father once a year when he takes the family to Montreal and Oakville for their two-week summer vacation. They visit with Mordecai and then drive westward to see Laura's parents. The rest of the year, Mordecai and Lewis speak briefly by phone about once a month. Sometimes Mordecai comes to Saint John for one of the Jewish holidays. "How did you know?"

"I have you on Google Alerts. I would have read it even earlier, but my phone was in my locker while I was working out." Lewis laughs despite himself. Mordecai approves of Lewis's reaction because he goes on to joke, "Usually you're making the news for your own building designs, not stealing those of others."

Lewis stops laughing. "I didn't steal anything."

"I know, Lewis."

"Neither did Drescher." But Mordecai doesn't respond this time because Lewis doesn't sound nearly as definitive.

Mordecai waits a moment before asking, as kindly as he can, "Do you need any help with the lawsuit?"

"No. I mean, I'm okay."

Mordecai waits a split second too long before replying, which Lewis knows means he doesn't believe him. "Okay. Good to hear." More silence. When he senses he needs to be, Mordecai is as patient as he is direct. He's never been someone who has to hear his own voice. And he never stops thinking.

Lewis doesn't have the heart to tell Mordecai about what else is keeping him up at night. He hopes Mordecai's next Google Alert doesn't show his only son being escorted to Saint John's court in handcuffs, charged with exposing himself to a gaggle of adolescents. And he can't bear the thought of telling his father he has been thinking — just thinking — about suicide. Since the incident in the park, Lewis has always thought of the group of teenagers as a "gang." Lewis is too distracted to notice, but after five minutes of speaking with Mordecai, the "gang" has unexpectedly transformed itself in his mind into a "gaggle."

"I assume you're looking elsewhere. Any irons in the fire?"

Lewis wants to lie to his father, but he can't bring himself to so he says, "Not really, Dad."

Lewis senses Mordecai nodding at the other end of the line, taking in his son's response, making up his mind. "Okay. I'm coming out to visit you tomorrow."

"Tomorrow? You don't have to do that. How are you going to get a ticket so fast?"

"Who's flying? I'm going to drive. Be there for *Shabbos* supper." His father's little joke. The Mortons never had a proper Sabbath meal in their lives. "Besides, there's an exhibition of your mother's work at the Beaverbrook. I never miss one." Split-second pause. "Actually, it's a joint exhibition with Jones. The curator's even given it a highfalutin title: 'Jones and Mortinsky: Reciprocal Muses.' It opens Saturday. I thought we could drive down to Fredericton together to see it."

"That would be fine, but I'm supposed to go hunting on Sunday with some friends, so we will only be able to spend Friday night and Saturday together."

"Hunting? Since when did you take up hunting?"

"It's a long story."

"No doubt. Well, I'm still coming down."

Lewis has never been to one of Miranda's exhibitions. But just as he visited her every day when she was in the hospital, Mordecai has remained faithful to Miranda even in death. Lewis always assumed that Mordecai had girlfriends after Miranda, but if he did he never said. And he certainly never brought any of them home. It is fitting, Lewis thinks, that Jones is being featured along with Miranda. It was he who single-handedly made Miranda famous after her death.

TWO MONTHS AFTER Miranda's suicide, André Jones came to see Mordecai. He asked to see all Miranda's paintings, and Mordecai obliged. He spent three hours looking at every one. At the time of her death she had sixty in total. It had taken two years, but she had managed to finish the painting in which she depicted herself and her family as deer. Jones studied each work in silence, with the occasional "*Incroyable*" or "*Tabarnak*" muttered under his breath. Halfway through his viewing he said softly, "I never knew."

When Jones was done, Mordecai offered him a Scotch in the living room. Jones downed it one gulp before declaring, "I want to make Miranda famous. May I have your permission to borrow some of the paintings and do so? *S'il vous plaît?*"

Mordecai wasn't sure what Miranda would have wanted. But in his practical way he concluded that if she had taken the time to paint sixty pictures she would have been happy for people to see them. He didn't know what Jones could accomplish for a dead unknown artist, but he decided to let him try. And if he ever had any concerns about the relationship between Jones and Miranda he never let on.

With Mordecai's permission, Jones leapt into a one-man frenzy of marketing and promotion. Like a travelling salesman, he paid visits to his contacts in the art world with two or three of Miranda's paintings in tow. He offered to write catalogue copy, to make opening remarks at any exhibition, even at the beginning to underwrite shows. Everyone in the gallery business respected Jones, but nobody wanted to invest the time and effort in a dead woman nobody had ever heard of. At least not at first.

Finally, a new gallery downtown on Sherbrooke looking to make its reputation agreed to hold a small exhibition. Jones made sure every single one of Montreal's art critics was in attendance and gave a personal guided tour of the sixteen paintings that were hanging within close proximity of each other on the white walls of the small space. The reviews were unanimously ecstatic. From there the exhibition was invited to Toronto, and within two years museums and private collectors across Canada were bidding on paintings for their permanent collections.

Mordecai had always enjoyed Miranda's paintings, but still he was pleasantly surprised that the art world was willing to pay for them. Together, he and Jones worked to manage Miranda's healthy posthumous career and sales. They knew they were dealing with a finite amount of work, so they had to avoid letting it go too quickly, and they were careful about to whom they sold and for what price. Mordecai didn't need the money, but he was proud each time one of Miranda's paintings sold for a decent sum. After every sale, Mordecai paid Jones a commission and went home alone and had a Scotch. With one hand he raised a silent toast to Miranda, and with the other he wrote a cheque for the remaining proceeds of the sale to one of his three favourite mental health charities.

TRUE TO HIS word, Mordecai arrives the next day just in time for Friday night supper. The children hear the distinctive rumbling of their *zayde*'s Porsche accelerating up their quiet hill of a street. They rush to the door and give Mordecai a hug. Even Judah, on the cusp of standoffish adolescence, gives his *zayde* a warm, unself-conscious embrace. Laura makes him comfortable in the living room and hands him a glass of the expensive whisky they keep in the house just for his visits. Lewis sits primly in his chair, but Mordecai slouches in his, not because he is old and can't sit up straight but because he is still strong and flexible and slouching makes him feel young. He is a very young seventy-seven.

"*L'chaim.*" Mordecai has just raised his glass in the traditional Jewish toast, to life, and Lewis has barely taken a sip of his two-percent-alcohol fruit beer that he and Laura discovered on a European trip a few years ago when four-year-old Samuel runs into the room.

Lewis's third child bends to one knee, extends his right arm, and slides halfway across the floor, slamming into Mordecai's feet. Mordecai doesn't seem to notice. He doesn't even try to rearrange his legs.

"Look, *Zayde*, my new Spider-Man pyjamas."

With Samuel at his feet dressed as his favourite superhero, Mordecai can't resist an opportunity to build some Jewish pride. After giving Samuel the thumbs-up, he says, "You know those superheroes?"

"What about them?" asks Samuel, suddenly stationary and interested in this long-haired elder who is showing an interest in his obsession.

"They're all Jewish." Mordecai nods solemnly. "Invented by Jews."

"C'mon, *Zayde*, Jewish?" says Samuel, suddenly a very serious, skeptical Spider-Man. "You're joking me."

"No, seriously. Here, sit on my knee." *Zayde* Mordecai lifts "Spider-Sam" onto his still sturdy seventy-seven-year-old knee. "You know where 'The Batman' got his name? That was his original name, by the way. Not just Batman but *The* Batman. He was originally from Russia. Small-town Russia. Sort of like us. Real name Batmansky. First name Hyman. Hyman Batmansky. But when his family immigrated to the U.S., the customs agent on the pier in New York said, 'Batmansky? What kind of American name is that? People won't be able to pronounce it. Don't you want to fit

in? Don't you know we're a melting pot here?' And then he asked
them the usual question 'Tell me, Mr. Batmansky, what did you
do back in the Old Country?'

"'Well, sir,' Mr. Batmansky said, 'I was in charge of getting rid
of bats in the old churches.' Great job for a Jew if you ask me,
Spider-Sam, but I digress. 'Well, then, The Batman it is. Welcome
to the United States of America, Mr. Batman.' And then he stamped
his passport."

Samuel looked at Mordecai skeptically.

"No joking, *yingele*. No joking." Mordecai solemnly crosses his
heart. "Look, cross my heart and hope to die."

For Samuel, who is clearly too young to pick up on the irony
— and just possibly the blasphemy — of a Jew crossing his heart,
his *zayde* swearing with the promise of such serious consequences
that he is telling the truth is more than enough. And this confidence that his four-year-old grandson is showing in him is
sufficient encouragement for Mordecai to launch into true profes-
sorial detail, rhyming off on his still strong, slender, and just slightly
hairy fingers.

"Superman — created by Joe Shuster and Jerry Siegel. Batman
was the brainchild of Bob Kane and Bill Finger. Jack Kirby was
fruitful with his pen and pencil, like one of those biblical patriarchs:
Fantastic Four, Incredible Hulk, and X-Men. Jack Kirby and Joe
Simon were the proud daddies — yes, Samuel, you can have two
daddies — of Captain America himself. And of course, you have
the stealthily named Stan Lee, who invented the superhero whom
I somehow think is your favourite: Spider-Man. Whose original
name was Spieder-Man, by the way, before he changed it."

Mordecai is in free, creative, and *meshuga* flight now, having
shamelessly invented the last factoid, reminding Lewis that the
best inventions are always partially grounded in reality. "Making

up superheroes was a way for young Jewish guys who probably couldn't get hired doing anything else to show how Jews could assimilate into American society — think of the Clark Kents, the Peter Parkers — while still retaining their Old Testament God-given ability to fight evil. And I know, Lewis, you don't like me to talk about the Holocaust because you think the kids are too young, but there was no shortage of evil in the thirties and the forties."

Of course, Samuel has to ask at this point what the Holocaust is, but Mordecai sails on. "Funny enough, most of these guys came from homes where they were doing okay but then lost everything in the Depression. So, you have all these superheroes whose parents have been murdered or, in the case of Superman, their whole planet has been blown up. It's also a metaphor for the immigrant experience where people leave their worlds or families or whole lives behind and have to start completely over. And if you read this Fingeroth guy who wrote a whole book on this stuff, the superhero idea of someone who appears weak but is really powerful is proof that Jews really do control the world. He joked that his book was of most interest to Jews and anti-Semites."

"What do you mean, *Zayde*?"

Lewis feels compelled to jump in at this point. "Okay, Sam, that's probably enough superhero history for today. You better run along and shoot another web before you forget how to." This is good enough for Samuel, who jumps off Mordecai's knee and runs away, pivoting this way and that as he shoots invisible webs from his little wrists.

Mordecai has finished his whisky and stands up on his way to pour himself another when he turns to Lewis. "What was the name of the architect again? The one who's suing?" Lewis's forehead wrinkles. Mordecai pats Lewis on the shoulder on his way to the kitchen. "Through some of my friends and clients in Montreal I know a few people in New York. I might be able to ask around and learn something that would help."

Lewis doesn't want Mordecai's help. He hasn't wanted anything from his father since Miranda died. And he certainly doesn't want anything to do with any of Mordecai's legal or business contacts. But he has also never refused to answer one of Mordecai's direct questions. "Abercrom. Maurits Abercrom."

Lewis can't help grimacing as he pronounces the name, but Mordecai nods and grins as he walks toward the kitchen with the gait of a young man.

21

THE BEAVERBROOK ART Gallery looks like a particularly unimaginative architect's vision of a 1950s high school. But when Lewis walks through its glass doors, he feels a brief shiver, as if he is crossing the threshold from one world to another. Mordecai is right there beside him as they cross over. Mordecai who, despite his well-tailored suit, moves and looks like a pirate with his long, wavy grey hair and dark eyes. And then they are inside. Lewis hasn't set foot in an art gallery for nearly twenty-five years. Miranda was still alive. In all that time, Lewis hasn't looked at one of his mother's paintings.

A small crowd is already gathered in a rough approximation of a line, even though the show doesn't open for another fifteen minutes. New Brunswick really is a small place, and up ahead Lewis sees the soft contours of a back he recognizes. The owner of the back is wearing a well-tailored suit that hides imperfections well, but the round body and pink neck of Alex Flandergast is unmistakable. Lewis didn't know Flandergast was an art fan. Like many architects, Flandergast espouses a hierarchy in which art is the afterthought: art is what other people hang on walls after architects design the building. Flandergast's ample arm is being tightly held by a taller woman whom Lewis assumes is his wife, Jane. Like uxorious husbands everywhere, Flandergast is faithfully supporting his wife's interest in the softer things in life tonight. And is that Bob Fielding just beyond him? But the crowd is moving now, and Lewis can't be certain.

Mordecai exchanges their tickets for two glossy souvenir exhibition catalogues for himself and Lewis. *Jones and Mortinsky: Reciprocal Muses.* It is a captivating story: the model turned fellow creator recognized only after her untimely death. Mordecai has previously seen the giant Salvador Dali in the Beaverbrook's permanent collection and so he pauses only briefly in the lobby on the way to the show he has come to see, but Lewis stops, transfixed. The huge painting that welcomes all visitors to the gallery is resplendent in its saturated blues and enthusiastic depiction of Spain's patron saint astride a white horse. Santiago El Grande ushers Christ upwards while in the background an atomic bomb explodes. Two or three minutes go slowly by and Lewis moves off in search of Mordecai.

Wisely, the curator has not divided Miranda's and Jones's paintings into distinct sections or placed them on separate walls. They are all here, in one large room, intermingled. The canvases have been arranged so viewers can see for themselves how the two painters influenced each other. Mordecai has quickly walked off at a diagonal into the room because one of the paintings further on has caught his eye, leaving Lewis to start at the beginning.

But before Lewis can begin his orderly viewing, his line of sight is interrupted. The man Lewis saw earlier must have been Bob Fielding because there he is, standing in the centre of the room. Yet he is conspicuously alone and awkward. Bob's body is twisted in place, pinned equidistant between two paintings of a naked Miranda hanging on opposite sides of the room. His shackles are invisible, yet he is tied down as firmly as an over-reaching hero being punished in a Greek myth. But Bob is no Tantalus. Judging by the look in his eyes he is a nervous Odysseus trapped between Scylla and Charybdis.

Lewis blinks and the mythological aura lifts, leaving Bob an ordinary well-groomed mortal ill at ease in his suit and tie, the way Lewis knows he himself would look if he stood in the middle of a hockey rink, the players swirling around him. This is the second time Lewis has seen Bob uncomfortable. The first was at Tom's cocktail party when he didn't know how to tell the story of Elspeth in the park. Tonight, Bob is not a treasured, well-off friend of Tom's having a difficult moment among a familiar crowd. He's a man who's found himself mistakenly invited to the wrong party. He's clearly never seen anything quite like the art hanging on the walls. Lewis is confused for a moment, wondering what has brought Bob to the exhibition, but he remembers something Bob said at the cocktail party. His wife is on the Beaverbrook Board of Governors. What is her name: Jocelyn? Jennifer? Janet? Something that starts with a "J." The world tonight is full of loyal husbands accompanying their artsy wives.

Lewis feels no responsibility to rescue Bob from his social malaise. Bob hasn't yet seen Lewis, and Lewis turns away to face the first painting on the wall. It's Jones's famous study of a naked Miranda, save for her red necklace, standing in the doorway of her bedroom, trying to make up her mind whether to come or go. As Miranda became famous not as a model but as a painter, critics speculated about the relationship between her and Jones. Some argued the painting depicted a woman struggling to decide whether to remain in her marriage or leave. But most critics cited Miranda's well-known struggles with depression to promote their view that the painting was about a woman caught in the throes of making up her mind whether life was worth living or not. A visual version of "To be or not to be." The last time Lewis saw the painting he was fourteen years old. Less than four years later, Miranda would succeed on her final suicide attempt.

Miranda's eyes are bright in the painting. Her hair is blond. She can't make up her mind and is clearly confused, but she is beautiful as she pauses. Her lips are almost as red as the necklace. Her body is framed in the doorway. There is something about the painting that reminds Lewis of the famous Botticelli, Venus and the giant seashell. But this painting is not idealized. The woman in it is real. She is not standing for the pleasure of the viewer. Perhaps the intervening years have desensitized Lewis to his mother's primary artistic obsession, or he's been so worried for so many weeks about being arrested and losing his architect's licence that there's no room left in his brain for any other concerns. Maybe Miranda has been dead long enough. Or, who knows, it could be that Lewis is finally growing up after turning forty. Lewis has no idea. All he knows is that for the first time in his life he is not embarrassed by his mother's nakedness.

Lewis finally turns to the next work. It is titled *On Top of the Mountain* and is one of Miranda's. Jones saw it for the first time when he went through Miranda's work after her death. Much to his surprise, the painting depicts him naked. Jones never posed for Miranda, but she had seen enough of his naked body in his own work that she was able to carry off enough of a likeness. Miranda painted him standing like King Kong on Mount Royal, the large cross visible beside him, the skyline below him. In front of him a pale female deer and a giant red bull are running toward each other. Miranda depicted them almost at the moment of contact. In the painting Jones is reaching out his arms and placing a hand on the back of each animal. The deer and bull are lifelike. There is no question they are real and alive in the context of the painting. But when Lewis looks at Jones's hands, he sees a paintbrush in each one. Jones isn't just placing his hands on each animal. He is painting them, willing them into being with his brush. In his teenage years Lewis was sufficiently familiar with art criticism and had heard enough about Jones's bisexuality to know that the two animals represent the female and male principles, and that Miranda was also commenting on the creative process.

For the third painting, the curator has selected one of Miranda's most famous works: *Deer Family*. When it's not being loaned out to shows in the provinces, it hangs in the National Gallery of Canada's permanent collection where it attracts crowds of repeat visitors. Miranda, Mordecai, and Lewis in the forest with their own bodies but the heads of deer. Lewis has tried hard over the years not to think about *Deer Family*, but in spite of himself it has always been his favourite. Tonight, Lewis lingers over the painting. How has Miranda managed to portray such affection between the three humans with their deer faces, even though none of the three is close enough to touch the others, and even though the forest around them is dark and menacing?

Lewis skips the next painting, by Jones. The one after is pure Miranda. There is no family inside the frame. Her only subject is herself. She is running through a forest. Of course, she is naked. It has been over twenty years since Miranda committed suicide. But in the painting, she is still very much alive.

At first Lewis doesn't hear the whispering behind him. A woman's hurried, breathy, certain voice, kept low but not quite low enough. "Beth, I have to tell you: I don't get …" The words trail off followed by a moment's pause.

Someone else might be asking in another whisper, "Why not?"

Miranda's white skin looks even brighter against the dark green of the pine trees, each needle seemingly rendered in specific detail.

"I know art is highly subjective, but to be honest, I think the work is ..."

"Really?"

"Actually ... not the right word. More like deranged."

Miranda appears to be running toward the viewer, but there is something about her expression and the way her torso is twisted and one of her legs slightly angled. Miranda has created the impression that she is having a last-minute change of mind and is about to veer off to her right, back into the forest.

Return whispers, clearly now another woman, but this second whisperer is more discreet, and Lewis can't make out the words. But then it's back to the first.

"... I can sort of get my head around his ... it's the Mortinsky woman that I think is absolutely crazy. I've never seen anybody who was so ... so fascinated with seeing herself naked." Giggle. Pause. The first woman listening. "Exhibitions are obviously the CEO's responsibility but ... have to tell you ... embarrassed to be on the Board of Governors." The whisper is getting louder as if the owner of the voice feels the need to distance herself from gallery decisions. "... I even told Bob I didn't want to come. But you know Bob ... always big on duty," followed by hushed, girlish laughter.

Miranda is clearly suggesting what is about to happen on the canvas before it does.

The woman whispering must be Bob's wife. What is her name again? Starts with a "J." Lewis remembers it's three syllables ... works in French ... Jacqueline. It's Jacqueline! When Jacqueline Fielding is not serving diligently on the Board of Governors of the Beaverbrook Art Gallery and being Bob's wife and sharing her unvarnished opinions about artists with her friends in loud confiding whispers, she is the proud mother of one Elspeth Fielding, *Girl from the Park*.

And of course, what is supposed to happen in the painting never does.

Lewis's unthinking body desires movement, but he is afraid to turn around. He doesn't want the two women to catch him eavesdropping. So, he turns around slowly, as if he hasn't heard a thing, and begins to move toward the next painting. He keeps his direct gaze averted, but out of the corner of his eye he sees the two women, middle-aged, well-dressed. Despite his best efforts to appear innocuous they have noticed him. By the way one smiles, open and confident and friendly, he knows she was the one whispering about his mother. Jacqueline Fielding, wife of Bob, mother of Elspeth. Lewis keeps walking, struggling to keep his limbs steady. As he moves he notices that Drescher's suit feels, for the first time, tight on him, especially around the chest. He unbuttons the jacket and lets it hang loosely against his flanks. He's still warm, but at least he can breathe now.

THE TWO WOMEN have stopped whispering, and even if they haven't, Lewis is already out of earshot in the crowded, noisy room. Ten feet away, a man with a pale face and long, greasy black hair falling over the collar of a shiny, ill-fitting suit is standing in front of *Garden of Eden*. It's the painting Miranda did of herself, Mordecai, and Lewis posed in their backyard Westmount garden. It's one of Miranda's few paintings where everyone is wearing clothes. The forever ten-year-old Lewis stares out at the viewer with an even gaze. He is not yet worried about Miranda's suicide attempts, not yet having nightmares about his house disappearing. His hair is blonder than it is today, and the contrast between his bright hair and calm, dark brown eyes is even more startling than it is now.

And of course, Miranda has exaggerated the contrast to make a point.

The pale, long-haired man is staring intently at the painting. He tilts his head to the left, holds the pose for half a minute, and slowly straightens his neck. But he is not done with *Garden of Eden*. Narrowing his eyes and squinting, he rubs the wispy hairs on his chin. He's obviously trying to grow a beard and failing, much as Lewis is with his post-Park disguise.

Even seen only in profile, something about how the man is studying Miranda's painting is off-putting to Lewis, The man's gaze strikes him as intent but naive. It's the gaze of someone accustomed to only looking out at the world from inside, from behind a layer of old, distorted glass. But it is also powerful and unsettling, as though the long-haired man is reaching certain far-reaching conclusions that will have consequences.

Miranda painted Lewis in the foreground sitting cross-legged on the grass. His parents are slightly behind him. Mordecai is sitting with his right leg crossed over the other on an old-fashioned lawn chair, and Miranda is standing with her hand on his shoulder. But Miranda has subverted the typical portrait studio pose by painting herself looking to the viewer's right while Mordecai looks left. From the way the long-haired man is looking slightly downward, he appears to be focusing on the foreground, on Lewis. Even though Lewis is almost thirty years older than he was when Miranda painted him, and even though the long-haired man is staring at the painted Lewis and not the real one, Lewis feels he is being visually dissected. But as much as it bothers the real Lewis, the painted Lewis is oblivious to the man's stare. Finally, the man shakes his head and turns away, but not before pulling out his phone and taking two photos of *Garden of Eden*.

The long-haired man looks distracted now, almost exhausted

from his viewing, and he backs away slowly from the wall of paintings. Lewis watches him turn around and walk aimlessly into the centre of the room, which is where he comes face to face with Bob Fielding standing with his arms crossed. Bob Fielding who is waiting out the show, waiting for Jacqueline to be done. And here something funny happens. The long-haired man extends his hand for a handshake, and Bob clumsily releases his right hand to meet it. Bob clearly knows the man, which is odd because Bob does corporate law, and the long-haired man looks anything but corporate. More like someone in need of a public defender. He is exactly how Lewis imagines he himself will appear once charges of indecency are brought against him.

But despite the look of mutual recognition that passes between the two men as they shake hands, Bob's face is not relaxed. He glances around the room, a frightened rooster looking to escape a gang of gallery-going hens. Shifting on his well-shod feet, hand-made Italian loafers if Lewis's guess is right, he angles his body slightly so he is not facing the long-haired man directly. The handshake doesn't last long enough to be brief. As soon as Bob makes contact he pulls away. He doesn't recross his arms but holds them self-consciously at his sides.

The two ill-matched men are making small talk as Bob relent-lessly scans the room. He's looking for someone, anyone, to come to his rescue. The effect is humorous because Bob is tall and athletic and dressed in professional armour: a well-tailored suit. And then his eyes alight on Lewis. In that split second, before he has time to steady his gaze, the tough corporate lawyer's eyes can't conceal a sequence of thoughts and emotions. *I know this man. He's an architect. I met him at Tom's cocktail party. We talked about hockey and hunting, although he didn't seem interested in either. I told him a very personal story about Elspeth. Fuck. And then I read in the paper that's he's facing a lawsuit for copyright infringement. What the fuck is he doing here?* And then Bob's mind clears and he slips the social mask back down over his eyes, and that's good for him because Lewis is now walking toward him and the long-haired man. Lewis is not sure if he is walking further away from the women whispering about Miranda or toward Bob because he doesn't want to be standing alone and thinking about what Bob's wife has just said about his mother, but ten steps later he finds himself standing in front of Bob and saying hello.

Lewis knows Bob is too polite to ask about the lawsuit. That would be more Flandergast's gossipy style or even guileless, curious Tom's. But by the way Bob is looking at him, Lewis knows Bob knows. Normally this would upset Lewis, but tonight, surrounded by his mother's naked paintings, he doesn't seem to care what Bob or anyone thinks about the lawsuit. Bob extends his hand, almost as reluctantly as he did for the long-haired man, but there is a little more familiarity and warmth in the gesture. Perhaps Bob, even though he is a lawyer sworn to uphold the law, is like most people and finds it secretly thrilling to meet someone bold enough to break taboos. Few people like violence, but everyone roots for a clever white-collar criminal, especially when the only victims are rich people who can afford to lose their money.

Bob opens his mouth to introduce Lewis to the long-haired man and can't hide a relieved smile. After making the introduction he will leave the two men and move on. Out of politeness Lewis is already extending his hand. But when Lewis makes eye contact with the long-haired man and shakes his long, pale hand, the man quickly shuts his blue eyes. He rubs them slowly with what Lewis can't help noticing are the long fingers of his other hand. These fingers and their fingernails are smudged with something dark. It could be dirt, but it looks like charcoal. Does the man never wash?

Lewis worries he's going to give himself pinkeye. But the pale, long-haired man is not worried. His eyes are wide open now, and he is staring at Lewis with pride and pleasant disbelief.

This is a look Lewis has seen many times before. At least he's seen something like it. Whenever she finished a painting, Miranda would put down her paintbrush and drop her smock and stare for twenty, thirty minutes at what she had done. If Lewis was there he'd watch her, fascinated, but then get bored and leave her, and sometime he would miss how the look in her eyes would change. At first it was pride: *What I saw in my mind's eye I have put down on paper for others to see as clearly as I do.* But halfway through her silent standing, the look would change to *I can't believe my hands are capable of capturing on canvas the vision in my mind.* With the pale, long-haired man the effect is similar but different. The same mingling of pride and disbelief, but disbelief comes first in the man's blue eyes. Pride follows quickly, but when it does it falls over his face slowly. Lewis's first split-second realization is that the man's sequence of emotions is the reverse of Miranda's. Whereas Miranda was proud before feeling surprised that her art was equal to her vision, this long-haired man is initially surprised and then proud that what he has just seen is equal to his art.

For Lewis's second realization, following quickly on the heels of the first, is that he is staring into the blue, discerning eyes of the police sketch artist who has taken Elspeth's impressions from the park and created a portrait that corresponds uncannily to the reality that indirectly inspired it. And because Lewis is mostly unable to keep a poker face, the pale, long-haired police sketch artist knows he has been made at the same time the thought occurs to Lewis.

Still, in a last-ditch, brainstem-driven effort to ward off the inevitable, Lewis narrows his eyes so his brown irises are harder to make out and stoops, taking a full inch off his six-foot-two frame. But the effect is only helpful to a point: now the two men are practically the same height, and the pale, long-haired man can see directly into Lewis's eyes. At this, the other man blushes, and even though he holds Lewis's fate in his dirty hands, the effect is charming, even to Lewis, because the pale, long-haired man doesn't look like the kind of man who blushes at anything.

By the time — two seconds later — when Bob's words come, they are unnecessary. "Lewis, I'd like you to meet Simon Turner. Simon, Lewis Morton. The two of you probably have a lot to talk about: you're both in the arts field. Simon is a police sketch artist, and Lewis is an architect." Bob says all this in slow motion, attaching great import if not innuendo to each word, as if he isn't sure whether he's speaking to people of lower intelligence or those in possession of the same secret.

Lewis wants to escape again, but now that he's been recognized there's nowhere for him to go. And Simon Turner hasn't just recognized Lewis's face. He has his full name. It's only a matter of time before Simon Turner turns Lewis in. Who knows, maybe this pale, long-haired police sketch artist will even channel his inner Dirty Harry and make a citizen's arrest in the middle of the show. Isn't it true that every artist secretly dreams of being a man of action? But even if Simon Turner lets Lewis leave the Beaverbrook a free man, he will report his stunning find, and tomorrow Detective Blunt will come to knock loudly on Lewis's beautiful wide front door. Perhaps Detective Blunt will show Lewis the courtesy of not cuffing him in the presence of his distraught family, delaying the placement of the cold manacles around his slender wrists until just before he shoves him into the back of his unmarked cruiser.

But not even the near certainty of being arrested by the end of day tomorrow prepares Lewis to be standing face to face with

Jacqueline Fielding. Bob, mystified by the strange glances passing between the two men he has just introduced, has summoned his wife over with a tilt of his head. She must not have recognized Lewis from behind as the man who overheard her making disparaging comments about the exhibition because she is now by Bob's side, wearing her smile like an accessory. It is the fixed expression she saves for the public, and as Lewis looks closely he can see it is a smile backed up by Botox. But she is composed, asking Lewis how he is enjoying the exhibition and pretending that nothing has happened. She is a member of the Board of Governors, after all. And members of the board have a certain dignity and gravitas that protects them from all embarrassing situations, like a social force field.

But Lewis, usually so accommodating, is no longer prepared to slink away or let Jacqueline off the hook. Now that he has been positively identified by the talented and observant Simon Turner, Lewis has nothing left to lose. The gently rebellious side of him, the one that doggedly questioned Mordecai about his work years ago over breakfast and the more recent reckless one that talks back to Laura when she's on her environmental high horse, is being irrevocably if subtly goaded into action.

After admitting he is enjoying the exhibition very much, thank you, Lewis politely asks Jacqueline for her opinion. She falters only slightly because even she is not geared up to baldly lie. But she hasn't been named to the Board of Governors for nothing, so she soldiers on. "As a board member I appreciate all our exhibits." She's happy with her answer, but the skin on the surface of her cheekbones is tight as she smiles. She looks like a well-fed skeleton.

Lewis smiles too and says, "I thought I heard you offering some criticism of the artists. The Mortinsky *woman*, in particular."

Jacqueline's smile has been replaced by a grimace. This isn't how the game is played. Judging from the look in Bob's eyes, as he glances from Lewis to his wife and back again, he isn't sure what is going on. There is a noticeable undercurrent, but Lewis's voice is even and light. So far, what Lewis and Jacqueline are engaging in is still acceptable gallery-going conversation. Undaunted, Lewis continues. "I think the word you used was 'deranged.'" Lewis says the word slowly but avoids inflection. Bob doesn't know whether to look at Lewis or his wife, so he looks at both. His legal brain still can't fathom what is going on beneath the surface. Simon Turner is not even attempting to make sense of the dialogue in front of him, let alone pass judgment. He is rapt, like someone watching a blockbuster movie.

But Jacqueline's face now takes on a look of horror even more frightening than her distorted smile. Having gone so far, Lewis can only continue. Again, he speaks slowly, evenly. "That Mortinsky *woman*, as you referred to her, was my mother."

As Lewis stands there, unmoving, waiting for Jacqueline's reply, the woman in front of him blurs into his childhood neighbour Mrs. Staunton, into Monsieur Louis St. Pierre drawing Miranda at Chez Nick, into Lewis who has secretly agreed with Jacqueline's snap assessment of Miranda his whole life. Indeed, Lewis has lived with the fear that his mother was crazy and therefore by extension so was he, and so Lewis is talking as much to himself as he is to the disconcerted woman standing in front of him who happens to serve on the Board of Governors of the Beaverbrook Art Gallery and is also the mother of one Elspeth Fielding, teenage witness to Lewis's temporary descent into insanity. Lewis is at last defending the woman who brought him into the world, and so he is defending himself.

At Lewis's revelation, Bob's straight jaw drops. He glances away and his now uncharacteristically unlawyerly gaze bounces wildly around the room, at all the paintings, all the naked flesh, and back to Lewis, but he doesn't know where to rest his eyes. His usually successful face tries on several expressions in quick succession. Jacqueline, to her credit, looks mortified. And now that she is no longer smiling or horrified her face goes soft and almost liquid, and the effect, while not quite flattering, makes her look more human. She has the good grace to say, "I'm sorry," and Lewis has the reciprocal good manners to accept her apology. And now there is a moment where anything can happen.

But long-haired, artistic Simon Turner, who works for the police and is still standing beside Lewis, will no doubt call Detective Blunt tonight. And now that Lewis is momentarily occupying the moral high ground with the Fieldings, he logically if also swiftly concludes that the conditions are as favourable as they're ever going to be, and he decides to drop his bombshell. So, surrounded by paintings and memories of his naked mother, his mother who would have never given a second thought to what anybody thought of her paintings, no matter on how many boards they sat, Lewis girds his spine and lifts his chest. He fully opens his brown eyes and runs his hands through his still close-cropped but still blond hair. He plants his feet and stands his little piece of ground.

Without pausing to choose his words or take a question, afraid that if he stops he won't be able to continue, Lewis proceeds to tell the upright, respectable parents of one innocent Elspeth Fielding, happy Rothesay teenager with her youthful confidence and leadership potential, that he is the man who accidentally exposed himself to their daughter. Neither Bob nor Jacqueline says a word as Lewis tells his story. Both are speechless for perhaps the first time in their lives. But their eyes are hyperactive. Jacqueline can't help herself — she sneaks a quick look at Lewis's groin when he seems to be looking at Bob — and Bob studiously avoids taking his eyes off Lewis's face.

Lewis describes what happened that morning at East Riverside-Kingshurst Park. He doesn't dispute any of the details in the police report, doesn't deny any of his actions, doesn't renounce any of the visuals that so upset young Elspeth. In fact, he admits them freely. Where Lewis differs in the telling of the story that the Fieldings have heard already from their beloved daughter is not in describing anything that Elspeth saw but only in the context, in his intent. In the fact he was urinating, not masturbating. That he meant to apologize, not frighten. Lewis speaks matter-of-factly and fluently. He is concise. He doesn't falter or speak in run-on sentences. He is no longer embarrassed. To his surprise, he is no longer afraid. When Lewis is done and when according to the conventions of conversation it is the Fieldings' turn to speak, neither of them knows what to say.

22

THE FOUR OF them — Bob and Jacqueline Fielding, Simon Turner and Lewis — are standing still, as attentive and carefully arranged as the students in Rembrandt's *The Anatomy Lesson of Dr. Nicolaes Tulp*. The two Fieldings and Lewis are raw, exposed, as though an X-ray has just been taken of their emotions and they can see through each other. But why be derivative? The group of them could be in their own painting called *Lull in Conversation at the Exhibition*, for each is as unmoving as any of the figures in one of the works of art that hang on the walls and that have brought them together. The stillness is not allowed to break of its own accord.

Bob opens his mouth to speak, not because he has anything particularly coherent to say but because he feels he has to say something to defend his daughter. But he is too late. An excited whisper runs through the crowd like a command, and like a well-trained army battalion wheeling in formation to face a new opening in the front, almost everyone, including the four people in their little tableau, turns toward the entrance to the exhibition room. A man has just appeared. He isn't tall or particularly handsome, but he is striking with his ridiculously expensive black suit, black

T-shirt, and black designer glasses beneath thick white hair combed back from his forehead. And he is standing unnaturally straight, like a stylish palace guard.

The many loud conversations in the room from just a few seconds ago have all turned to near silence. The newcomer looks around slowly, benevolently, bestowing his gaze on each group of people, if not individuals, with only the slightest trace of amusement in his large bright eyes, and he waves. It isn't quite a royal wave. There is an element of warmth and kindness in it, although his gaze is all restrained sharpness, like a sword being used to grant a knighthood. Then he turns away and everyone is politely dismissed. Superstar Dutch-American architect Maurits Abercrom, having made his entrance and acknowledged the crowd, is now just another gallery goer, if also a generous patron of the Beaverbrook and a wealthy collector, out to enjoy one of his favourite painters, Miranda Mortinsky.

But Alex Flandergast is in attendance, and he is not prepared to let Abercrom go easily. Like Bob, Flandergast is not a big art fan, but his wife, Jane, is, and so tonight he is too. In the aftermath of Abercrom's entrance, Flandergast spots a gap in the crowd and rushes to introduce himself and his wife to Abercrom. In his enthusiasm to impress both Jane and the great man, Flandergast almost bows, bending his soft round body. Abercrom is gracious and makes small talk with Alex and Jane. When Abercrom learns Flandergast is an architect too, he says something complimentary about Fredericton's collection of beautiful heritage buildings. After this, Abercrom turns to go, but Flandergast has seen Lewis just a few short feet away, and he can't resist. He will pretend he's forgotten about the lawsuit.

So Flandergast, with just the faintest inkling of a smile, waves Lewis over and introduces the international superstar to the regional practitioner he is suing. Lewis responds because despite his recently induced bravery he is happy to escape his impending reckoning with the Fieldings. The copyright infringement lawsuit is still abstract compared to the police visit that will be coming tomorrow. Abercrom is a welcome diversion. Abercrom, to his credit, has correctly summed up Flandergast, and once the introduction is made he dismisses him by turning his back and brings Lewis over to the wall, in front of Miranda's painting of herself running naked through the forest.

Despite his fame, Abercrom is used to uncomfortable social situations, and speaking to the man he is suing doesn't seem to faze him. He treats Lewis like an honourable opponent in a legal joust. Soon they will be armoured and arrayed against each other on the legal field, but for now they can be gentlemen. After the initial pleasantries are trotted out and dismissed, Abercrom speaks first. "And what brings you here?" His voice is mid-Atlantic, cultured, cosmopolitan, and somehow down to earth at the same time. Despites the traces of a British accent it is a very American effect.

Lewis's first impulse is to say it was Mordecai but thinks better of it and instead says, "My mother."

Abercrom's finely trimmed eyebrows rise. Most of the men he knows don't talk much about their mothers.

Lewis adds, "My mother is Miranda Mortinsky." Clears his throat. "Was."

Abercrom nods. He is now interested. Or maybe this is just the manner of a great man, appearing mildly fascinated by the lives of others. "Tell me about your mother. What was she like?"

In some barely acknowledged part of his brain Lewis has never stopped asking himself this question, but nobody has ever asked it of him. Certainly not a stranger. Now that the question is out in the open, Lewis is not confident he even knows where to begin.

He turns to look at Miranda's paintings, but the answer isn't there. Lewis doesn't know if he owes Abercrom an answer, but he is polite. If he will answer a lawyer's questions he will also answer a fellow architect's. But his reply is not effusive: "She was a painter." He corrects himself immediately: "A great painter. She suffered from depression. She was my mother." Lewis feels dumb and exposed, like a child in a play who has forgotten his lines or an adult speaking with people who are far more educated, experienced, and powerful. He is also feeling hot again. Lewis can't imagine what Abercrom, still cool and immaculate in his suit will think, but he takes off Drescher's jacket and folds it over his right arm.

Abercrom appears to realize he has asked too big a question, or at least he has asked it far too early. Abercrom is rich and famous but seems sufficiently self-aware to know that not all his questions deserve to be answered. So, he smiles and shrugs as if to say it doesn't really matter and asks an easier one. "All right, what was her favourite colour?"

Lewis laughs despite himself. This one is easy. He doesn't have to turn to Miranda's paintings for confirmation. "She didn't have one. She loved them all. She always said life was too short to have only one favourite colour."

Abercrom smiles and nods before turning to look at the painting of Miranda running through the forest, and says, not for anybody's benefit, but just for himself, and maybe also for Lewis, "How wise."

Abercrom is still absorbed in the painting and Lewis's answer when Mordecai returns. He inserts himself and stands sideways between Abercrom and Lewis, with his face turned to his grown-up son. Lewis has seen the same look of concern in a stranger's eyes thirty years ago. He was ten years old and found himself surrounded by a gang of aggressive boys a year or two older in

Vendome Metro station. Lewis had been alone and before he knew it this swarm of kids had crowded around and started pushing and taunting him. But a teenage boy standing on the platform about twenty feet away had seen what was happening and looked at Lewis the same way Mordecai is looking at him now. When the teenager walked over to ask, "Hey, are these kids bothering you?" the other boys assessed the newcomer's height and dispersed, but tonight Abercrom is not so easily dismissed. Mordecai looks like a boxer in a suit, and Abercrom has seen enough of Miranda's paintings — he owns two — to know that he's standing beside Miranda's widower and one of her favourite models.

Mordecai waits for Abercrom to address him, and finally he does. For once Mordecai isn't smiling in a social situation, but Abercrom is. "And you must be Mordecai." As if he has been absolutely dying his whole perfect life to meet him. Mordecai reluctantly shakes hands but doesn't say anything. Instead he turns his back on Abercrom and speaks to Lewis as if he were one of his clients. He doesn't refer to Abercrom by name.

"Lewis, in my professional capacity I have to advise you not to speak to this man. I hope I don't have to remind you, but he's suing you. You might think you're having an innocent conversation, but you could severely damage your case. I can assure you that anything you say will be used against you."

Despite the strain that Miranda's illness and suicide have put on their relationship over the last twenty-five years, Lewis is a good son, and as a good son he doesn't ever want to take another man's side against his father. But he doesn't need Mordecai's help. Now that he has already confessed to what happened in the park, he can easily speak to any accusation of which he is innocent.

"Thanks, Dad. I'll be fine." And he speaks around Mordecai to Abercrom. "I didn't steal your design. Drescher shared the basic

232 ◆ DANIEL GOODWIN

design with me and then I added details."

For once Mordecai looks uncertain. It's clear he doesn't like the idea of Lewis speaking directly to the plaintiff, but he also can't find any fault with what Lewis has said or how he's said it. And yet he's still uncomfortable. He's never doubted his son, but he's also been through enough to know that truth in law, unlike in art, doesn't always triumph.

After Lewis's declaration, Abercrom gives him a look that says prisons are bursting with men who proclaim their innocence. But then he smiles, and his teeth are perfect, and he shakes Lewis's hand. "It was a pleasure to meet you, Mr. Morton." He has not yet let go of Lewis's hand. "Or shall we say, Mr. Mortinsky." And at this he winks and lets go. He doesn't shake Mordecai's hand but nods again, this time solemnly, and before he has a chance to move on to the next painting the crowd has parted for him and then he is gone.

It has been years since Maurits Abercrom has had to work a room — the grandest of rooms open themselves widely to him, and he flows through them on the continually rolling wave of his fame that precedes him and announces his presence. But he has always been a social creature, and he makes the rounds. Within ten minutes he is in deep conversation with a shaken Jacqueline Fielding. By this time Lewis and Mordecai have left and so Lewis doesn't notice Jacqueline grabbing on to the well-tailored sleeve of Abercrom's suit and whispering loudly into his ear while Bob looks on, disbelief etched on his usually confident face.

MORDECAI AND LEWIS drive the hour and a half back to Saint John in silence. Lewis doesn't want to answer any questions and Mordecai doesn't feel the need to ask them.

Unlike Drescher, Mordecai doesn't speed in the darkness. Thanks to the moose fence that a forgotten premier once installed along the stretch of highway between Fredericton and the Port City of Saint John, the risk of hitting a deer, or far worse, a moose, has been reduced but hasn't been eliminated.

Mordecai is driving efficiently and calmly, yet Lewis knows his legal brain is racing ahead. No doubt Mordecai has multiple contingencies in mind for how his friends in New York will make the fancy architect's troublesome legal action disappear. Luckily for both father and son, Mordecai doesn't seem aware of Lewis's earlier confession to the Fieldings. It shouldn't be this way, but for once in his life, Lewis is the one who is calmer than his father.

Lewis is no longer standing on the edge of reality. Now that he's already jumped into space with his double confession at the Beaverbrook and begun to fall toward his destiny, he should be feeling desperate. But his feelings of anxiety are leaving him like fog being burned away by the sun. With the prospect of prison looming closer and closer, Lewis is paradoxically less inclined to imagine its enclosing walls, the commingled smell of frustration and stale testosterone, the fear of rape in the shower. Now that he has said his piece to the Fieldings and Abercrom, Lewis has done his part. Although he is falling, Lewis can see the future clearly, and he doesn't have to imagine it anymore because it is happening and he has initiated it.

AT HOME, LAURA shuts down her computer when father and son return, and she makes tea for Lewis and herself. Mordecai declines with a soft shake of his head and a smile and pours himself a Scotch. Laura wants to know how the exhibit was, and both her husband and father-in-law give her minimalistic masculine answers. Good turnout. Well curated. Met some people they knew. Laura, usually perceptive, mistakenly assumes they are both overcome with emotion after seeing Miranda's work. When it's time to go bed, Lewis and Laura make love quietly, and when Lewis falls asleep soon after he doesn't dream a thing. Mordecai, on the other hand, never shuts his eyes.

23

WHEN DETECTIVE BLUNT rings the doorbell insistently the next morning at 8:00 a.m., Lewis quickly tracks down his children and gives them each a secret goodbye kiss while Laura, after realizing Lewis has no intention of answering, frowns and goes to the door. The scene is already deviating from the way Lewis has imagined it so many times before. Blunt is supposed to bang the knocker loudly. Lewis expects the children to be surprised because he has never kissed them before when the doorbell rings. But each child confounds Lewis's paternal expectations.

Skye is upstairs, stretched out in the graceful slumber of a not-yet-two-year-old. She gets a kiss on her forehead and doesn't wake. Luckily for a twelve-year-old who already doesn't always appreciate kisses from his father, Judah is sleeping over at a friend's. Samuel and Alexandra are playing kitchen together in the family room. They don't know why Lewis is suddenly interrupting their play, but they are patient with their father and hug him back and enjoy the rough feel of his two-day stubble on their cheeks. Even Alexandra doesn't try to read too much into it or ask any questions. Lewis is happy to see she assumes kisses out of nowhere from her tall, sometimes awkward father are no more than her due. And Samuel, he safely keeps his eyes on the imaginary meal he is cooking on the toy stove that Lewis assembled two years earlier for Christmas.

When Lewis finally makes his way to the foyer he wants to kiss Laura too. He assumes he will be allowed one last kiss with his wife before he is taken away. Even in her exasperation with Lewis because he has wandered all over the house rather than answer the door, Laura looks beautiful, and Lewis knows he will miss her while he is in prison. Lewis is so distracted by Laura that it takes him a few seconds to realize that the man standing beside her in hunter's camouflage is not Blunt. Was his transgression in the park so monumental that the police called in the Army Reserve? But it is not even the friendly Canadian militia standing before him. It is Tom. Lewis is supposed to go hunting today. It's only 8:00 a.m., but Tom is tipsy. He wears it, like he wears everything, well.

"Tom, I'm so sorry. I forgot. I'm not able to go."

"That's okay, Lewie." And because Tom is feeling relaxed this morning, he lets a friendly expression of pity, understanding, and relief cross his clean-cut face as he turns to leave.

Lewis is also relaxed, so when Tom calls him "Lewie" it annoys him less than usual. He makes a mental note to correct Tom when his friend is more likely to remember it. But Lewis is not ready to let Tom go. "Tom, is Bob with you?"

Tom gives Lewis a strange look, as if somehow Lewis should already know the answer. "Bob called late last night after your mother's exhibit. He's unable to make it." And then Tom can get back to what Lewis assumes is Fred's big black pickup truck idling in the driveway.

Because Mordecai hasn't slept, he decides to stay another day. The children are all excited, and Mordecai promises to take them to the New Brunswick Museum downtown to be enriched by bleached whale skeletons and old machinery while Mordecai admires the small permanent collection of paintings.

LATER THAT MORNING, after Mordecai and the children have left, Lewis googles "art store Saint John" and finds ESL Art Supplies on Union Street in the uptown. He is waiting outside fifteen minutes before it opens. The store is just a few blocks from the Drescher & Drescher office. Lewis is not sure why Blunt is biding his time, but he decides to put him out of his mind. He buys the biggest piece of canvas he can find, and a frame to stretch it over. He wrestles briefly with the choice of paint, but in the end he decides on oils, Miranda's favourite. Watercolours will be too weak, too pale for what he knows he has to do. And acrylic is too flat, too modern. He grabs a set of the most expensive paintbrushes and pays for everything before rushing home, barely stopping at stop signs. He has already cleared a place for himself in the study. Remembering how strong oils can smell, Lewis opens his window as wide as he can and props it up with a book. He mixes his paint without too much thought.

He sketches the scenery first. A dark, mature forest. The trees a mix of cedars and pines. A small clearing in the centre, but the forest surrounding it is thick on the sides and in the background. The tree branches resemble arms with gnarled hands. Lewis starts painting the figures before he will fill in the rest of the scene. He begins with Miranda. He paints her running across the canvas from left to right, her long blond hair streaming behind her. She is running quickly, away from the viewer and the heavy forest with the trees with arms reaching for her, trying to hold her back. She's looking over her shoulder at the viewer, a clearly accusatory look in her pale blue eyes.

Lewis paints himself as a young child sitting in the foreground at the front of the clearing. He has been playing with some small stones, but something has caught his eye. He is lifting his head and looking in the direction of Miranda running but also off to the far left of the painting. There, a tall cedar tree rises to the top of the canvas. The viewer has to look closely, but a man is hiding behind the tree. Only his head, a shoulder, and two arms are visible. His hair is long, black, and wavy, swept back from his forehead. His face is tanned. It is clearly Mordecai. He is still, holding his breath. His eyes and arms are steady. He holds a bow and arrow and is preparing to shoot in the direction of the viewer. Anyone looking at the painting would be torn between Miranda's frightened eyes and the point of Mordecai's arrow. It is the gaze of pursuer that Lewis has chosen for the viewer.

As Lewis paints, he finds he is a bit rusty. He can capture the bodies and shapes, but his colours are a bit off. Yet as he steps back and looks at the painting, he sees that it is fine. The vaguely off-balance colours add a slightly surrealistic look to what is a realist psychological painting. The forest is dark and vibrant at the same time. It is clearly alive. But it is the humans who stand out, as small as they are, as different and distinct each of their actions. Miranda is running away. Mordecai is preparing to shoot whoever is pursuing Miranda. Yet despite Mordecai's obvious concentration, his intent to kill, Lewis has also somehow managed to convey the love between the humans.

The three human figures form a triangle on the canvas. Miranda is running toward Mordecai but also away from him. The young Lewis is motionless in the middle. Both Miranda and Mordecai want to be with Lewis, but they each have something to do first. Miranda has to try to save herself, and Mordecai has to try to save her. And after painting both his parents, Lewis gives himself an

THE ART OF BEING LEWIS ♦ 239

important role. Lewis paints himself holding a gun. It must have been lying there out of sight all along. The painted Lewis has picked it off the forest floor. It's very much a gun, the kind of silver-plated, ivory-handled revolver boys play with when they're young. It looks big and heavy in Lewis's hand, and Lewis is holding it as if he means to use it.

It is just the three of them in the forest, which is cruel, arbitrary, and alive, but they are not alone. They have each other. There is an energy their bodies are giving off: the light emitted by their skin, their clothes, their lifelike eyes; the illusion of rapid movement that Lewis has somehow conveyed in unmoving lines and colours and shapes on the canvas. The viewer of the painting will see that Mordecai is about to loose his arrow, and Lewis is about to fire his gun. Thanks to both of them, Miranda will be saved. The parents will grab hands and rush toward their boy and take him in their arms.

The painting is clearly a tribute to Lewis's posthumously famous mother's most well-known work. But it is not an imitation of Miranda's style: it is fully realized and his own. Lewis isn't sure what has come over him, but when he is done painting for the day, and without thinking about what it means or whether it is a good idea, he grabs a narrow brush and signs himself Lewis Mortinsky.

EVERYONE ENJOYS THE museum, and Laura makes hot chocolate when they return. This time Mordecai accepts the hot drink but insists on adding a shot of rum. Laura gives him an oversized mug, and eventually even the physically disciplined Mordecai has to go the bathroom. The downstairs one is occupied by Samuel, as it often is, and so Mordecai goes upstairs.

After Mordecai asked for rum Lewis also added a splash to his hot chocolate, and he is enjoying the drink while sitting beside Laura on the living room couch. When Laura hears the upstairs bathroom door close she leans over and whispers, "Your dad looks tired. Is he okay?"

For the first time in his life, it occurs to Lewis that he has never worried about Mordecai. He was always too busy worrying about Miranda and then about himself. "I think so." But after Mordecai doesn't return from the bathroom, Lewis starts to wonder about him. As far as Lewis knows, Mordecai is one of the few men over seventy who doesn't have prostate trouble. But Mordecai isn't one for sharing his problems, so Lewis probably wouldn't know even if he did. Has he had a quiet heart attack on the toilet? Has he died alone while Lewis was waiting downstairs? Lewis is afraid of what he might find, but he can't put off the inevitable. So, he climbs the stairs with a mild sense of dread, imagining a separate terrible scenario with every step, each possibility becoming more outlandish as he climbs toward the second floor. But when he reaches the landing, the bathroom door is wide open and Mordecai isn't there. Lewis is bewildered, and thinks Mordecai, like a magician, has disappeared. But then he sees the light on in the study that Lewis used earlier as a makeshift studio.

Lewis treads softly on the old floorboards, trying not to make them creak. And when he reaches the door he sees his father standing in front of his half-finished painting. In fact, he has only just begun. Lewis walks into the room so he can see his father in profile. Mordecai hears Lewis's footsteps, but he is not yet ready to look at his son, not yet ready to take his eyes from the painting, at least not just yet. Mordecai is standing tall and light on his feet. He is looking proud, happy, and tolerant at the same time, but a tear is slowly sliding down his handsome septuagenarian face.

Lewis doesn't know what to say, so he says nothing and waits for Mordecai to be ready to leave the painting. When he is, Mordecai walks over to Lewis with his light stride and embraces him. Mordecai, who always seemed so tall when Lewis was a child, has shrunk a bit, despite his best efforts to remain young. Lewis can see the top of his head. To his surprise, the smallest of bald spots is just barely visible. But his hair is still thick, and Mordecai will die with a full head of hair. Lewis and Mordecai have not hugged each other since Miranda's funeral, but it all comes back to Lewis now, and for the first time Lewis is holding Mordecai with a firmer grip than he is being held.

Lewis is surprised that Mordecai is weeping quietly. Slow-moving, dignified tears are welling up in his eyes one by one like soldiers being called up to the front. The tears are spilling over and running down Mordecai's olive-skinned cheeks that are still mostly unlined. Lewis can feel Mordecai gently shaking against him, his chest heaving slightly. No son wants to see his father cry, and Lewis fears that Mordecai is going to break down bawling. Just when this fear is greatest, Mordecai pulls away and Lewis can feel his father's whole body shaking and then Mordecai is a full foot and a half away from him and now Mordecai has his hands on Lewis's shoulders. Lewis shuts his eyes, afraid of seeing his father losing control. He straightens his back and prepares himself for Mordecai to faint or have a heart attack and to have to catch him.

Mordecai squeezes Lewis's shoulders — it must be a heart attack — and still Lewis doesn't open his eyes and so Mordecai squeezes harder. Lewis opens his eyes, and only now does he see that Mordecai is no longer just crying but also laughing. He is laughing so hard that his tears, tentative before, are now pouring down his cheeks, and Lewis, without knowing why or caring, hugs Mordecai and laughs along with him.

MICHAEL MILKMAN CALLS two days later. "Lewis, I have some news. Mr. Abercrom has withdrawn his lawsuit." There is no trace of a smirk in his voice. If anything, he sounds slightly anxious and surprisingly respectful.

An image of Mordecai playing pinochle and laughing in faraway Montreal appears suddenly in Lewis's head. "Did he give a reason?"

"Technically, he doesn't have to. But he did communicate through his lawyers that in light of Drescher's death and the sale of the firm he has decided to move on."

"Hmm."

"Well, goodbye, Lewis."

"Goodbye."

AS SOON AS Lewis puts down the phone it rings again, and Lewis answers automatically. He assumes Milkman is calling back to say he was just joking, that the lawsuit is still on.

"May I please speak with Mr. Lewis Morton, also known as Mr. Lewis Mortinsky?" The voice at the other end sounds like a highly successful lawyer. Well-informed too, because he knows the family's former name.

"Speaking."

"Mr. Mortinsky," and from the way Maurits Abercrom now says it, like a teacher playfully chastising his favourite pupil, Lewis somehow knows this is not going to be a terrible call. But it's clear from Abercrom's next handful of sentences that it's not going to be an easy one either.

"I'm phoning this morning — by the way have I caught you at a bad time?" And unlike Montcalm, Abercrom waits for Lewis to respond, "No."

"Good. I'm phoning this morning to ask you to please intervene with your father, Mr. Mordecai." Abercrom is obviously familiar with the former and current surnames in Lewis's family. But for some reason he is choosing to use Mordecai's first name preceded by an honorific.

"My father?"

"Yes, the one and same. It appears he has been attempting to stir up some trouble for me if I don't drop my lawsuit."

Lewis can only imagine what Mordecai is up to. He wants to ask, but he is afraid. Abercrom seems to correctly read Lewis's silence through the ether because he helpfully continues. "Earlier this week certain gentlemen residing in New Jersey paid me a visit at my office. They were very subtle, all things considered. A few businessmen talking to another one, if you get my drift." The word *drift* sounds funny coming from Abercrom. He makes it sound like a dirty word. "They seemed to suggest — and who knows, I could very well be wrong — that if I didn't drop my lawsuit, it might somehow become a little more difficult for my clients to construct my buildings. Labour unrest, defective materials, delays, that sort of thing. We all know construction is complex, and these kinds of difficulties are not unknown in the business."

Lewis refuses to believe what he is hearing. He hopes he is hallucinating. Not only will he be fighting a lawsuit for the rest of his life after he pays the price for the incident in the park, he and Mordecai are going to be charged for blackmail and making threats. Yet another consecutive prison sentence. Just when he was getting used to the idea of going to jail for indecent exposure. He has to fight a sudden angry urge to cry, and he is even more ashamed, if that is possible, when he bursts into crude, miserable tears. To have lived through the anxieties of the last few

244 ♦ DANIEL GOODWIN

months — actually, for most of his life — to have come clean at the Beaverbrook, to have done all that only to have it all end like this, especially when he didn't steal anyone's design?

But Abercrom doesn't notice. And as Lewis waits for the next blow to fall he wipes his eyes and is astonished when the back of his hand comes away dry. He is confused, and it takes him several seconds to realize he is not crying at all. Angry and stunned and ashamed but not crying. The loud sound in his ear is Abercrom laughing. Abercrom is laughing so loudly that Lewis has to hold the phone away from his head. Abercrom is clearly laughing at his enemy's expense, like a deranged villain in one of those Hollywood movies that Lewis prides himself on never watching.

Time slows for Lewis, and finally Abercrom is done with his amusement. "Lewis, I like you. But your father is crazy. Completely *krankzinnig*. That's a good Dutch word for 'crazy,' by the way. As his son, you need to talk some sense into the guy." Just like *drift*, Abercrom puts his own sophisticated twist on the word *guy*. "I like your mother's work, but I really like you. I don't think you stole my design. My guys have done their research, and I know you worked on the MAC Building's details. Which made the building great, by the way. But I didn't come up with any details. And Drescher, well, he's dead. So, I'm dropping the lawsuit. But it's important you know this: it's not because of your father. It's because of you. Please speak to him and, as they say, knock some sense into him. For his own sake. He's too old to be playing these sorts of games."

Lewis says something he already doesn't remember, but it's evidently enough for Abercrom because he changes the subject. "And just to show you my heart's in the right place, I had a little discussion with Mrs. Jacqueline Fielding. At your mother's show."

"Oh." Lewis wishes he sounded more articulate, but at this point he can't manage more than one syllable.

"She filled me in on the rather unfortunate experience of her daughter in the local park."

"Oh," again. Lewis has lost all imagination. Abercrom is clearly a sophisticated sadist who has spared Lewis the minor indignity of a copyright infringement lawsuit in exchange for seeing him do hard time as a convicted pervert.

"We spoke about your mother, about you, about my affection for both of you, and about the small but delicate matter of a not insubstantial donation I planned to make to the Beaverbrook. If the fine and unusual good name of my friend Lewis Morton-Mortinsky were to be unnecessarily dragged through the mud, this is a gift that I would unfortunately be forced to reconsider." Lewis is not sure that he is hearing correctly. "I explained that what happened in the park was nothing more than an honest misunderstanding. I even apologized on your behalf." Pause. "One of the finer rewards of fame, Lewis, is that people listen to you when you speak. Mrs. Fielding and I, along with her husband, Bob, reached an understanding under the wise eyes of your mother. Miranda was looking down on us all the time."

And while the phone call continues for a few minutes and includes an invitation from Abercrom to visit him at his famous Long Island home, the conversation ends then and there for Lewis.

As soon as Lewis gets off the phone, he calls Mordecai.

"Hi, Lew." It sounds like Mordecai has been expecting his call for a couple of days.

"Abercrom withdrew the lawsuit."

"That's a lucky break. Good for you. Look, *yingele*, I'm in a bit of a rush now so can't talk, but I'll be driving down this weekend. I'm leaving early so will be there mid-afternoon on Saturday. We can chat then. Bye." And Mordecai hangs up on him.

MORDECAI ARRIVES THAT weekend. After the nine-hour drive from Montreal he leaps out of his Porsche. It is 4:00 p.m. and Lewis wants to talk to him in his study, but Mordecai insists they go for a walk by the river. "It will help me work out the kinks in my back."

As they walk down the hill, it is clear Mordecai is going to leave the first word to Lewis. Lewis waits until they are walking along Rothesay Road with traffic as background noise before he speaks. "Did you not want to talk on the phone because you thought our phones might be tapped?"

"Mine, definitely. Yours, probably not. At least not yet." But Mordecai shrugs his shoulders and turns his hands over in a "you-never-know" gesture.

Lewis shakes his head.

Mordecai shrugs again and looks away at the far shore of the Kennebecasis. It appears to be the other side of the river, but it is actually a long, narrow island. It too is called Long Island.

"Dad, I don't know if I should be angry or embarrassed."

Mordecai keeps his gaze on Long Island before finally turning back to face Lewis. "What about just being happy?"

"I have no idea whether Drescher stole Maurits's idea or not. But I didn't do anything. I didn't need help. And certainly not the kind of help you provided."

"You know you didn't do anything and I know you didn't do anything. But nobody else knows. And you know what, Lew? No-body else cares."

"But, Dad, you broke the law. You asked people to threaten someone." Lewis can't say the word *blackmail*. He feels like a kid again. Even out on Rothesay Road with nobody and nothing around them but the river and a few cars going by, he is being careful to whisper. Although it is a loud whisper.

"Oh fuck, Lew. I didn't do anything. I made a call. Talked to some old friends. That asshole Abercrom and his lawyers and even Milkman were going to ruin your life. Milkman was hired to defend the firm, not you. He was being paid to figure out how you could take the fall while Drescher & Drescher emerged with minimal damages." Mordecai pokes Lewis in the chest of his down-filled coat with his finger. "Abercrom didn't care whether you were guilty or innocent. He just wanted redress." Lewis looks away across the river at the stone cliffs rising on the other side. The setting sun is reflecting off the water.

"Do you not remember anything about the Bible I taught you when we were studying for your bar mitzvah? Ours is not the Christian way, Lew. It's not turning the other cheek. It's an eye for an eye. It's justice. But it's more than that — it's doing what you have to do to protect your family. God will forgive a lot of things. Sending your best friend into the heat of battle so he can get killed and you can finally sleep with his wife. Arguing with Him. Laughing at Him. Making war. But there's one thing He most certainly will never forgive: not taking care of your family. If you don't keep your little tribe from getting lost in the desert or being overrun by your enemies, you're lost. That's the only lesson of the Bible. The rest, the Ten Commandments, the six hundred and thirteen laws, the beautiful language, it's just filler." Mordecai now has the setting sun at his back. It surrounds his head like a burning halo. "I lost Miranda. I wasn't going to lose you."

Mordecai can tell from Lewis's expression that his son is not sure he agrees with what he is trying to tell him. So, he tries to help him understand in a different way.

"Lewis, how old are you now?"

"Dad, you don't know?"

"Come on, Lewis, give an old man a break." Lewis never thinks of Mordecai as old — he has always seen him somehow as his contemporary — but he is seventy-seven. Mordecai turns back, and Lewis falls into step beside him. "By the way, do you know how you know if you're getting old?"

"No, Dad."

"When you want to reread books you've already read. Anyway, forty or forty-one? I know it's one or the other."

"Forty, Dad."

"Okay, so if you believe the actuaries and what they say about average life expectancy — which I don't, by the way — your life is just a little over half over. I think men get to seventy-eight or nine, depending on which province they live in." If so, Lewis reflects, Mordecai is almost done. Luckily, he isn't average in any way. "Women get a couple of extra years on us men. I suppose it's fair, their reward for putting up with us for all those years. Do you know how many days and nights that gives you, if you get to eighty?" Lewis has never thought about it before. "Guess. No, no, don't try to do the math in your head. Just guess."

"Fifty thousand?"

Mordecai shakes his head. "Way too many. Way, way too many. If you live to eighty years old you live twenty-nine thousand two hundred and twenty days and nights." Mordecai taps his temple with his right index finger. "That includes the twenty extra days for leap years. Twenty-nine thousand two hundred and twenty days to design new buildings, meet with clients, play with your kids. Twenty-nine thousand two hundred and twenty days to read books, watch TV, go for walks, go to the gym, be happy. Twenty-nine thousand two hundred and twenty nights to sleep, to dream, to have sex with Laura, to kiss her good night when you go to bed and kiss her awake when you get up and know you have one less day and night to go. Less than twenty-nine thousand two hundred and twenty nights, actually, to sleep with Laura because you didn't meet her until what, you were twenty? So, take off a quarter of that, what does that leave you with?" Mordecai starts to do the math in his head. "Something like twenty-two thousand, and you've already used up about seven thousand of those." Lewis is staring at his father and admiring his amateur math. "The point is, Lewis, you only have so many days and nights. You have a responsibility to be happy, you know? If not to God or yourself, then to Laura and the kids."

The sun is dying and spilling its red splendour across the river, and Mordecai is unrepentant. Lewis knows he will never believe that Abercrom withdrew the lawsuit on his own. Mordecai wants to believe he has saved his son. And so, Lewis lets him.

TWO DAYS AFTER the story about the lawsuit being withdrawn, Montcalm calls Lewis. It is Laura who answers. With a winning frown she passes him the phone and, hand over receiver, whispers Montcalm's name.

"Lewis, how are you?" And before Lewis has time to formulate an answer, Montcalm has moved on. "Look, I hope all is well. I'm calling because now that all the unpleasant business with the lawsuit is over, we'd love to have you back. The firm just isn't the same without you."

A thousand thoughts stream through Lewis's brain, but he quickly distills them all into one that he articulates. "I'll think about it."

Montcalm is used to always getting his own way, at least in the end, and is unfazed. "Yes, yes, of course. You do that. Take your time. I'll call to check in on you next week."

Epilogue

SIX MONTHS LATER, Lewis, Laura, and the children drive to Montreal to attend the wedding of Lewis's second cousin Julia, whom he hasn't seen more than twice in over twenty years. Anya's daughter. After her mother's suicide, Julia grew up intelligent and kind and normal, and the Morton family is looking forward to seeing their relatives. Lewis hasn't gone back to Drescher & Drescher. Instead he has set up his own firm. He's not yet enjoying the same level of success he had working with Drescher, but he has already completed a design and is now working on two other commissions. Even though not one of his designs has been built yet, every single one of them is fully his own. He is the only partner — Mordecai is not an architect, Lewis has no brothers, and his children are still too young to even think about becoming architects — and he hasn't changed his name. But Lewis has decided to call his firm Morton & Mortinsky. And he is painting again.

THE NIGHT BEFORE they left for Montreal, Lewis was trying to pick out a suit. Without the twin spectres of an indecent exposure charge and a copyright infringement lawsuit hanging over his head,

Lewis no longer craves a few minutes every day immersed in the tight comfort of one of the fifteen suits he inherited from Drescher. He doesn't have to feel the suit jacket pulling snugly over his ribs whenever he has an anxiety attack, the fine Italian wool draped over his shoulders, chest, and back like a doublet, restricting the air flow to his lungs and brain as effectively as a paper bag given to someone hyperventilating.

During his period of crisis, Lewis wore almost every suit of Drescher's at least once. But there was one, an off-white, light-weight, linen summer suit, that Lewis never wore. The suit always seemed too lighthearted, casual, almost frivolous for Lewis's heavy moods. It was inappropriate for a job interview or even a humble coffee meeting. Yet that night Lewis wanted to put it on, not because he was anxious but because he felt a burden had been lifted off his shoulders and because it might be suitable for a spring wedding.

Lewis pulled on the pants that did not require a belt. He put on the jacket over a white shirt. He buttoned the top two buttons of the jacket and threw his shoulders back so his airways opened fully. The suit on his torso and his hips and legs felt good, as if he was both wearing it and wearing nothing. But as Lewis looked down at himself he saw the light material of the right side of his jacket bulging just ever so slightly over his lower chest. When Lewis patted himself on the chest he felt resistance and heard the unmistakable gentle crinkle of folded paper. Lewis had always assumed Miriam carefully checked all the pockets before giving away the suits. She must have found at least one of the crumpled fifty-dollar bills Drescher insisted on carrying around without a wallet, or a tissue. Maybe even an affectionate note from her? Perhaps she had missed going through this particular suit.

Lewis reached into the tight, well-tailored chest pocket and felt a piece of neatly folded paper. When he pulled it out and unfolded it, his eyes went first to the gold logo at the top of the page. Beneath the logo, spreading across the page in dark blue ink, was a hastily but finely executed drawing. It was clearly an early version, and it looked different in real life, where one couldn't miss the red rock and blue slate, the more pronounced iconic wave shapes, the tall windows that reflected the Atlantic Ocean and the Maritime sky.

Many features of the final building were not at all present in this first iteration. But the blue ink drawing on the Fairmont Southampton's stationery was unmistakably the design for the Macdonald Arts and Culture Building. Lewis didn't have to see a signature at the bottom to know the drawing had been made by Maurits Abercrom. He had seen enough of Drescher's drawings to know without a doubt that it had not been Drescher's hand that had held the pen.

THE WEDDING IS not as big as Lewis anticipated. It is simple, really: the ceremony outdoors in an inner-city park ringed by unremark- able houses, mostly semi-detached and duplexes, the park a wel- come blend of curved paths and gentle hills, so you can't see from one end to the other. The surrounding trees are only semi-majestic but wholly beautiful in the early weeks of a warm Montreal May, a man-made pond nestled amid the man-made hills, the *huppa* white and swaying in the gentle breeze. The smell of lilacs and freshly mowed grass floats on the hint of the smell of sunburned flesh only two generations removed from crowded European ghettos.

Drescher's summer suit is a perfect choice for both the weather and the matrimonial occasion. It is light on Lewis. As he feels the fine material against his skin, he knows that his younger self would have never worn the suit after discovering the proof of Drescher's theft. The young Lewis would have given the suit away or hidden it at the back of his closet, would have put it out of his mind. Lewis tried hard to understand but still has no idea what would have driven Drescher to steal another architect's design. As far as Lewis knows, it was the one and only time it ever happened. But today he doesn't dwell on his disillusionment. He doesn't blame Drescher for committing the intellectual theft and then dying in a car accident, leaving Lewis to potentially bear the weight of the lawsuit. The forty-one-year-old Lewis forgives his dead friend and mentor.

Lewis and Laura can't watch the whole ceremony, certainly not at the same time, because their youngest daughter, Skye, now a two-year-old who never stops moving, has to get up and dip her hands in the water, has to feel her sturdy legs moving beneath her, has to wave her arms, hear her musical voice. Lewis and Laura take turns getting up from the ceremony and walking around with Skye, although Lewis, who wants to serve Laura, happily shoulders the brunt of the care. When Skye is ready to sit, Lewis sits down with her at the furthermost edge of the pond and watches the ceremony from afar, the two small figures, one in white, one in a navy suit. Lewis watches the couple holding hands, the bridegroom stepping on glass, the solemn exchange of rings.

The blond ring bearer reminds Lewis of the day over thirty-five years ago when he was the ring bearer at one of his older cousins' weddings. Even though the father of the bride told him he could sit down, and even though the flower girl sat down because the ceremony went on forever for a five-year-old, Lewis refused to sit. He remained standing until he passed the ring to the groom to give to the bride even though by that time his legs were shaking. Today the rabbi is looking solemn, then suddenly he is smiling as the bridegroom lifts the veil and kisses the bride and the guests clap happily. Everyone is joyful, even though Anya is no longer with them.

Then it is all over, and Lewis and Laura are reunited with all their children and Mordecai. Before they know it, they are sitting inside the synagogue at dinner and eating, or trying to eat because they have to help Skye with her food. Between bites they are speaking loudly with Lewis's relatives whom they haven't seen for years, and soon it is time for dancing.

Lewis has not danced for years, although he remembers dancing from his childhood. One of his parents' rituals, usually after supper, sometimes when Lewis was awake and sometimes when they thought he was asleep. Mordecai would take Miranda by the hand, no matter what she had been doing, reading, watching TV — the only rule was that he would never disturb her when she was in the midst of painting — and lead her to the centre of their living room. He would hold her in his arms and start to dance with her. They would slow dance like a couple of teenagers, except there was no music.

Lewis watched them more than once from behind the banister at the top of the flight of stairs that led to the second floor. Miranda would lean her head against Mordecai's chest, and Mordecai would hold her lower back, sometimes her upper buttocks, and with his other hand he would stroke her hair. Sometimes they would kiss. They would dance this way, slow moving, eyes closed, so they looked like they were both asleep, not anxious the way teenagers are but content with each other, with who they were, secure in their mutual knowledge that after their dance they would sleep together again, over and over again.

This was a ritual that was never suspended, never interrupted, even when Miranda was descending into depression or was slowly coming out of it after being officially discharged from the hospital. Sometimes Miranda would open her eyes and stare at the wall or out the window for a moment, and then she would close her eyes again. As far as Lewis could tell, Mordecai never opened his eyes once they started dancing until it was over. Mordecai and Miranda never spoke to each other at these times, either.

When he was six, Lewis started to cut in, squeezing his way between Mordecai and Miranda. They would always welcome him, and often Mordecai would pick Lewis up and hold him so he was nestled between Mordecai and Miranda and he could smell their flesh and sometimes after a long day their sweat, and the three of them would dance slowly together and Miranda would often nuzzle Lewis's hair and whisper, "My sweet, sweet boy."

Today, over thirty years later, everyone crowds into the large room next door to the dining area and forms circles and circles within circles. The bridegroom dances in a circle with his male friends and relatives, and the bride dances in a separate circle with hers. Mordecai is dancing wildly with the groom, but Lewis, who has not really danced since his late teens, stands at first like a sober middle-aged man at the edge of the dance floor with Laura and their four children beside him.

But without thinking, Lewis grabs Laura, Alexandra, Samuel, Judah, and Skye by their hands and starts to dance with them. He finds himself picking up Skye and gently throwing her in the air, and she is shouting happily. Soon Lewis and his whole family are dancing and laughing. They form and dance in a circle of their own, and Lewis is sweating. The sweat is rolling down his face, and Laura has the flush she gets when she drinks wine. Alexandra is pulling Lewis down to her level and telling him she wants to dance with the bride. Lewis looks across the room and sees the bride dancing with her groom.

They are whirling and whirling in circles and then friends and relatives put both groom and bride on chairs and lift them up. Lewis doesn't know how they hold on, both of them laughing and screaming. Lewis can see in the expressions on their faces and the tension in their arms that they are holding tightly to the edges of their chairs as they are carried around the room like a god and goddess on a tide. This is when Lewis lifts up Laura and kisses her. He feels Samuel and Skye push their way in between him and Laura, jealous of the attention their parents are showing each other. Lewis picks up Skye, and Laura picks up Samuel even though he is starting to become heavy at five years old. The four of them dance as one and pull Judah and Alexandra in.

When Lewis looks over again to the centre of the room, the bride and groom are now sitting on a tabletop. Their male friends and relatives are holding up the table and dancing with it around the room, and Lewis feels he is witnessing not a Jewish wedding but the pagan celebration of a king and queen. Close to the centre of it all is Mordecai. Lewis doesn't know how he is managing it, but Mordecai is one of the men holding up the table. Mordecai's face is flushed, and Lewis worries he will have a heart attack and ruin the wedding, but Mordecai is laughing like a young man. By now the bridegroom has taken off his jacket and thrown away his tie, but the bride is still fully dressed in white, and Lewis can see the sweat dripping down her face. Lewis doesn't hear his oldest daughter at first — the music and the singing and the dancing are so loud — but seven-year-old Alexandra is shouting at him, and finally Lewis understands she still wants to dance with the bride. Lewis tells Alexandra to wait a bit, that now is not a good time because the bride is still balancing on the table.

Five minutes later the bride is back to earth, separated now from her husband. The groom is dancing again with his friends while the bride dances with her bridesmaids, and soon she is surrounded by her younger relatives, the flower girls. They all dance in a circle, and the flower girls take turns dancing with the bride. She pulls them in to her in turn and dances with one flower girl at a time while the others dance around them.

Lewis looks down at Alexandra to tell her it is still not the right time, but she is already gone. Lewis becomes frantic, even though he is surrounded by much of his family. He looks for Alexandra and then he sees her, his little daughter walking determinedly through the crowd of adult bodies swirling around her. There is no fear, no hesitation in her walk. She walks right up to the bride and stands in front of her. She waits until the bride has finished dancing with one of her little cousins. Then it is Alexandra's turn, and the bride reaches out to her. They begin dancing together, and Lewis moves closer and steps behind the bride so he can see the look in his daughter's eyes. He can smell the cologne that men still wear abundantly in Montreal and the perfumed sweat around him and he watches Alexandra dance with the bride.

As Lewis stands and watches, Laura comes to take his hand. Lewis feels tears swimming in his eyes and everybody around him blending into one heaving body, and Lewis feels himself go. He begins dancing slowly with Laura, the remaining three of his children by his side, and the room keeps spinning around him, but this time everything isn't spinning away from him. Instead, the whole world is spinning toward him. For just an instant, Lewis sees the scene as a painting that he knows he will paint at some point, but for now Lewis has stopped thinking. He is letting himself be taken away, and finally he no longer regrets the past nor fears the future but is fully in the moment, and in that moment he feels like he can keep dancing forever.

Acknowledgements

This book ended up being a personal journey as much as a literary one. I wrote the ending and what I thought was the beginning while still living in Saint John. I continued writing while living in Ottawa and only figured out how Lewis becomes who he is meant to be after moving to Calgary. Now, with Lewis safely out in the world, I am back in Ottawa. A number of people played a part along the way. Thanks to my friend John Smith for all the conversations about writing over food-court lunches, and for helping me think through some of Lewis's more intractable problems. My cousin Jack Gaiptman for the book on architecture. My editor and publisher Marc Côté for his extraordinary literary midwifery. Angel Guerra for the brilliance of the cover. My wife Kara and our children for the space and time to write the book and more importantly for their love. Our friends in Calgary for making us feel at home. Pete and Anke Eadie for all their support, and for being the best in-laws. My brothers Eric and Jesse — and belle soeur Marie Hélène — for their confidence. My mother Sandra for her art and affection. My late father William for his example in the art of living. Everyone who had coffee with me in 2010 when I was looking for work.

We acknowledge the sacred land on which Cormorant Books operates. It has been a site of human activity for 15,000 years. This land is the territory of the Huron-Wendat and Petun First Nations, the Seneca, and most recently, the Mississaugas of the Credit River. The territory was the subject of the Dish With One Spoon Wampum Belt Covenant, an agreement between the Iroquois Confederacy and Confederacy of the Ojibway and allied nations to peaceably share and steward the resources around the Great Lakes. Today, the meeting place of Toronto is still home to many Indigenous people from across Turtle Island. We are grateful to have the opportunity to work in the community, on this territory.

We are also mindful of broken covenants and the need to strive to make right with all our relations.